CATCH ME

WHEN

YOU CAN

CATCH ME
WHEN
YOU CAN

A NOVEL

J. PHILIP DAVIES

FIRST EDITION

ISBN 979-8-9926268-1-0 (eBook)
ISBN 979-8-9926268-0-3 (paperback)
LCCN 2025904591

Catch Me When You Can
www.catchmewhenyoucanbook.com

Published by The Accidental Press

Illustration and layout design by Jenny Menzel — jennymenzel.com

Original AI-generated imagery by Christian Davies & Harrison C. Davies

Printed in the United States of America

For my brother, Steve Davies (1952-2024),
who is somewhere out there in "the field," no doubt,
watching a star being born.

CONTENTS

INTRODUCTION

Two very similar brutal murders occur a thousand miles and three weeks apart. A suspect is quickly arrested in the town of Hightower, Missouri, where the second murder took place. George Maybrick, a merchant seaman visiting his family in Hightower for the holidays, quickly confesses to the murder in New York City and his hometown, as well as several others in various ports around the world. It should be an open-and-shut case, but there is something about the confessed serial killer that doesn't add up. Dr. Richard Crane, a psychiatrist, is called in to see if he can help the suspect with his chronic nightmares and to evaluate him to determine if he is mentally competent to stand trial for murder. To his dismay, he encounters a cold-blooded killer who is a brilliant self-taught artist with a passion for the writings of the Welsh poet, Dylan Thomas. As he begins exploring Maybrick's lifetime of horrific nightmares he discovers that he has a clinical profile unlike any he has ever experienced before. He calls upon a fellow psychiatrist, Dr. Shoshana Liebman, an internationally recognized expert on past life regression therapy. Maybrick agrees to undergo past life regression therapy in the hopes of alleviating his tortuous nightmares, which have plagued him since he was a very small child.

As the past life regression therapy progresses, the impending trial date gets closer. During his sessions, the suspected serial killer and two psychiatrists revisit Whitechapel in East London in the late summer and fall of 1888 where a series of brutal murders of five prostitutes occur, the work of the first serial killer in modern times. Under hypnosis, Maybrick recalls in uncanny detail each of the murders, forcing the psychiatrists to confront a perplexing reality that neither of them could have ever been prepared for. Was George Maybrick a cruel, manipulative, pathological liar or a copycat serial killer? Or could he possibly be the reincarnation of the infamous Whitechapel serial killer? If so, will they be able to solve the greatest murder mystery in modern crime history—the real identity of Jack the Ripper?

CHAPTER ONE

New York City, present day

The exterior of the abandoned warehouse near the port, layered with decades of soot and pollution, stood out among the bleak structures that dotted the waterfront. The late October overcast sky made the decaying red brick structure with jagged remnants of broken glass in the windows and refuse strewn about appear even more dark and foreboding. Off in the distance, the bellowing horn of a towboat pierced the air. By the time the detectives pulled up to the warehouse two patrol cars had already responded. The detectives exited their car rapidly and entered the warehouse. One of the responding officers cupped his hand tightly across his mouth and swiftly exited the building. A few seconds later, the two detectives heard the sound of retching.

"Some lunch he must have had," veteran New York Detective Francis Declan Finn O'Meara—a name his very Irish mother had insisted on—said sarcastically.

"Yeah, probably street food," his partner, Joe Santorini, added.

"Where are you guys?" O'Meara called out.

"Over here in the back of the building, Frank," a disembodied voice replied.

"Goddam, it smells awful in here. What the hell is that?" Joe asked.

"Death," O'Meara replied, reaching into his overcoat, pulling out a wadded-up handkerchief, and strategically placing it over his nose and mouth.

"Son of a bitch!" Joe exclaimed.

In over twenty-eight years of homicide work, O'Meara had never seen anything quite like this one. The woman had been dead for a few days, if not longer. Solid walls and the absence of a window in the corner room of the warehouse intensified the putrid smell wafting from a bloated, decaying corpse. The body lay face-up on a worn-out mattress darkened by dried blood. Flies buzzed all around it, alighting quickly and then flying away, only to return a few seconds later. A large rat that had probably been gnawing on one of the corpse's feet maintained his hungry vigil a distance away.

The scrawled writing on the wall caught O'Meara's attention nearly before the ravaged corpse.

CATCH ME WHEN YOU CAN.

He read the words aloud.

The perp must have used the victim's blood to write the message. So much blood that several of the letters had a trail of dried rust-colored blood running several inches below them.

As O'Meara instinctively began scanning the crime scene looking for anything that might have been used to scribble the message, he pulled a cigarette from a crumpled pack of unfiltered Lucky Strikes, lit it, and took a deep drag. "Have you ever seen anything like this, Joe?" he asked his partner.

"Never! This was some sick bastard," Joe replied.

The victim, a woman who looked to be in her mid-to-late thirties, was lying on her back on the bloody mattress, both arms extended with the hands palms up. Her left leg was straight with the foot dangling over the end of the mattress while her right leg was bent. A large gash across her face had left a deep wound in her cheek. The slash had been so forceful that it severed the end of her nose and part of her right ear. Her throat had been cut, and she had been stabbed repeatedly in the chest. A huge gash ran from the perineum to the breastbone with a horizontal cut across her waist. She'd been disemboweled, and her intestines had been removed and deliberately positioned over her right shoulder. The killer had cut a piece of the intestine nearly two feet long and placed it carefully between the body and left arm.

"Where's the damn medical examiner?" O'Meara asked brusquely as he spotted several crushed cigarette butts scattered on the floor.

"Finishing up a homicide over on Wooster Street," one of the uniforms responded. "A lover's triangle that got ugly. Should be here anytime now."

While his colleagues surveyed the carnage, O'Meara went to work. He'd always possessed an uncanny visual memory. He could recall a crime scene he had investigated a decade earlier and rarely missed a detail. That skill along with his ability to analyze the facts and evidence in a case had made him one of the most successful homicide detectives in the city. He held the record for the most murder cases solved by any law enforcement officer on the entire force. New York City averaged hundreds of murders a year, and he'd invariably been assigned to investigate the most difficult and often the most gruesome cases.

Detecting was what he did, and all that he did. A third-generation cop, he'd grown up in a household listening to his grandfather—a cop for forty-three years who had walked a beat in Soho when the area was known as Hell's Hundred Acres—tell stories of New York during prohibition. Frank had loved to hear those stories growing up. His father had followed in his grandfather's footsteps, and Frank had continued the tradition, creating an O'Meara family legacy.

Now, in his late fifties, with an ex-wife who'd left him years ago because he was married to his job, police work was all that he had. He worked twelve-hour days, often on weekends, and spent evenings unwinding at Donovan's Pub on shots of Bushmills with an ever-present unfiltered Lucky Strike dangling from his lips. He walked with a slight limp. He told people he had arthritis, but it was really a bullet wound from his days as a patrolman. His partner knew the real source of his uneven gait but thought it best not to ask why O'Meara always offered a different explanation when asked. Every twelve to eighteen months, his division captain insisted he use his accumulated vacation and take a few weeks off. So, O'Meara would grab up a pile of cold case files, sometimes decades old, and hole up in his apartment reviewing them.

Once he started investigating a cold case he never stopped. He might not look at it for months or even a year, but he never stopped thinking about it. Applying current forensic technology unheard of fifteen or twenty years ago, he'd managed to get several cases reopened.

"Every case can be solved if there is enough time to study the clues," he always told his colleagues.

CHAPTER TWO

"Whaddya got for me, Joe?" O'Meara asked the next morning as he pulled out his desk chair while juggling a bagel slathered with cream cheese in one hand and an oversized cup of black coffee in the other.

"One big goddam mess! Happy Halloween," he replied.

"Anything on the autopsy yet?"

"Yeah, a preliminary report. I just looked it over."

"Anything promising?"

"A couple of things. The victim was probably strangled first and then had her throat cut. That's what killed her. The ME believes that whoever carved her up probably had some knowledge of anatomy."

"Doctor...or med student maybe?" O'Meara suggested.

"Possibly. Whoever it was, he worked very methodically. The autopsy doesn't suggest it's the MO of some kind of crazy slice-and-dice killer worked up in a frenzy."

"How about the writing on the wall?"

"It looks like the killer used a make-up brush he took from the victim's purse. The crime scene guys found it several feet away from the body. It appears that the killer intentionally tossed it there. The lab is confident the blood on it belongs to the victim. We'll know for sure this afternoon."

"Well, it doesn't take a rocket scientist to figure that out," O'Meara replied dryly. "What about the murder weapon?"

"A very sharp knife, six-to-eight-inch blade with a hell of a point on it, is the medical examiner's best guess."

"Any evidence of sexual assault?"

"The ME said he couldn't be sure just yet," Joe said. "When I spoke to him this morning, he said he hadn't seen anything like this in thirty years, and it would take time to sort through everything trying to isolate body fluids. He hoped to have it in the final report, but he couldn't promise a definitive answer. There's just too much blood everywhere to be certain."

"And the cigarette butts?"

"The crime scene guys found a load of cigarette butts but most of them had been ground into the floor pretty good and had blood all over them, so I'm not sure what they're going to tell us."

"I want to know everything about those cigarettes that the lab can find out. Brand, who makes them, who smokes them, everything. I've got a hunch about those butts...something strange about the filters. Didn't look like any I've ever seen. Can't quite put my finger on it just now, but something tells me..."

"Tells you what, Frank?" Joe asked.

"Let's just wait and see what the lab guys turn up. In the meantime, we can run a check and see if there have been any recent murders with the same MO in the last, say, six months. I'm betting this wasn't his first time. It wasn't some spur-of-the-moment whack job. The murder scene was too deliberate. And he'll kill again. You can bet your ass on that."

"Right," Joe agreed. "You know it could be anybody. That warehouse is close to the docks. There are hundreds of people coming and going in that area every day."

"And nobody's seen anything, of course."

"Nothing. We've had uniforms canvassing nonstop since yesterday and they've turned up *nada*."

"Did we get a time of death, at least?"

"The autopsy report says the victim was probably killed early in the morning on Tuesday. She'd been dead for around seventy-two hours when they found her."

"Any ID?"

"Yeah, but it's fake. We ran it. Nothing checked out."

"Hooker, maybe?" O'Meara suggested.

"Possibly. They did get a couple of partial prints off the victim and are running them now."

"Nothing from the killer, I assume."

"Nothing, unless we get a break on the partial prints. Looks like he was pretty careful."

O'Meara narrowed his eyes. "How do you figure? What about the cigarette butts?"

"Like I said, they don't look promising."

O'Meara shook his head slightly. "Doesn't add up. Some guy brutally murders a hooker and writes a message in blood on the wall, making sure he leaves no prints, but tosses his butts on the floor?"

"Maybe they're not the killer's cigarettes?"

"Maybe."

"Yeah, very strange. The psych people are working up a profile, but it won't be ready till the middle of next week."

"I'm gonna get this son of a bitch," O'Meara announced in an angry tone. "I don't care what it takes. This bastard's gonna kill again, and when he does, I'm going to be there to catch him!"

CHAPTER THREE

Hightower, Missouri, present day

A steady easterly wind was blowing across the frigid Mississippi River and chilling the air. Clumps of the naked trees that dotted the river's edge were weighed down by a huge flock of starlings. A lone towboat sounding its foghorn sent annoying sonic vibrations across the water that could be heard for miles.

Once a thriving river community with a vibrant marine industry servicing the towboats and barges on the Mississippi, the last thirty years had not been kind to the small Missouri town of Hightower. Most of the local river commerce had dried up, along with the jobs that supported it. Those who were able to found work ninety miles upriver in St. Louis. As people abandoned the town, the once middle-class family neighborhood of Windwood devolved into several blocks of decaying homes, flop houses, and an occasional crack den. The townspeople sardonically referred to the area as Deadwood and avoided it whenever possible.

Even the petty criminals and undesirables didn't stay in Hightower very long if they could help it. For a while, a couple of meth labs had operated on the edge of town but had moved on for lack of business.

The irony did not escape Detective Chris Stanford as he raced to Windwood on a battered road paralleling the wide river. Hightower was a town dying a slow death, and along with it, the volume of criminal activity. Since it witnessed few homicides, Chris handled any serious cases, working under a special investigations unit which consisted of himself and his partner, Detective Harry Caulfield. They investigated maybe one or two homicides a year. When they weren't involved with murder investigations, they handled any other cases that came up in the small town of eighteen hundred inhabitants.

Nursing a hangover from too much Thanksgiving football and beer from the day before, Chris's head pounded as he strained to keep his eyes focused on the road. He could see just a hint of the wide river off to the right through the grey rain.

"Don't let anybody go inside until I get there," he barked into his police radio.

"It's bad isn't it?" Harry asked nervously, sitting next to him in the car.

"Sounds pretty grim. Best to prepare yourself."

Chris wondered what they would find. A veteran detective of ten years, he'd never intended to spend his law enforcement career in a podunk place like Hightower. After completing his degree in criminal justice, he'd sat for the entrance exam for the St. Louis Police Department. It had never occurred to him that he might fail the exam…which he had. Confidence diminished, he'd looked around for a small department where he might get some experience and study to retake the exam. His boyish appearance back then had made him worry that people would not take him seriously. Nevertheless, his degree attracted the attention of the Hightower chief of police, who'd told him he was overqualified with a college degree, but had hired him, nonetheless. Four-and-a-half years later, Chris had made detective, a modest achievement at best in a department of nine.

As he glanced again at the river, he wondered why he had never left. There really was no reason to stay in Hightower. His wife, Julia, whom he'd married a few years after moving to the fading town, would be happy to move on. When the subject came up from time to time, his son and daughter complained mildly about leaving their friends, but nothing substantive. Chris chided himself for settling for less than he was capable of and allowing himself to become too comfortable as one of Hightower's finest. He sometimes imagined he might break a big case and that would be his ticket out of Hightower. But after ten years of detective work, even the few homicides seemed routine.

Maybe this would be it, he told himself as he drove. When the call came in, the initial report was of a brutal murder in an abandoned house in Windwood. Brutal murder. How brutal? Maybe it would make the St. Louis newspapers, he thought to himself.

An aging patrol car already sat parked on the street at 1342 Riverbend Drive as Chris pulled into the driveway of the abandoned house. A uniformed officer stood sentry at the wrecked entrance to the house, ashen-faced and visibly shaken. His hand quivered almost imperceptibly as it rested on the handle of his holstered firearm with the thumb break unfastened. The front door, weathered and shattered from being assaulted a long time ago, hung precariously on one rusted hinge.

"Anybody go in, Gene?" Chris asked brusquely.

"Only to verify the body and make sure it was dead, Detective," the patrolman responded, his voice trembling.

"It? What the hell does 'it' mean?" Harry asked.

"You'll have to see for yourself, Detective Caulfield. It's impossible to describe. I wasn't sure exactly what I was looking at."

"What kind of bullshit is that?" Harry demanded.

"It's like I said, Detective. You'll just have to see for yourself," the officer repeated. "The medical examiner is on her way and should be here any time now," he added.

"And the victim?" Chris asked.

"Back bedroom, just to the left off the kitchen."

After donning protective gear, Chris and Harry moved slowly through the entrance hall. The sound of scampering rats could be heard from various spaces in the house.

As they walked by what had once been a kitchen, Chris spotted bloody footprints on the yellowed linoleum floor. "Oh my God," he muttered as he stepped through the bedroom door and stopped dead.

Harry took one look and immediately averted his eyes.

The crime scene had been meticulously laid out. And the degree of mutilation made it impossible at first glance to determine the sex of the victim.

Chris scanned the room intently for several seconds, then closed his eyes for a moment before walking toward the victim.

"You'll have to go this one alone, Chris. I can't handle it," his partner said.

"Bullshit! You've got to hang in there, Harry. It's going to take both of us to work this crime scene."

"I'm sorry, buddy. I can't. This ain't like anything we've ever seen before. I think I'm going to puke."

"Okay...okay," Chris muttered. "Go out, puke, catch your breath, do whatever you have to do, and then get your ass back in here."

Overtaken by nausea, Harry exited the room and raced out the front door. His partner could hear him throwing up Thanksgiving leftovers onto a pile of garbage.

Chris walked farther into the room, traveling in the reverse of the bloody footsteps leading toward the front door, careful not to compromise the scene. A feeling of dread unlike anything he had ever experienced overcame him. His body tensed and he struggled to catch his breath. He felt as though he had somehow in a few measured steps crossed over onto a different plane of reality.

The female victim lay nearly naked on the bed, the upper body twisted somewhat to the left, clothed only in the remnants of a shredded beige blouse. Her head rested on its left side. The neck appeared to be severed nearly to the backbone, and the face was hacked beyond recognition. The badly mutilated left arm ended abruptly in a stiffened clenched fist. The lower part of the body twisted to the right and the legs were spread open. Largely stripped of its skin and muscle, much of the left thigh bone was exposed. A huge gash ran the length of the calf from the knee to the ankle. The chest had been cut open and the abdominal cavity emptied of all its viscera. A large wound on each side of the chest was layered over in dried blood.

Feeling dizzy, Chris paused, turned his head to one side, and drew in a deep breath. Heart racing and his palms sweating profusely, he turned and took a few steps, retreating from the room, then stopped.

Do your damn job he told himself.

He closed his eyes, breathed deeply, then once again moved toward the bed, forcing his eyes to focus on the body, beginning at the head. Although difficult to see clearly with only the light from a broken window, he could make out some of the organs and a severed breast under the head. The intestines lay on the right side of the body, with another organ he couldn't identify on the left. The liver had been placed between the feet and the other breast, muscle still attached, rested near the right foot. On an old shipping crate next to the bed lay three large flaps of flesh that had been cut from the chest and thigh. Just over the head, on the wall someone had written in large bloody letters.

FROM HELL.

Chris repeated the words quietly to himself.

"My God!" The voice of the medical examiner startled him and he jumped. "What is this?" she asked.

"You tell me," Chris said.

"Never in my life…" Dr. Sarah Anjali, the medical examiner, replied, her words trailing off in horror. Her day job was as an emergency room physician and she routinely witnessed blood and gore, but this seemed to shock her.

"I'm back now," Harry announced, reentering the room. "I've called Chief Monroe for some help. I told him what we've got here, and he's sending two more officers over to help check things out. What do you think, Dr. Anjali? Looks like a medical examiner's nightmare."

"This looks like everybody's nightmare," she replied with a grimace.

"All right let's not miss a thing on this one. Whatever it takes. We need to make sure we get every shred of evidence. I don't care if there's mouse crap in the corner. Bag it," Chris said emphatically.

"We're going to need more light. The window's not enough," she advised.

For the next four grueling hours, Chris, Harry, the medical examiner, and Hightower PD's makeshift version of a crime scene unit went over the entire murder scene plus the rest of the house. The HPD didn't have its own photographer so one was called in from a nearby town. Collectively, they gathered dozens of bags of potential evidence, including a large number of cigarette butts.

"I'll hopefully find something useful when I get the body to the lab and get a closer look," the ME told Chris. "And there's something else that is pretty bizarre."

"What's that?" he asked.

"It looks like the victim's heart is gone. It's not anywhere in the room."

"Jesus," he growled. "You've got to be kidding me. Harry, we're going to have to search the whole damn neighborhood, just in case."

"But we've only got three guys," his partner protested.

"Then get on the horn to Chief Monroe and tell him we need some more uniforms," Chris ordered.

When the crime scene had been gone over meticulously for a second time, he directed the photographer to shoot another round of photos just to be sure everything had been documented. He didn't want to take any chances. He noticed the doc standing at the bedroom door looking pensive, her chin resting on her clenched fist. "What's the matter Dr. Anjali?"

"I don't know quite how to proceed. I've dealt with some messy situations, but I've never had to gather up so many body parts in a manner that doesn't compromise the autopsy or the police investigation when I get back to the lab. Maybe we should bring someone else in, Detective Stanford. A routine autopsy or a gruesome accident I can handle, but maybe you don't want a small-town emergency room physician in charge of this autopsy…"

"Looks like it's already half finished," Harry drawled.

"For crissake Caulfield," she responded indignantly. "Let's not forget this is a real person here."

"You're right. I'm sorry," Harry apologized sheepishly. "Cop humor."

"I know you can handle this one, doc," Chris said. "I realize it's a horrible mess, but you've got the skills to do it. How long before I can get a report?"

"Give me a couple of days at least to do a thorough autopsy."

"Sorry, I really need it asap. The trail is getting cold. The killer may have already left town. Time is of the essence. Can you do better? Please?" he pleaded. She had to know time was working against them.

Dr. Anjali looked at her watch. "Okay. I'll get started this afternoon and work late. But it's going to take a good twelve to fifteen hours. With some assistance and no surprises, I may be able to have something for you by this time tomorrow. But it'll be a preliminary report at best."

"Thanks, I really appreciate it. It scares me that the perp—"

"Or perps," she interjected.

"Why do you say that?" he asked.

"This is a lot of cutting. I'm just guessing, but this amount of carnage would have taken someone at least two to three hours to do working alone. Looking at the left eye, which is still intact and the temperature, I'm guessing she's been dead for about ten to twelve hours. That puts the time of death early in the morning. It's been chilly for the last twelve hours, so I'm guessing on the *algor mortis*. I could be off an hour or two."

"Will you be able to give me an exact time after you do the autopsy?"

"I should be able to get pretty close," she responded.

"It scares me to think that the person who did this might still be here, walking around town." He recoiled at the thought of another gruesome murder taking place in the town that he had sworn an oath to protect.

"Meanwhile, we have another problem, Detective Stanford," she said. "Unless you find some form of ID, the victim is going to be tough to identify. Her face has been substantially mutilated. You might be able to get some prints, but unless we can match them in the police or federal database it could take days, maybe even weeks. Facial recognition is going to be all but impossible. Let's hope she's a local and someone reports her missing."

"Let's hope she's not," he responded in a somber tone.

"What about going to the media?" one of the officers suggested.

Chris shook his head. "Stall them for twenty-four hours. I don't want any of this getting out, at least until I get the autopsy report," he said sternly. "Tape it off and put a uniform on guard around the clock. No one gets in or out until we find out what went on here."

"The chief isn't going to like that. You know what a pain-in-the-ass he is about overtime," Harry reminded him.

"I don't give a rat's ass about overtime! We've got a real psychopath on our hands, and we don't know where he is or when he might kill again."

"And he will kill again," Dr. Anjali added emphatically. "Somebody like this doesn't kill because they want to. They kill because they *have* to."

CHAPTER FOUR

Chris sat at his desk motionless, chin cupped in his hands, replaying the images seared into his memory from the day before. Every time the phone rang, he jerked it to his ear hoping to hear Dr. Anjali's voice on the other end of the line. He toyed with the idea of going over to the morgue and waiting, but he realized he would just get in her way. At around three thirty he got the call. "Finished?" he asked. "Great! I'll be right over."

The short drive from the station to the hospital morgue where the local autopsies were performed seemed interminable. He wondered whether she had turned up anything that would help solve the murder. As he rapped on the glass door to her office, he could clearly see the strain and exhaustion in her expression.

"What do you have?" he asked anxiously.

"Where do you want me to start?"

"How about the cause of death, and we'll go from there."

She nodded. "As far as I can determine, there is no bruising on the arms or wounds to the hands, which means that the victim didn't have any opportunity to resist and was probably killed where she was found. The cause of death was asphyxiation. The contusions on her neck, swollen lips, and tongue indicate that she was initially strangled, but that's not what killed her. It was probably just enough to make her lose consciousness. The cause of death was the slash across the throat which severed her carotid artery and her windpipe. Death would have been nearly instantaneous, thank God. It was only one cut, but the neck was severed all the way through to the vertebrae. I'm guessing the killer was left-handed. The cut was from right to left, consistent with a left-handed person. It was slow and deliberate, as evidenced by the ecchymosis."

"What's ecchymosis?" Chris asked.

"Bruising around the wound," she explained. "The killer used such force that the fifth and sixth vertebrae were deeply notched by the knife."

"Would that require a great deal of strength?"

"Absolutely," she replied.

"What can you tell me about the murder weapon?" He asked.

"An extremely sharp knife. I would guess a six-inch blade, maybe a little longer, about an inch wide, with a point," she replied holding her two index fingers about a half a foot apart.

"Time of death?"

"I'd say two a.m., give or take a half hour."

"Anything that might help us identify the killer?"

"I suspect the person who did this is a real head case. You need to pull out all the stops on this one, Detective. It's terrifying to imagine the person who did this wandering the streets of Hightower. I know resources are tight but get a profiler on this right away if you can. The person who did this knew what he was doing. This is a killer who has a pretty good knowledge of anatomy."

"How so?"

"He was efficient," she said as she pulled some photographs from a large envelope. "Look at the abdomen. The skin and tissues from the costal arch to the pubes were removed in three large flaps. Those are some of the remains we found on the crate beside the bed. Very methodical. And all the organs... they knew exactly what they were cutting out."

Glancing between the photos and the cadaver while listening to Dr. Anjali's explanation, the initial sense of dread that Chris had experienced when he first encountered the victim returned. Lying on the cold stainless steel table, the victim's body, now cleaned, looked even more grotesque. The veneer of dried blood had been removed, revealing every gash, puncture wound, and place on the body where flesh and organs had been removed. The face was disfigured beyond recognition.

Chris had to force his attention back to the doc's explanation. "Are you suggesting our killer might be a doctor?"

"Maybe. Or a med student, or possibly even a butcher. But he could be anybody with some understanding of human anatomy who's also adept with a knife."

"Why do you say he?"

"I wouldn't ordinarily rule out a woman as a suspect. In this case, however, when you look at how long and how much strength it would take to mutilate and carve up the body, I'd say our suspect is probably a male. Whoever did this was very deliberate and took their time."

"What about the heart? Any sign of it?"

"No. The left lung was intact, and the lower part of the right lung was torn away—maybe when the killer was trying to get at the heart. There's one clue, though."

"What's that?" he asked optimistically.

"You know, the dead will usually speak to you if you treat them with respect and promise to listen carefully. In this case, the victim was a heavy smoker. She was relatively young, mid-to-late thirties or early forties, but her lungs were already partially blackened."

"Would that explain all the cigarette butts we found at the scene?"

"I doubt it. I don't think the killer gave our victim enough time to smoke even one cigarette. I'm betting they belong to the killer, or a homeless person who might have used the house for temporary shelter."

"Well, that's something to go on."

"Two other things that might be helpful," she said.

"What's that?"

"I honestly don't know how they found them in all the mess, but forensics identified two strands of hair on the body that don't belong to the victim." She produced an evidence bag which she held up, allowing Stanford to view the hair samples. "They may belong to the killer, but obviously I can't say for sure."

"Any evidence of sexual assault?"

"Not that I could tell, but I can't be sure of that either. There was just too much blood everywhere," she replied. "To find any trace of seminal fluid, blood, or saliva left by the killer would be like trying to find a needle in an entire field of haystacks, and I say that with no exaggeration."

"I understand. Anything else that might help us establish who the victim is?"

"Nothing."

"Did you find anything in her purse?" Chris asked hoping against hope that something had turned up

"*Nada.* If the purse we found belonged to the victim, the killer emptied its contents and took them with him. Probably at the bottom of the river at this point."

Chris stood staring off into space, his attention riveted to a mental checklist of questions he always went through after an autopsy to make sure he'd covered all the bases. He was just about to thank Dr. Anjali when he thought of one more thing. "Did anything turn up in the victim's clothing?"

The doctor's face registered surprise, then chagrin. "Sorry, Detective Stanford. Examining the victim's clothing got right by me. I was so focused on the autopsy I didn't even think about that."

"No need to apologize. I know you've had your hands full and probably haven't had any sleep for twenty-four hours. Can we just take a quick look?" he offered.

"It's a bloody mess, but certainly."

They each put on a pair of blue latex gloves and began meticulously examining the victim's clothing. A badly torn blouse, the only article of clothing found on the body, revealed nothing. Chris carefully examined the victim's black jeans, desperately hoping to find something.

And there it was. Dried blood from the victim had fused a small piece of paper to the inside back pocket of her jeans.

He looked around and grabbed a pair of surgical tweezers which he gingerly inserted into the pocket, gently removing the paper. It had been folded multiple times. He'd seen enough tickets from the local Hightower pawn shop to know what it was. Very carefully he placed the bloody piece of paper in an evidence bag.

Finally, something to go on.

CHAPTER FIVE

"Looks like we caught a break, Chris," Harry announced, grinning from ear to ear as he hung up the phone. "We got a name from the pawn ticket. And there's something else. A missing person's report came in this morning for the same name."

"Who is it?" Chris asked.

"A local. Donna Strickland. Worked as a waitress at the Dock Lounge, a dive bar over on Trinity Avenue across town."

"Who phoned in the report?"

"The bar owner. He says she hasn't shown up for work since Thanksgiving Day. He didn't know who to call, so he called the police."

"He got a name?"

"Stan Langham."

"Let's take a ride," Chris said, grabbing his coat. "Got an address?"

"Yeah, let's go."

When they arrived, the bar hadn't opened yet.

"This place has seen better days," Harry observed.

"Ya think?" Chris responded as he knocked on the old, weathered door covered in peeling yellow and purple paint.

An older gentleman, broom in his hand opened the door. "Sorry, we're closed."

"Are you Stan Langham?" Chris asked.

The man nodded. "Are you here about Donna?"

"Yes. I'm Detective Chris Stanford, and this is my partner, Detective Harry Caulfield. We'd like to ask you some questions."

"Sure, come in."

The bar owner appeared genuinely concerned about the waitress. He explained that she was an excellent employee and never missed work without calling. He suspected she lived alone because she never talked about a family.

"Can you remember anything unusual that happened on her last shift?"

Chris asked.

"That was Thanksgiving Day. We opened at three that afternoon and she worked straight through the afternoon and night shifts. Donna spent a lot of time waiting on a man who came in around ten thirty and stayed until we closed at one."

"Did they leave together?"

"Can't say for sure. Donna don't usually take up with customers. This can be a tough crowd. They did seem to be getting along pretty well. She told me he gave her a big tip. She took Friday off, but when she missed her shift on Saturday night I got a little concerned. That's not like Donna at all. Sunday we're closed. When she didn't show up for work on Monday, I knew something must have happened to her for sure. That's when I called you fellas."

"You wouldn't happen to have a photo of Ms. Strickland, would you?"

"Sorry, I don't, Detective Stanford."

"Did she have light blond hair by any chance?"

"Yeah," the bar owner answered. "Why do you ask?"

"Just curious," Chris replied. "Did she smoke?"

"Like a damn chimney! I tried to get her to give it up, but she just couldn't. I kept telling her it was going to kill her one day. All she would ever say was she had been smoking since she was fourteen and we all gotta die from something."

"Did you recognize the customer she waited on?" Harry asked bringing the subject back around.

"He wasn't no regular."

"Can you describe him?" he asked.

"Sure. He was kinda friendly. He had a couple of drinks at the bar before he settled into that booth over there. I'd say mid-to-late thirties. About five-eleven, medium build. Gray eyes, I'm pretty sure. Never seen anyone with gray eyes before. Wore a navy wool cap, but I could tell he had red hair. Otherwise, nothin' particularly remarkable about his appearance. Oh, except he had a birthmark that started on the right side of his forehead above his eye and disappeared under his cap." As he described it, Langham pointed to his head, showing where the birthmark began.

"Anything else?" Chris asked with a nod.

"Yeah, now that you ask. Something different about his hands. They showed hard work but seemed somehow…delicate. Hard to describe."

"Very helpful. Can you recall anything else, Mr. Langham?" Chris asked.

"Smoked a helluva lot. Donna emptied his ashtray twice."

Harry perked up. "Did you happen to notice what kind of cigarettes?"

"No, but they weren't no regular brand, Detective Caulfield."

"Why do you say that?"

"The pack was blue and larger than a regular pack of cigarettes, and the writing was in some kind of language I didn't recognize. The cigarettes didn't have a regular filter—more like some kind of cardboard tube he pinched together before he lit up. Not like anything I've ever seen before. Do you know who this guy is? Do you think he might have done something to Donna?"

"That's what we're trying to find out, Mr. Langham. Thank you for your time and cooperation," Chris said.

"Are you going to be able to find Donna?" the bar owner inquired, his voice heavy with concern.

"You read about the murder in the paper, right?" Harry asked.

"You mean the one over in Windwood last week?"

"Yes. Well, it's looking like the victim may have been Ms. Strickland."

The bar owner's eyes started to tear up. "Damn. I'm really sorry. She was a nice girl. I wish I knew if she had any family."

"You've been very helpful," Chris reassured. "Here's my card. If you can think of anything else give me a call. We'll be in touch."

"What kind of monster does that to a person?"

"One that belongs behind bars," Harry assured the old man.

Driving back to the station, Chris remained quiet.

"Something wrong?" Harry inquired.

"It all seems too easy."

"Whaddya mean?"

"Whoever this guy is, he's either careless and stupid, or he doesn't care if he gets caught."

Harry frowned. "How so?"

"Just think about it for a minute. Who spends a couple of hours at a bar where he can be seen by all kinds of people, gets friendly with his waitress, leaves the bar with her when she finishes her shift, and then brutally murders her?"

"Yeah, not smart. Not smart at all," his partner agreed.

CHAPTER SIX

The following day, Harry poked his head into Chris's office. "Looks like we caught another break."

Chris glanced up. "Yeah?"

"I did a little checking this morning. The day before the murder, Benny Sykes pulled a driver over for running a stop sign at Fifth and Columbia. The guy was in an old Buick with expired tags. The description of the guy matches our suspect. The driver was even wearing a navy blue wool cap. He told Benny his name was George Maybrick. No driver's license, but he had a Merchant Marine credential."

"What the hell is that?"

"An official merchant seaman's ID card," Harry explained.

"What about the car?

"He told Benny it was his mother's car, and that checked out. The car is registered to a Vera Maybrick."

"Got an address?" Chris asked.

"I tracked her down through public records. She resides at Riverview Assisted Living, that nursing home just outside of town on the bluffs. She's been there a year and a half."

"What do you say we go pay Mrs. Maybrick visit?" Chris suggested.

On the drive over, they talked about how they would approach the elderly woman.

"Leave the questions to me," Chris insisted.

"Fine. What are you going to do, ask the old lady if her son murders cocktail waitresses?" Harry replied sarcastically.

"And that's exactly why I'm going to ask the questions, you moron."

When they arrived at the nursing home they presented their badges at the front desk and asked for Vera Maybrick's room number. "We are working on an investigation and just need to ask Ms. Maybrick couple of questions," Chris explained with a smile.

"Her health is quite poor. She's in a very fragile state. Please try not to agitate her," the nurse instructed. "You'll find her in room 106, three doors down on the left."

Rapping very gently on the door, they opened it after hearing someone call, "Come in."

A very elderly lady was sitting in a wheelchair gazing out the window.

"Mrs. Maybrick?" Chris said.

"Yes," the elderly woman replied in a strong voice that belied her frail appearance.

"How are you today, ma'am?" Harry inquired.

"Fine. It's a beautiful day, considering we're getting into December," she responded, nodding toward the window.

Chris introduced himself and his partner, explaining they were detectives with the Hightower police department.

"Oh my, is something wrong?"

"No, not at all, ma'am. We just need to ask you a couple of questions."

"Sure, as long as nothing's wrong."

"Detective Caulfield and I are following up on a ticket issued to a car that is registered to you. Do you own a 2005 emerald green Buick LaSabre?"

"Yes. Or at least I used to. I gave it to my daughter after I moved here to Riverview. I don't have much use for a car these days. Heidi hasn't been in an accident, has she?" the old woman asked anxiously.

"No, no accident, ma'am. We're just trying to find the driver of the car," Chris reassured her.

"Maybe it was your daughter's husband who was driving?" Harry suggested fishing for information.

"No, I'm afraid her ex-husband left her years ago and lives in another state. It was probably George."

"George?" Chris asked, eyeing the woman carefully for her response.

"Yes. My son. He's in town for a couple of weeks."

Chris could see that the elderly woman was becoming agitated. "Nothing to worry about, Mrs. Maybrick. Can you tell us a little about your son?"

"There's a problem isn't there? I need to call Heidi."

"No ma'am, there's no problem," Chris replied quickly, trying to reassure her. He started perspiring over the unease he felt from upsetting the sickly woman, and even more over the guilt he felt from deceiving her. "Mrs. Maybrick, we think George might be a very important witness to something that happened, and we'd really like to talk to him."

"A witness?"

"Yes, he might have seen something and may not even realize it."

"Oh, I see," Mrs. Maybrick said smiling slightly. "You think he might be able to help you in your investigation."

"Exactly," Harry reassured her.

"You know, George can probably help you. He's terribly observant, you know."

"How's that ma'am?" Chris asked.

"He is very artistic. That's one of his paintings over there," she said, pointing to a nicely framed canvas on the wall by her bed. "Isn't it beautiful? That's how the river looked nearly thirty years ago. It's George's first painting. He did it the day after Christmas when he was only nine years old."

"It's wonderful," Harry responded. "Doesn't look like a kid's painting at all."

Chris didn't know much about art, but he found the woman's story hard to believe given the caliber of the artwork. Hardly the work of a child, he thought.

"You have a good eye, Detective. My George has a gift. He never took a single lesson, but he got a scholarship to one of those fancy art schools in New York when he graduated from high school. Can you imagine that? A full scholarship. His father always told him couldn't make a living as an artist and tried to talk him out of going, but George went anyway. Only stayed one semester, though. I was so sorry, but he didn't really like the big city. Then my husband died in a terrible accident and George came home and worked on the towboats for a year or so. Unfortunately, by then the boat business was already dying. One day he told me he had signed a contract to work a boat down to New Orleans. He ended up becoming a merchant seaman and took off to see the world. He's been doing it for over fifteen years."

"Do you know where your son is now?"

"Well, not for sure. George is a good boy. He visits me every day when he comes to Hightower, but he's not here much. He shows up once every twelve to eighteen months. He works the big tankers and cargo ships, sailing all over the world," she said and pointed to a straw basket on the nightstand filled with postcards from her son. "This week is the first time he's been home since my stroke. He's such a good son. When he's in town he comes to see me every day," she repeated. "George will be sorry he missed you. He was just here about an hour ago."

"Do you know where George is now?" Harry asked again.

"He might be at Heidi's. She's my daughter, George's older sister. She and her two boys moved into my old house when her husband left her. My son doesn't have a place of his own because, like I said, he's not in town very much. You could try Heidi's. You say he might have seen something very important that could help you with your case?"

"Yes ma'am." Chris nodded.

"Well, try my daughter's place. I'll write the address down for you," she said, pointing to a pen and paper on a small desk across the room.

"Your daughter's name again please, Mrs. Maybrick?"

"Heidi Carson."

"Does anyone else reside at the house with her?" he asked and handed her the pen and paper.

"No, she lives alone, except when George is in town. She raised two sons all by herself, but they're grown now and have moved away. Her good-for-nothing husband cheated on her and left her to raise those boys while he ran off and married some woman in Kansas City. My daughter and grandsons hardly ever heard a word from him again. Could be dead for all I know." She sighed and handed Chris the address. "I don't think Heidi ever stopped loving him. I kept telling her he wasn't worth it. She never remarried. Worked double shifts as a nurse's aide at the hospital to give my grandsons a decent life. My husband and I helped as best we could, but we didn't have much. When Walter died, it was just Heidi, the boys, and me. George would sometimes wire Heidi and the boys money from overseas to help out."

"I see," Chris said quietly, not sure quite how to respond. "Well, we really appreciate you meeting with us, Mrs. Maybrick. You take care of yourself and thank you for your time."

"I hope you have a blessed day, Detectives.

CHAPTER SEVEN

Heidi Carson opened her front door and panicked as soon as Chris and Harry introduced themselves as police officers. "Look, I can explain about the car. I never realized the tags had expired. My mother had a stroke and gave me the car. I just assumed the registration would be good for a while. I would never have driven the vehicle otherwise. I had no idea George had no driver's license. He told me the policeman gave him a ticket for running the stop sign and driving without a license, and a warning for the expired tags. My brother is going to pay for the tickets before he leaves town, and he'll lend me the money to get the tags renewed." Pausing to catch her breath she must have read the confusion on their faces. "Oh. You're not here about the car, are you."

"No, Ms. Carson, we're not," Harry said.

"Then why are you here?"

"We're looking for your brother."

"Has he done something wrong?"

"We just need to ask him some questions."

"I don't think he's here right now. He left this morning to go visit our mother and he's not back yet. What's all this about?" she asked nervously.

"You mean you don't know if he's at home?"

"No. He doesn't live in the house when he visits. He stays in the old cottage in the back. He's not here much. George is a merchant seaman and most of the time he's away working cargo freighters and oil tankers."

"Yes. We know."

"How?"

"Your mother told us," Chris replied.

"My mother!" she exclaimed.

"Yes, we went to see her this morning. We traced her through the plates on the car. She told us where you live and that we could find your brother here."

"You didn't upset her, did you? She's very ill!"

Chris and Harry could see the concerned expression on her face. "No, not at all," Chris assured her. "We told her that George might have witnessed something and we needed to talk to him. Do you mind if we check to see if he's here?"

"If the car isn't parked in the drive, he's still out." Nevertheless, she led them around the back of the house to a ramshackle cottage. The small red brick cottage, desperately in need of a coat of paint, had been a garage many years ago. The converted building badly needed fixing.

Chris was taken aback by its state of disrepair. "Is this where your brother stays when he comes to visit?"

"Yes. Why do you ask?"

"I would think the house would be a lot more comfortable."

"Let's just say my poor brother has terrible sleep issues and prefers staying here when he visits and leave it at that."

Ms. Carson's vague explanation only made Chris more curious, but he decided not to pursue the issue. Despite no green Buick in sight, he asked if they could knock on the door just in case."

Ms. Carson was becoming quite nervous and agitated. She kept trying to pin them down for more specifics, but they remained circumspect.

"Mind if we take a look around inside?" Chris asked as he turned the knob on the cottage door.

"Just what is it you're looking for, Detective?"

"Anything that might help us identify a murder victim," he answered, trying to provide as little information as possible.

"Murder! Is my brother dead?" she cried.

"No! Sorry, I didn't mean—"

"And he is no killer!" she said with wide eyes.

"I didn't say that Ms. Carson," he replied, trying to calm her down.

"Wait. Is this about that murder last week over in Windwood?"

"Afraid so, ma'am," Harry replied.

"Detectives, my brother has had his share of problems, but he's no murderer. I can promise you that."

Chris held up a hand. "We're not accusing him of anything. We just want to talk to him as a witness. He may have been one of the last people to see the victim alive. Would you mind if we took a look in the cottage?"

"Don't you need a search warrant or something?"

"We can do it with your permission. But if you feel like your brother might be hiding something, well, then…"

"What could he possibly be hiding?" she said indignantly.

"Probably nothing, but we'd like to be sure by checking inside the cottage."

She stepped in front of the door. "I think you'd better leave now, and don't come back unless you have a search warrant."

"Very well, Ms. Carson. I'll be back in a couple of hours with a warrant. Detective Caulfield will stay here in case your brother shows up. He'll make sure nothing is disturbed in the cottage."

"Look, I'll be honest," she said after a hesitation. "The only time I ever go in there is to clean before George visits, which isn't very often. The last time he visited was July last year. Once we didn't see him for over two years. Sometimes I'll use the place for storage. My brother's hobby is painting, and he's quite good. He leaves most of his books and some art supplies here—an easel and such. He takes his other belongings with him. Go on in if you're going to get a warrant anyway but try not to disturb his things. I don't want my brother to know I let you in. He could be back any time now."

"Thank you, Ms. Carson. We shouldn't be too long," Chris assured her.

Entering through a side door, Chris noticed that all the lights were on. A wall of stale air—a concoction of nicotine and linseed oil—immediately invaded his nostrils. Art materials and several partially painted canvases in an impressionist style were strewn about. Near the lone window stood a heavy wooden painter's easel with a Monet-like seascape, nearly completed, that might easily have hung in a high-end New York City gallery. Hundreds and hundreds of books were stacked several feet high along two walls.

"Must like to read," Harry muttered.

A small paint-splattered dining table with two wobbly chairs contained several well-used sketch pads and an open carton of foreign cigarettes. Chris didn't recognize the brand on the blue carton. He looked at it carefully. "Cyrillic alphabet, probably Russian-made cigarettes, would be my guess," he told Harry.

Two bone china bowls, one flecked with dried oatmeal and the other the final resting place for countless cigarette butts, sat on the table in front of one of the chairs.

"Some breakfast," Harry joked, but neither Chris nor Ms. Carson laughed.

A large coffee-stained mug stenciled with National Line rested on a tattered copy of *18 Poems* by Dylan Thomas.

As they explored the tiny living quarters, it was clear to Chris that Heidi Carson was as curious as they were and seemed completely unfamiliar with what took place in the cottage while George lived there. Beyond the dust and clutter, nothing seemed out of the ordinary.

Harry lifted the mattress slightly and began running his hand under the edge. When his fingers hit an object tucked between the mattress and box spring, he lifted the bedding and retrieved a thick sketch pad. "Let's see what we have here," he announced, clearly pleased with himself as he glanced at Chris to see his reaction.

Chris and Ms. Carson immediately walked over and stood on either side of him to look. As Harry began paging through the hefty sketchbook, the drawings prompted an expression of horror on Ms. Carson's face. "Oh my God," she cried. "This can't be George's. He would never draw such awful things. All his art is beautiful...just look around!"

Chris's mind flashed back to the grisly murder scene from the previous week and felt an instant replay of the same sense of dread.

The well-worn sketch pad contained several dozen graphite pencil sketches. Viewed in order, each one was more violent than the other. Some of the initial sketches portrayed women bound and gagged, the artist taking great care to render the fear in their faces with striking detail. Further in, the drawings revealed women who had been brutally murdered, mostly from multiple stab wounds. The last half dozen images were reminiscent of the scene Chris and Harry had witnessed in the abandoned house in Windwood. Each sketch depicted a female victim, her throat cut, and disemboweled with the organs strewn about. In some, the faces had been lacerated nearly beyond recognition.

Chris couldn't imagine such brutality rendered so graphically using only a pencil and paper.

It was the last drawing that proved to be the most disturbing. A badly mutilated corpse lay face-up on a bed. All of her facial features had been cut away. Parts of the body had been skinned to the bone, and the internal organs lay strewn about. A light source in the corner of the drawing illumined the brutal scene, outlining the dark silhouette of the killer who stood gazing upon the results of his ghastly work. A knife with a long blade protruded from the clenched fist of the killer's left hand.

As they quickly stepped up their search for more evidence, the killer's sister sat sobbing at the small dining table. "Oh my God! This can't be George," she kept repeating.

But other than a few clothes scattered about and a couple more cartons of foreign cigarettes, nothing else seemed out of place.

"Ms. Carson, we really need to find your brother," Chris said gravely.

"I don't know where he is."

"Has he said anything about leaving town?"

"No. In fact, he said he wouldn't be leaving for New Orleans until after he saw the boys. I have two sons, and every time he visits, he brings them gifts from the places where he's traveled. They aren't really all that close because they haven't spent much time together, but the boys are grateful and make it a point to come see their Uncle George whenever he comes to town. They're due in this weekend." She started crying again.

"Can I call anyone for you, to help?" Chris asked sympathetically.

"No, I'll be all right. It's just that..." The sound of a car pulling up interrupted the sobbing woman.

Chris pushed aside the nicotine-stained curtain on the window slightly. "He's headed this way."

Seeing strangers in his apartment caught Maybrick off guard. He stopped walking immediately, looked over his shoulder briefly as if contemplating making a run for it, but then walked up to the cottage, slowly pushed open the door, and hesitantly walked in.

"Heidi, what's going on? Why are these men here?"

She replied by sobbing even louder.

"George Maybrick?" Chris asked.

"Yes."

"I'm Detective Chris Stanford and this is Detective Harry Caulfield. We're from the Hightower Police Department. We need you to come down to the station and answer some questions about a homicide over in Windwood last week."

"Am I under arrest?"

"No, but I can certainly get a warrant for your arrest if that's what it takes to get you down to the station," Chris replied matter-of-factly.

"No need, Detective. Let me just get a pack of cigarettes and I'll go with you." Maybrick turned to his sister. "Heidi?" he began, but she continued sobbing and he fell silent.

"Detective Caulfield, please escort Mr. Maybrick to the car."

"Yeah," his partner replied.

"And call the station and get an officer assigned to guard the cottage until we can get a warrant for forensics to check out the rest of the place."

Chris turned to the sister. "Ms. Carson, I'm sorry about this. I know it must all come as a terrible shock to you. But I'll have to ask you to leave the cottage for now. A uniformed officer will be here shortly. He'll be posted outside and won't let anyone in until we get a search warrant and a crime scene unit has given the place a good going over. I hope you understand."

The woman nodded, murmuring a faint, "Yes, of course," as he accompanied her to the main house. She paused. "Detective Stanford, please don't tell my mother about any of this. She's not well and loves my brother dearly. This would surely kill her."

"I understand, Ms. Carson. We'll do everything we can to keep your mother out of it."

CHAPTER EIGHT

"Where's the suspect, Wilkes?" Chris asked the desk sergeant when he got to the station the next morning after a long night at the cottage.

"Downstairs Chris," the sergeant replied between gulps of black coffee.

"Why downstairs?"

"We had to move him to the old spare holding cell in the basement last night."

"Why the hell did you do that?"

"Nobody could take it anymore. The guy's got some major sleep issues. He screamed like a goddam banshee half the night."

"What do you mean, screamed?"

"He's got some serious bad dreams going on. It started around twelve thirty last night. He was scaring everybody to death. Pete Finster was working the night desk and woke the guy up three times to try to get him to stop screaming. But he kept having nightmares. The guys in the cell next to his couldn't take it and complained loudly. Pete said it was the freakiest thing he had ever experienced. Every time he woke the guy up, he was so agitated and frightened that it even scared Pete. Yeah, Special Forces, three tours in Iraq and Afghanistan, he ain't scared of nothin'. Except this weirdo."

"How long did this go on for?"

"According to Pete, about two and a half or three hours. They finally moved him downstairs around three thirty in the morning, and that's where he's staying. Even Chief Monroe agrees."

"Anybody look in on him this morning?"

"Yeah, he seemed okay when they brought him breakfast."

The echo of Chris's footsteps bounced between the thick concrete walls of the stairwell. With the decline in the town's fortunes, the basement of the police station had morphed into a storage area, and the extra cell built when Hightower was a thriving town hadn't been used in years. Chris's first office when he made detective had also been downstairs. He glanced in as he walked by. It contained nothing but boxes stuffed with documents no one would ever read and several olive-green army surplus filing cabinets.

But there on his original desk, instead of a computer and a phone stood several trophies. Relics from the days when the Hightower PD boasted a softball team, the trophies now stood idly on the old desk, dusty, tarnished reminders of better times. A pretty good athlete in his day, Chris glanced at the largest of the trophies, grinning as he recalled a hot, muggy day in July when, as a twenty-something patrol officer, he'd hit a triple that won the game and delivered the Tri-County Softball League championship to the Hightower Police Department. The memory of his clutch hit brought an even bigger smile to his face.

He kept walking. He had nearly forgotten about the solitary cell downstairs that had been added for those occasions eons ago when multiple arrests on Friday and Saturday nights taxed the station's jail on the ground floor. As he approached the normally-abandoned cell, he found the prisoner resting on his back staring at the ceiling.

"What's going on, Mr. Maybrick?" he said conversationally.

"Nothing," the suspect responded in a fatigued voice as he went through a pattern of nervously clenching and unclenching his left fist.

"The sergeant told me you didn't sleep well last night."

"Last night. Hmm. I haven't had a good night's sleep in thirty-eight years," Maybrick replied in a tone of quiet resignation.

"Why not?"

"No idea."

"Do you want to call your lawyer, now?"

"I don't need a lawyer."

"Are you ready to talk?"

"Sure, but how about a smoke first?" Maybrick said.

"Sorry, there's no smoking in the building."

"Look. Slap some cuffs on my hands and feet and take me outside for a couple of cigarettes and I'll tell you whatever you want to know."

"Why the sudden change in attitude? Yesterday you wouldn't say a word."

"What about a smoke?" Maybrick repeated, ignoring Chris's question.

"It's against regulations. I could get into hot water with Chief Monroe."

"Please. I go through two and a half packs a day, and I haven't had a cigarette since yesterday. I promise I'll tell you whatever you want to know."

Chris reluctantly agreed but felt uncomfortable standing on the back steps of the Hightower police station watching a murder suspect in handcuffs smoking foreign cigarettes. He kept glancing nervously back into the building hoping his chief didn't see. Chris never smoked, but he could see that Maybrick relished each inhalation, taking each drag deep into his lungs as if he were storing it for later when his nicotine cravings came back.

"Thanks, detective. A whole day without a smoke. I haven't done that since I was twenty, and it was killing me. I can't thank you enough."

CHAPTER NINE

As they settled across the table from their suspect, Chris and Harry glanced briefly at one another and nodded.

Chris flipped on the video recorder and began. "You're entitled to have an attorney present, Mr. Maybrick. If you can't afford an attorney, one will be provided for you."

"I told you yesterday, I don't need a damn attorney," he replied.

Chris couldn't tell if his tone was one of anger or frustration. "Mr. Maybrick, I should tell you that you can certainly waive your rights and speak to Detective Caulfield and me without an attorney, but I don't recommend it."

The suspect clenched his jaw, his gray eyes rolling upward. For one final time, he appeared to weigh the risks and rewards of waiving his rights. For a brief instant, he patted his pocket as if feeling the urge to have a cigarette.

Anxious for a response, Chris sat motionless, the quiet whir of the video recorder and the clacking of a vintage ceiling fan directly overhead the only sounds in the room. Typically, black and white in his thinking, he felt ambivalent. He knew from experience that suspects who waived their rights usually yielded more information without the warnings and protestations of defense attorneys in the room. On the other hand, rights once waived sometimes yielded confessions that proved more vulnerable to legal challenges afterward.

"I don't want an attorney," Maybrick said emphatically.

"Are you sure?"

"I've never been surer of anything," the suspect replied.

"Very well, Mr. Maybrick. Detective Caulfield, could you go out and find us a witness?"

"What do you need a witness for?"

"Department regulations require that another witness or an officer not involved in the arrest be present when a suspect waives their rights," Chris explained.

Harry returned with a uniformed colleague a few minutes later. "Mr.

Maybrick, this is Officer Ken Johnson. He'll serve as an official witness to your rights waiver," Harry explained.

"George Maybrick, you have the right to remain silent," Chris began, then went through the legal litany. As he explained each of his rights, Maybrick replied in the affirmative. "Having these rights in mind, do you wish to talk to Detective Caulfield and me now?"

"Yes," the suspect answered.

They all signed a waiver-of-rights form, providing written confirmation of what Maybrick had verbally agreed to.

"You have a very interesting way of signing your name, Mr. Maybrick," Chris observed.

"Yeah, my handwriting is terrible. No one can hardly read it. Except me, of course."

"And your middle initial? What does the S stand for?"

"It's not an S, it's an L. My middle name is Lindfield, my mother's maiden name. My sister has the same middle name."

"Okay, Mr. Maybrick, we're going to ask you some questions now," Chris said. "If you cooperate with us in this investigation, it might help you if your case goes to trial. Do you understand?"

"Detective, I've done a lot of horrible things, but believe it or not, I've always been a man of my word. As I explained earlier, let me have a couple of smokes and I'll tell you whatever you want to know," Maybrick responded.

Chris saw a confused look on Harry's face. He started to say something, but Chris waved him off.

"How long have you been in Hightower?" Chris asked.

"A little over two weeks."

"And before that?"

"New York for several days. I've been out of the country since July last year. I worked on a tanker from the port in Houston to the Philippines. We had some hellacious weather. Had to layover in South Korea for three weeks having repairs made. Then I signed on in Manilla and worked a freighter all over the Far East and several ports in Africa. Another freighter took me on in Melbourne, and we did several turnarounds between Australia and Indonesia. I finally landed in the States in late October. After I blew through way too much money in New York, I caught a bus from the city to Hightower."

"A bus?" Harry asked. "Who rides a bus anymore?"

"I hate flying. I'd sooner weather a typhoon and a tidal wave on a junk in the South China Sea than get on a plane on a calm day."

"What did you do in New York?"

"I don't understand your question, detective?"

"Did you visit friends? Go to the museum? Catch a Broadway show? You tell me."

"I don't have any friends in New York. Quite frankly, I don't have any friends anywhere."

"Did you kill anybody there?" Harry asked matter-of-factly.

"Yes, I did," Maybrick said after a few moments of reflective silence.

"Did you say yes?" Chris queried, trying to hide his disbelief at the suspect's ready acknowledgment.

"I did," the suspect replied, "kill someone."

Maybrick's words caught them completely by surprise. Chris quickly tried to process the sudden unexpected confession. "Why don't you tell us about it," he suggested, trying to appear calm while his pulse raced a hundred miles an hour. He could not recall a time in his life when sixty minutes—thirty-six hundred fleeting seconds—felt like they would go on interminably, and yet the hour seemed to be over almost before it started. The surreal experience would be seared into his memory for the rest of his life.

The suspect related in grisly detail how he had murdered a prostitute in an abandoned warehouse off the docks near the Port of New York. They had met in a bar where he'd made sure she saw his wad of cash as he insisted on paying for each round of drinks. He'd promised her two hundred dollars if she would spend the remainder of the evening with him. "I could tell she was getting nervous when the cab dropped us off a couple of blocks from the old wharf. She said something about there being no hotels in the area. When we got to the warehouse she panicked and tried to run away, so I had to drag her inside. She screamed a couple of times, but there was no one around to hear her."

"Why did you choose that particular warehouse?"

"I'd checked it out a couple of days before. It was the perfect place—dark, abandoned, nothing around. I figured it would be a while before anyone found her, and by then I'd be long gone."

"Then what happened?" Harry prodded.

"I choked her till she started to pass out. I could see the fear in her eyes as she gasped for air. As soon as she fell to the ground, I slashed her throat. I knew she was still alive when I did it, but she had passed out from asphyxiation."

"What kind of weapon did you use?" Chris asked.

"A knife I bought years ago in London. It's an antique, actually, a Victorian-era postmortem knife well over a hundred and twenty-five years old. It's razor sharp and will cut through leather like it was a piece of paper."

"Why an old knife?" Harry asked.

"Several years ago, in London while walking through the Portobello Road Market in Notting Hill I ran into a dealer who collected and sold antique medical instruments. He specialized in Victorian medical collectibles. Everything he had was expensive. But I saw an old wooden box with a small sign on it. *Authentic Vintage Surgical Instruments CHEAP. Everything guaranteed to be at least a hundred years old.*

He told me it was stuff in poor condition or that had originally belonged to a set of surgical instruments but weren't nearly as valuable without the rest of the original pieces and cases. A knife in the box caught my attention. It turned out to be part of a set of postmortem surgical instruments made in the eighteen seventies. You could still make out the name of the company that made it. Louis Blaise and Co. The shop owner showed me a full set of instruments in their original wooden case that contained the very same knife." Maybrick looked pleased at the memory.

"Did you use that knife to kill anyone else, Mr. Maybrick?"

"I didn't buy the knife to kill anyone, Detective. I just bought it because I thought it was interesting. It sat hidden in the bottom of my seaman's bag for five years before I used it."

"I see. Can you tell us where you were Thanksgiving Day and early Friday morning?" Chris asked, wanting to shift the focus of the interrogation off London and back to Hightower.

"I was at my sister's on Thanksgiving Day. We went to have Thanksgiving dinner in the afternoon with my mother at Riverview Assisted Living, the nursing home where she lives. Later that evening I went out for a drink."

"Where did you go?" Chris asked.

"A place called the Dock Lounge."

"Did you leave the bar with Donna Strickland, one of the waitresses, after the bar closed?" Maybrick asked.

"Yes. She explained that she didn't socialize with customers, but she said she found me interesting. I asked her if she wanted to have a beer when she got off work, and she said yes. To tell the truth, she was not the one I was looking for."

"No?"

"My victims are typically prostitutes."

"Why is that?"

"Two reasons. I don't like prostitutes, and their work makes them easy targets." At his words, there was a pronounced shift in his demeanor. His grey eyes reflected a kind of dark intensity, his jaw tightened, and his entire body seemed to be on edge.

Chris knew they had hit a raw nerve. He had to make a snap decision. Should he let the interrogation move in this new direction and possibly gain a better understanding of the psyche of a cold-blooded killer? Or redirect him back to the events of the previous Friday morning? Rarely had he faced such a perplexing dilemma in the interrogation room.

It only took a few seconds for Chris to go with his gut feeling. "Why Windwood?" But he anticipated Maybrick's answer before he had even finished the question.

"I always plan things meticulously. It's been that way from the beginning. I scout around and find a place that's off the beaten path and there's no one around. Once when I was home, my mother had lamented that the only people who hung around Windwood now were crack dealers and criminals. I'd sometimes played there as a kid. But lately the place has gotten so bad that nobody wants to go there. My sister told me there's talk of bulldozing the entire neighborhood. Perfect. I drove through Windwood a couple of days after I got into town. It didn't take me long to find an ideal spot, an abandoned house near the back of the neighborhood on Riverbend Drive. After that it was just a matter of finding my victim, and I'd have all the time in the world."

Maybrick recounted in excruciating detail how he took advantage of Donna Strickland's confidence, drove her to the abandoned neighborhood, and brutally murdered her. Normally suspicious and predisposed to doubt the veracity of anything he was told—particularly a confession coming from a suspect—Chris knew intuitively that this killer was telling the truth. And the details were frighteningly similar to the murder in New York City three weeks ago which he'd just confessed to committing. Chris's mind darted from one murder to the other, making comparisons and recording mental notes.

"Donna Strickland wasn't a prostitute. Why did you kill her?"

"I can't really answer that. Crime of opportunity, maybe? We seemed to get along well in the bar, and she went with me very willingly."

"Did you know you were going to kill her when the two of you left the bar?" Harry asked.

"Yes."

"But you can't tell us why you killed her?"

"I've already told you I really don't know. Somehow, I feel like I'm getting revenge, but I have no idea where that feeling comes from."

"Did you write something in the victim's blood at the crime scene in Windwood?" Chris queried.

"Yes. *From Hell.*"

"Had you done that before?"

"Not until the murder in New York City."

"What did you write there?" Harry asked.

"*Catch me when you can.*"

"Why write in the victim's blood at the scene of the crime, Mr. Maybrick?"

"I have nightmares. That's why I'm in that shithole of a cell all by myself downstairs. In some of my nightmares I do horrible things."

"Like brutally murdering women?"

"Yes, Detective, like murdering women. In one of my dreams, I commit a horrific murder, similar to the one I committed in New York City. After I've carved her up pretty badly in my dream, I take a makeup brush from her purse and scrawl *From Hell* in the victim's blood on the wall above the body. I can't explain why, but I can tell you the impetus for doing so came from my recurring dream."

"So, you made your dream literally come true, Mr. Maybrick?"

"I guess you could say that."

The interrogation room fell silent for several moments as Chris wrestled with the language of the murderer's disturbing message. He'd felt that recurring sense of dread settle over the interrogation room as the back-to-back confessions unfolded. Glancing over at his partner, he knew that Harry's experience mirrored his.

Meanwhile, the killer offered up little more than a blank stare. Chris summoned up the courage to look directly into his eyes. He wasn't sure what he hoped to discover. He found the exercise both discomfiting and futile. And for a brief moment there was nothing he would not have bartered, perhaps even his own soul, to peer into Maybrick's mind to see what he was thinking and feeling.

Except he knew a sociopath felt nothing.

"What about the other message, Mr. Maybrick?" Chris asked, hoping the quiver in his voice went undetected.

Breaking the silence banished the suspect's blank stare and forced his attention back to the interrogation. "What?"

"Can you tell us why you wrote *From Hell* at the house in Windwood?"

"Can't say for sure. It certainly wasn't something I'd planned. I'd grown weary of killing and still hadn't been caught. At some level, I think I wrote that message to taunt the police. Make you angry, push you to use every ounce of energy and skill you have to catch me. I don't know if that makes sense or not, but it's the best I can determine. I'd never killed anyone in Hightower before. It always seemed too risky. Maybe that's the reason I did it this time, committing one last murder in Hightower with no freighter or tanker as a means to escape, so I'd get caught."

"Are there other victims besides the two you've mentioned?"

"Yes."

"So, you go out and find an innocent victim, kill her, and butcher her beyond recognition so you can get caught," Harry reviewed angrily.

"I can't talk anymore," Maybrick said. "Maybe tomorrow. At least you know that I killed those two women."

"Fair enough, Mr. Maybrick," Chris said. "I have just one more question for today. You said you can't tell us why you killed those women in cold blood. Something inside of you drove you to do it. Are you saying you had no control over your actions?"

"No, Detective. I knew exactly what I was doing. Something inside me pushed me to kill them, but I didn't have to do it. I could have chosen not to. I could have stopped myself."

"Why didn't you?"

He shook his head. "I don't know. The brutal reality of our conversation and the honesty with which I've answered your questions is completely shocking, even to me. I've often grappled with my shadow side in my conscience, but I've never spoken to another human being about my terrible dreams, let alone my crimes." Maybrick buried his face in his hands. "I just don't know, but there's more."

CHAPTER TEN

Chris sat quietly next to Harry, both trying to process Maybrick's confession.

Finally, Harry broke the silence. "That's one sick bastard."

"Never heard anything like it," Chris said, nodding in agreement.

"Do you believe him?"

"I do."

"Do you think there are other victims out there?"

"Yeah, you can bet on it."

"Think he'll come clean about them?"

"I don't know. We're in way over our heads with this guy."

"Still. We've got enough to fry him already," Harry said.

"Maybe."

"No?"

"I can't quite put my finger on it. He just doesn't strike me as the sadistic killer type."

"You gotta be kidding me," Harry said incredulously. "That guy carved up Donna Strickland like he was field dressing a goddamn deer."

"I know. I know. But something doesn't add up for me."

"Chris, you're a detective. Don't try to play armchair psychologist. You're overthinking this one, pal. Sadistic or not, the guy is a cold-blooded killer, and when he gets what's coming to him the world is going to be a better place."

"Yeah, you're right," Chris conceded.

"Should I give the NYPD a heads up?"

"Not just yet. Let's see what our killer has to say tomorrow first."

"Isn't that like withholding evidence?"

"One day's not going to make a difference either way. We've got the killer locked up. And at this point, it's not as if we're putting anyone in danger."

Twenty-four hours later Chris found himself standing in front of the basement cell. "I'm dying for a cigarette, Detective Stanford," Maybrick pleaded, his arms and hands extended in anticipation of being handcuffed.

"Yeah, fine. But we need to hurry. Chief Monroe's going to be here any minute." Chris looked at his watch anxiously. "He'll ream my ass if he catches us."

With no sun in sight and a cold December wind blowing in from a westerly direction, there was nothing on the back side of the police station to provide any protection when they got outside.

"I'm not used to this damn weather," the killer grumbled. He folded his arms close to his body for warmth, a cigarette dangling from his lips. "I haven't been home in December for six years. I'd forgotten how cold it gets here in the winter."

Chris kept his hands buried in his armpits as he listened to Maybrick's complaints, waiting for an opening to run an idea by him. As the prisoner ground his cigarette butt underfoot, an image of him doing the same thing at the scene of the murder popped into Chris's mind. "Ready for another?" he offered, shaking off the haunting image lurking in his consciousness.

"Thanks. I can't remember when a smoke tasted so good." Maybrick took a deep drag and held the smoke in his lungs for a few seconds before exhaling.

"Mr. Maybrick, I want to ask you about something. If you don't like the idea, just be honest with me. How would you feel about someone else joining us in the interrogation room today?"

"Another cop?"

"No, a doctor."

"A shrink, I'm guessing?"

"Yes, a psychiatrist," Chris replied.

"You think I'm crazy?"

"I didn't say that," Chris shot back.

"But that's what you're thinking. Isn't it? Well, the answer is no."

CHAPTER ELEVEN

As soon as the witnessing officer added his signature to the document acknowledging Maybrick's waiver of his rights, Chris, anxious to begin, hit the video recorder button and launched into the interrogation. He stifled his disappointment over Maybrick's threat to remain silent if anyone other than Chris, Harry, and the witness participated in the interrogation.

"Mr. Maybrick, yesterday you told Detective Caulfield and me that you killed a prostitute in New York last month and Donna Strickland last week. You intimated that there might be other victims. Were there others?"

A long silence hung in the air. Maybrick lowered his head, resting his chin on his chest.

Chris broke the silence. "Were there others, Mr. Maybrick?"

The prisoner sat quietly, remaining unresponsive.

"Have you killed anyone else?" Chris asked a third time.

Harry reached over and touched his arm as if to tell him not to press the question. "Okay, Mr. Maybrick," Harry said, "let me ask you about Donna Strickland instead. Why did you cut out her heart?"

"It was something different. I had never done that, but I had certainly thought about it before with some of the other women I've killed. I can't really explain it, only to say that it seemed to make the murder more powerful. I imagined how the medical examiner might react when they tried to put the victim's body back together and was missing a part."

"What did you do with the heart?" Harry asked.

"It's gone."

"Gone where?"

"In the river," the killer answered smugly.

"You threw the victim's heart into the river," Harry repeated with brows hiked.

"Yes," Maybrick responded.

After a moment, Chris said, "So, you thought about removing the heart of some of your other victims. The woman in New York maybe?" He wanted to get Maybrick to talk about some of his other victims.

But the killer just sat quietly for several minutes, eyes downcast.

Unable to stand it any longer, Harry blurted out angrily, "How many women have you killed, you bastard?"

Maybrick continued to sit in silence.

"Okay, I think we're done for today," Chris said. "Detective Caulfield, please have the prisoner taken back to his cell downstairs."

"No wait!" Maybrick said loudly. "I want to finally get everything off my chest."

"Then how many women have you killed?" Harry demanded.

Chris focused every ounce of his mental energy watching the suspect—his body language, facial expression, vocal tone—for any clue that might explain his mental state. Although he didn't know what he should be looking for. At times the confessed killer seemed dispassionate, at others genuinely sad and remorseful. Chris wondered if anger or rage had fueled Maybrick to brutally murder and butcher his victims, but at that moment he showed no sign of anger. Chris surmised that something hidden inside Maybrick, something dark that he could not comprehend, was trying to escape from deep within the wilderness of his subconscious, but the killer seemed incapable of bringing it to the surface.

Then Maybrick began to speak in a subdued voice. "I can't say for sure. It's been going on for a while."

"How long?" Chris asked.

"Seven or eight years."

"How many women?"

"Maybe half a dozen before I came back to the States this time."

"That's bullshit!" Harry declared. "If you'd been killing women in this way for eight years, we'd have heard about it by now on the news."

"Ah, but you haven't killed anyone here in the States before now, have you, Mr. Maybrick," Chris stated with certainty. It suddenly all made sense. A merchant seaman traveling all over the world could kill at random, disappear, and not be seen again for months, maybe years, before he returned to the scene of the crime. If ever.

Once again Maybrick looked smug. "You can't catch a killer if he's nowhere to be found, Detective."

"You haven't killed in this country before now?" Chris repeated.

"No. In different ports around the world, but never here. Not until New York."

"All right. I'd like you to think about when and where you killed your first victim. Let's start there. Okay?" Chris prompted.

Maybrick closed his eyes. "I remember the first one very well. It took a long time for it to happen. I'd had thoughts...fantasies, about killing for as long as I can remember, but I'd never acted on them. I told you that some of my recurring nightmares are about me committing brutal murders. Unfortunately, working on the ships was like the perfect storm. In the maritime industry, time is money. Unless a ship puts in for repairs, you're never in port for very long. Ships unload and leave as quickly as possible, especially the oil tankers. They never pick up other cargo. I would wait until the last night the ship was in port to kill my victims. The next day I was gone."

"Tell us about your first victim."

"A prostitute in Amsterdam. I avoided the red-light district, too many people. I always kill in the same way. I choke them till they nearly pass out, then cut their throats. That first one was too easy. Though it hadn't been my intention to actually kill anybody. I just enjoyed making plans, setting everything up. I found an abandoned building down by the West Harbour of the Amsterdam port wharves. The last night in port, some of the crew had invited me to go with them down to the De Wallen, the famous red-light district, but I went out by myself instead. I had just eaten at an Indian restaurant and was headed back to the ship when a woman approached me. I could tell she was a prostitute. At first, she didn't want to go with me anywhere but her place. But I guess she really needed the money. You know the rest."

"Did you use your knife on her?" Harry asked.

"Yes, cut her up pretty badly, but not like the others later on."

"Why kill her, Mr. Maybrick?"

"You keep asking me that question, and I keep telling you that I can't really explain the compulsion. You found the sketch pad at my sister's. For a long time, that was how I channeled the feelings. I spent so much time thinking and dreaming about killing a woman that I drew pictures of it. It was how I dealt with my anger and urge to kill. I had all these horrible dreams about killing. Who the hell knows where they come from? Then I started planning, but I never imagined I would actually carry out my plans. And then one day I just kind of snapped. I started bringing my sketches to life. It made so much sense in my mind. The drawings then became rehearsals for the real thing. I suppose in some respects my art, something that I truly love, betrayed me. Instead of helping me work through my urge to kill, the drawings became studies for a canvas that I would eventually paint in living blood."

"Did you enjoy taking your victims' lives?" Chris asked.

"Enjoy is not a word I would use. Well...I'm not sure. Maybe in a way I did. But mostly I felt a sense of retribution and relief at the same time."

"Can you explain what you mean by that?" Chris asked.

"It's like I told you yesterday, Detective. I have this animus, this intense anger, that lives inside of me. I have no idea where it comes from."

"Did you ever sexually assault your victims?"

"No, never. It was never sexual."

"And yet, weren't all of your victims prostitutes?" Harry asked.

"Mostly, but not all of them. A couple were strippers, one in Bangkok as I recall. I think most were prostitutes, but I can't say for sure. They all were more than willing to take a walk with me when I flashed some cash."

"If not sex, was there another reason you targeted prostitutes?" Chris asked.

"You asked that question yesterday. It's like I told you. I don't like prostitutes and they are easy targets."

"Do you remember your second victim?" Harry asked.

"Yes. It was about 14 months later in Osaka. I was working on a supertanker. It took several days to unload the oil. I picked up a girl in a dive the night before the tanker left port. The place had a funny name...the Below Sea Level Bar, I think. I'd spent three days scouting the area near the port looking for an abandoned building. I couldn't find one. So, I ended up killing her right on the street. Then I disemboweled her and scattered her organs near her. It was about three in the morning and no one was around. I couldn't believe I had gotten away with it. After that, I got braver. I would try to find an old abandoned building, but if I didn't, I'd simply kill my victim late at night on a dark street where there wasn't anybody around."

"Are you saying you cut up a woman right on the street?" Harry asked in disbelief.

"Yes. I'm sure you can find something about it in the papers, though it was a while ago."

"The medical examiner's report on Donna Strickland suggests that the person who killed her might have some medical background. He appeared to know what he was doing—knowledge of the organs, and where to cut. How did you become so adept at using a knife?" Chris asked.

"I don't know. I got pretty good at using a knife working at sea, but it has more to do with human anatomy than skill with a knife. I'm an artist. You can't draw what you don't understand. It's impossible to render the human form with any accuracy without knowing every muscle, bone, and organ in the body. I've studied anatomy for years. As an art student in New York, I even took a class in it. We sketched the human body inside and out for an entire semester. I could illustrate a medical textbook if I had to." He reached for Harry. "Detective Caulfield, please give me your hand."

Harry hesitated for a long moment pondering the request.

"Don't worry. I'm not going to hurt you," Maybrick assured him.

"All right." Harry placed his hand palm up in Maybrick's.

Despite working for years as a merchant marine, the killer's hands looked delicate to Chris, even with their callouses. Each of the long fingers was tipped by clean, carefully filed nails. Hardly the hands of a brutal serial killer. Still. Appearances were often deceiving.

"There are twenty-seven bones, thirty-four muscles, and over a hundred ligaments and tendons in the human hand," Maybrick said, and for several minutes he gave an impromptu lecture on the complexities of the human hand, including a disturbing sidebar on how to render a thumb or finger useless with a calculated slice of a tendon, pointing things out on Harry's hand. Then he moved Harry's index finger to just below his right ear. "This is the carotid artery. If I start cutting here, I can sever your artery, your windpipe, and half of your neck muscles. With enough force and a very sharp blade, I can reach your vertebrae. Death is nearly instantaneous."

Harry jerked his hand back.

"That's enough for now," Chris announced.

He was emotionally drained. The last ninety minutes with the confessed murderer felt like the longest hour-and-a-half interrogation he'd ever endured. Nothing in his experience—cop or not—had prepared him for these disturbing encounters with George Lindfield Maybrick. When an officer came to take Maybrick back to his cell, at the door he turned, looked over his shoulder, and said, "Detectives, from now on, I'd like you to call me George."

The two detectives just stared at him.

"Seriously?" muttered Chris.

"Totally over the top," Harry agreed.

"Jesus," Chris said. "And I thought we were in way over our heads before."

"Yeah. Can't wait to see what tomorrow brings," Harry said, shaking his head.

"Don't know about you, but I've still got more questions than answers," Chris said.

Over the next three days of interrogation, Maybrick confessed to killing several more women. He insisted he couldn't remember exactly how many in all, but he was able to remember murdering victims in four other port cities. The MO was nearly always the same. The only difference was that each murder was grislier than the previous one. He had never killed anyone in the States until New York City, or even in the same port city, which explained why he had managed to elude capture.

"Do you think Maybrick's insane?" Harry asked after the final interrogation.

"I don't know Harry," Chris replied. "Maybe. But—"

And then it hit him.

CHAPTER TWELVE

"I was wondering when you were going to reach out to me, Detective."

Chris tilted his head smiling at the man sitting in his uncomfortable wooden visitor's chair, Dr. Richard Crane, a psychiatrist and the Director of Percy County Mental Health Services.

"Why would you think that?" Chris said with a smile, feigning ignorance.

The Hightower PD could barely keep its patrol cars running, let alone afford a forensic psychologist on staff. When the need arose, they called on Dr. Crane. The erudite, impeccably dressed psychiatrist had a deep interest in forensic psychology. And it didn't hurt that no attorney or dissenting expert witness had ever successfully challenged him on the witness stand.

"I don't live in Hightower, but I can read a newspaper," Crane said with a raised brow.

Chris grimaced. "It scares me to think you rely on information about our little town from the *Percyville Dispatch* or *Hightower Ledger*, Dr. Crane."

The psychiatrist laughed. He had consulted with the HPD on a number of occasions, and Chris shared a mutual respect with him...along with a dry sense of humor.

Chris waved a hand. "Besides, you cost too much. The last time HPD brought you in on a case, everyone including the chief had to give up days of paid vacation to cover your consultant's fee." He made a face. "Maybe if you didn't spend so damn much on your fancy suits we could afford you more often."

Crane grinned. "I keep telling you, Detective, dress for the job you want, not the job you've got." He scanned Chris's wardrobe with mock distaste. "Where did you get that tie? I keep telling you to stay out of thrift stores."

Chris snorted. "Very funny. I can tell you've been practicing your stand-up routines for the patients at the hospital. Talk about taking advantage of a captive audience."

"Good to see you again. It's been too long," Crane said, shaking his hand with a warm smile.

"I agree. I had every intention of calling you after my first chat with our kill—er, suspect. But I couldn't get him to agree. He told me in no uncertain terms that if I brought in a shrink he'd clam up and we'd never get anything else out of him. As you can see in the report, he had a lot to tell us, so I couldn't risk it. After five interrogation sessions with George Maybrick, I'm thinking this guy is way off the grid."

"What makes you think he'll talk to me now?"

"Nightmares."

"Nightmares?" Crane asked, confused.

"Maybrick has nightmares three or four nights a week. It's like nothing you've ever seen. They're so bad he screams and yells for hours. The first night in jail he scared the hell out of everyone—cops and inmates. After a few hours, they moved him downstairs to an old overflow cell in the basement."

"And what is it you think I can do?"

"I don't know...talk to him? Tell him you can help him get over his bad dreams. Maybe you can write him a script for something to help him sleep. If you can win his confidence, you might be able to get him talking and learn enough to be able to figure this guy out. I can't stonewall much longer. I think the Percy County DA is personally going to serve as the prosecutor, and he wants to get things rolling quickly. He's giving us another week or two, three max, before he starts moving on it. He'll shoot for first-degree murder. In Missouri, that means he's got to seek a grand jury first. I'm sure he's very confident of an indictment, given the evidence."

"Nice to know that the wheels of justice move quickly in our little corner of the world," Crane replied dryly. "Is Maybrick expecting me?"

"No," Chris said sheepishly. "If I told him you were coming, he might refuse to talk. Did you have a chance to go through my notes?"

"I read them last night,"

"Initial thoughts?"

"As a preliminary diagnosis, I'd guess he's probably a psychopath. Most serial killers are. I suspect trauma early in childhood, probably from within the family."

"Well, I'm not a psychiatrist, but I think you may be wrong, Dr. Crane. There's something...different about this guy. I can't put my finger on it, but he doesn't strike me as being a hardcore head case."

"But you just said he was off the grid."

"Yeah, but that doesn't mean I think he's nuts."

"Then what exactly did you mean?"

"Honestly? I'm not really sure. Why don't you talk to him and see what you think," Chris offered.

"All right. I must admit I'm curious." Crane winked. "And I've already spent a half hour talking to you. If I can get your suspect to talk for another hour, I'll rake in some real money off Hightower's finest." He grinned. "I'm officially on the clock."

CHAPTER THIRTEEN

Richard followed Detective Stanford down a poorly lit stairway to the basement cell where the prisoner was reclining on a neatly-made bunk.

"Good morning, Mr. Maybrick."

"Morning, Detective Stanford," Maybrick said glancing up.

The detective was right, he looked rough. Richard hadn't quite believed the severity of the nightmares, but he was revising his opinion.

"Tough night?" Stanford asked.

"Are you taking me out for a butt this morning?" the prisoner asked anxiously as he rose and walked quickly to the bars.

"It's ten degrees outside with the wind chill factor," Stanford said. "You don't wanna freeze your ass off for a lousy cigarette."

"Come on, Detective, you know I'm dyin' for a smoke," Maybrick whined in agitation.

"Sorry, I can't today. The chief's getting heat from all sides and he's running around the station raising hell with everyone. Maybe later."

"Son of a bitch," Maybrick muttered.

"Cheer up, I've got someone I want you to meet. Maybe talk to for a little while. This is Dr. Richard Crane, a colleague and a friend of mine."

"I feel fine, what do I need a doctor for?" Maybrick peered suspiciously at Richard.

"I'm a psychiatrist, Mr. Maybrick."

"A shrink?" Maybrick arched his left eyebrow as he studied Richard.

"Yes, a shrink. Although I don't particularly care for that term. Likely you wouldn't either if you knew where the slang word came from," Richard said lightheartedly, thrusting his hand through the cell bars to shake with the reluctant inmate.

"I know why you're here," he announced in a monotone, as he walked back to his bunk, and sat down.

Richard nodded. "That's good. Detective Stanford tells me you're having a lot of bad dreams and trouble sleeping."

Stanford had found a folding metal chair somewhere and set it up close to the bars of the cell. "Take a load off, Dr. Crane. I'll excuse myself and let the two of you talk." He nodded at them both, turned, and headed off down the basement hallway.

Richard took a seat. "So, lots of bad dreams and insomnia, Mr. Maybrick?"

"That's right. But talking to a damn shrink isn't going to help." Maybrick studied Richard's face with disconcerting intensity from his perch on the bunk.

"Have you talked to a psychiatrist before?"

"No!"

"Then how do you know I can't help you? If I could just ask a couple of questions…" Richard didn't wait for a reply. "How well do you remember your dreams when they awaken you, Mr. Maybrick?"

"Depends," the prisoner responded curtly.

"On what?"

"The dreams I have over and over again I can remember every detail."

"Good." Richard nodded. "What about other dreams?"

"Some of the ones that don't repeat I may remember with some detail when I wake up, but after that they become kinda vague."

"Hmm. Do you think much about the kind of dreams you have?"

"Not anymore. I did for a long time, but it never did me any good. Now I just wake up frightened, sometimes in a cold sweat. I even cry occasionally."

Richard frowned. "Have you ever taken any medication to help you sleep?"

"Yeah, over-the-counter stuff. Waste of time and money. I tried alcohol, but it didn't stop the nightmares. More alcohol didn't work either. I just woke up scared shitless with a hangover," Maybrick groused.

"Would you be willing to share some of your dreams with me?"

Richard had long ago grown accustomed to silences when talking with patients. He shifted back and forth in the hard metal chair searching for a comfortable position. After about five minutes he glanced at his watch—a vintage Rolex Submariner that made him smile every time he looked at it— gave up and got up to leave. "Well, have a good day, Mr. Maybrick."

"No, wait," wafted out from the cell, but he continued down the hallway. A few seconds later the same plea came in a louder voice. "Wait, Dr. Crane!"

Richard paused for a few seconds, erased the hint of a smile from his face, and returned to the hard folding chair to resume his vigil.

"So, are you here to find out if I'm crazy?" Maybrick asked, dragging a heavy metal chair to a spot on the other side of the bars from Crane.

"What do you mean by crazy?" he asked.

Maybrick dropped raggedly into the metal chair. "Answering a question with a question, that's pretty damn lame, Dr. Crane."

"Hardly my intention. I think we both know I'm here to try to get some sense of your mental state, but Detective Stanford thought I might be able to shed some light on your sleep issues and perhaps be of some help. He said you're experiencing very disturbing chronic nightmares with some frequency. Is that true?"

"Yeah."

"Do you want to talk about them?" Without giving him time to answer, Richard asked, "How long have you been having these bad dreams?"

Maybrick's head receded between his shoulders and he slumped down in the chair. "I can never remember not having them," he replied sullenly.

"Even when you were a child?"

"Yeah."

"Do you remember when they started?"

"No. They've always been there," Maybrick replied. "I just told you. I can't ever remember not having nightmares."

"That's very unusual. Nightmares don't typically start earlier than age three." Richard sensed he was beginning to engage the reluctant inmate.

"Well, I can definitely tell you my nightmares started long before I was three."

"That's very interesting. Let's talk about your dreams. Where do you think we should start?"

"You're the doctor. You tell me."

"Okay, how about this. Did you have a dream last night?"

"Yeah."

"Can you describe it to me?"

"Not really."

"You can't or you won't?"

"What's the point?"

"It might help you to sleep if you get it off your chest."

"Gimme a break. Nothing's going to help me sleep," Maybrick fired back angrily.

Richard detected a feeling of despair underneath the angry tone in the prisoner's voice. "Why do you say that?"

"Dr. Crane. Do you know anybody who's been to hell and come back?"

The question took Richard by surprise. "Define hell," he said, fumbling for a response.

"My life. My life is a living hell and there's no way anybody or anything is going to change that."

"That may be true, but since we're both sitting here, why don't you tell me about the dream you had last night? What do you have to lose?"

"Tell you what. Get me out of here for couple of smokes, and then we can talk."

"I don't think I can do that."

"Detective Stanford gets me out every once in a while. Why can't you?"

"If you tell me about your dream, I'll see what I can do about getting you out of here for a cigarette or two."

"Promise?"

"I'm a medical doctor. I've taken an oath never to lie to patients."

"But I'm not your patient," Maybrick reminded Richard. The guy was quick.

"As a rule, I try not to lie to anyone."

"Even serial killers?"

CHAPTER FOURTEEN

George sat staring intently at the psychiatrist. He knew he had backed the shrink into a corner and casually awaited a response.

"Everyone deserves the truth."

George pondered Dr. Crane's response for a few moments, then nodded and pulled his chair up closer to the thick metal bars.

He started talking. "Well, I'm walking down a street, a cobblestone street. It's very dark with an occasional gaslight. There's a winter chill with a heavy fog rolling in. I'm looking for my ship which is leaving port at first light. I've been out drinking most of the night. I'm getting anxious because I can't find the berth where my ship is docked. I know the captain is going to be pissed. The cold, damp air is going right through me. I'm walking at a rapid pace, and suddenly I recognize the outline of my ship in the distance. Ahead of me, I see the silhouettes of three men standing under a light. They appear ghostlike in the dense fog. For a minute I think about trying to find an alternative path back to my ship. Too late. They see me, so I decide to walk past them. As I pass by, one of the men with a pipe hanging from the side of his mouth asks me if I have some matches. I don't know what to do, so I reach into my pocket for some matches. Then one of the other men asks me, 'Matelot are you?'"

"Matelot?" Dr. Crane asked.

"Means sailor. So, I tell him, yeah, I'm on my way back to my ship. Heading out early in the morning to the Caribbean islands."

George closed his eyes and kept talking, letting the dream play like a movie in his mind.

"'Drinking and whoring?' one of the other men asks me. 'No, just a couple of pints,' I say. 'How 'bout a couple of bob for some thirsty wharf rats?' he says. I say 'Sorry, I spent my last three pence on a pint and a shot of gin.' He comes back with 'If you're skint, mate, you won't mind me checking your pockets.' I feel a hand in my pocket. I grab his arm and push it away. I realize they're going to rob me, so I start to run. I see my ship ahead in the fog. I'm only fifty yards away. Just when I think I'm going to make it, I'm tackled from behind. All three men are beating and kicking me, then one of them hits me on the head with a leather truncheon. I can feel the blood running down my face."

George lifted his hand and pointed to the side of his forehead at his birthmark. It sat about an inch over his right eye and disappeared into his red hair. It looked just like blood dripping down his temple.

He continued, "Then everything becomes a blur. I hear the heels of my boots dragging across the cobblestones. 'Bet the bloke swims like a rat,' one of them says. 'I'll wager he bloody sinks like ballast from a ship in a storm,' says the third. I try to scream but I can't. I feel weightless and totally disoriented for a few seconds. They've thrown me off the dock. As soon as I hit the cold water I'm shocked to my senses. But it's too late." The fear in his voice was palpable, even to him.

"Why is it too late?" Dr. Crane asked.

"My heavy woolen coat and trousers suck up the freezing water like a sponge. I never come back to the surface. The strong current carries me along as I sink. For a fraction of a second I see the light from the dock, then I'm surrounded by cold, wet darkness. I scream in pain and fear. The freezing water feels like I'm being stabbed all over my body. It fills the empty spaces in my lungs. It's ten seconds of unspeakable terror." George buried his face in his hand in despair and mumbled, "Night after night, I live it over and over and over again."

A long moment later, he opened his eyes.

Dr. Crane sat motionless, pulled into the nightmare, a residue of horror on his face.

"See why I don't sleep? That nightmare haunts me at least two or three times a month. It's been like that ever since I can remember."

"You've dreamed like that since you were a child?"

"No, not like that. I've dreamed that very same dream," George corrected him emphatically.

"But how is that possible? As a young child, you wouldn't have had any frame of reference for that kind of experience."

George sank into himself. He'd known all along talking would be useless. Stupid. "You don't believe me, do you?"

"That's not what I said. It's just…highly unusual."

Yeah, sure. "Welcome to my hell. I could really use that smoke now, Dr. Crane."

The shrink got up and left without saying a word. He returned several minutes later with Detective Stanford, a Bic lighter, and an open pack of unfiltered Pall Malls. George immediately held up his hands and motioned the detective to cuff him. "Thanks, Dr. Crane," he said with a flood relief. "You're a man of your word."

As they trooped outside, icicles glistened from the eaves of the station roof. A penumbra of bright white snow had transformed the ugly asphalt parking lot into a serene thing of beauty even he could appreciate.

George broke into a big smile as the detective cupped the lighter in his hands and lit his cigarette. With the first puff, deep pleasure and calmness flooded his whole body. By the time he stubbed out the butt of his first cigarette on the heel of his shoe, he was in a state of nicotine nirvana. He didn't give a flip about the cancer warnings he was always getting from his mom and sister. The health consequences of his addiction were well worth the sense of well-being that expanded within him with each inhalation.

He glanced over at the doctor and the detective, his strange bedfellows. They made a curious trio huddled on the back steps of the Hightower Police Department. A passerby would never have guessed who they were, or the circumstances of their gathering, if not for the steel restraints on his ankles and wrists.

"Feels good out here!" Dr. Crane exclaimed.

George rolled his eyes. "You actually like the cold weather?"

"I grew up in upstate New York. You either learned to love the winter, moved, or suffered interminably."

George made a face. "I once took a ship into Sweden in the dead of winter. It was five degrees below zero with the wind chill factor. On a bet, I stripped down to my shorts and T-shirt and stood on the deck for ten minutes. The crew thought I was crazy, but I made almost three hundred bucks on the wager. I damn near got frostbite on all my extremities, if you know what I mean. I have to say, it was one of the most exhilarating experiences I've ever had. But I've never cared for cold weather after that."

The doctor and detective both laughed out loud.

"I hope you don't feel the need to strip here," Detective Stanford said, still laughing. "I don't think I could explain that to Chief Monroe."

George took a final drag on his cigarette. He exhaled the smoke slowly, reluctantly, as though parting with an old friend. "I'm good now," he announced, crushing the butt of his third cigarette underfoot. "Thanks guys."

CHAPTER FIFTEEN

Richard found George Maybrick's description of his dream nearly as disturbing as the murder confessions he'd read in Detective Stanford's notes. His mind kept returning to the birthmark and the blow on Maybrick's head. His intuition told him there was a connection. Maybe he had created the dream to explain the unattractive birthmark he had probably been mercilessly teased over as a child, and no doubt hated. Richard didn't know what to make of his insistence that he had been having the dream since he was a toddler. Clearly, he was either lying or confused. A very young child couldn't entertain what was obviously the dream of a much older person.

He decided to visit the killer again. Maybe gain more insights.

"Dr. Crane, what a surprise. What brings you here again?"

"I thought we might talk."

"You want to know more about my dreams, don't you?"

"I do."

"How about a smoke first?"

"Sorry, Detective Stanford is out and won't be back for a couple of hours. But I'm sure he'll take you outside for a couple of cigarettes when he returns. You do know those things will kill you, right?"

Maybrick shrugged. "Yeah, but not as fast as drowning."

Ouch. "So, the desk sergeant said you slept okay after we talked, but last night was pretty bad."

"Yeah."

"The dream you shared the other day was pretty disturbing but talking seemed to help. If we talk about some of your other dreams, it might help. Maybe we could figure out what they mean," Richard suggested. "Often when we figure out what our nightmares mean they lose their power over us, sometimes ceasing altogether."

"No matter. It won't change anything," Maybrick stated matter-of-factly.

"It might. I had a patient once..."

"Don't jerk me around, Dr. Crane. I'm not your patient. And besides, it doesn't matter. We both know where I'm headed."

Maybrick's belligerence caught Richard off guard. He had felt very positive about the way their conversation had ended three days earlier on the back steps of the police station. He tried again. "You don't know that for sure," he suggested.

"Cut the crap!"

He ignored Maybrick's hostile response. "How often do you have these dreams, George? Can I call you George?"

"Whatever you want. Sometimes three or four times a week. Depends. Maybe less if I'm painting."

"What are some other things you dream about?"

"You don't want to know." There was a sadness in the killer's voice. "I'll tell you what, Dr. Crane. I'll swap you one dream for a cigarette break. Come visit, get me out for a smoke or two, and I'll share one of my dreams with you. But fair warning, you're not going to like them."

"Why not?"

"If I told you, you'd probably change your mind. But if you got the stomach for it and a pack of smokes—real cigarettes, not the ones with filters—I'll tell you my dreams." He paused for a few seconds "Have we got a deal?"

"Deal," Richard said, pleased with Maybrick's unexpected, if unconventional, agreement.

"Oh. Could I ask for one other thing? They turn the lights out at ten every night and it gets really dark down here. Could you have them leave the lights on in my cell and the hallway? It would help me sleep better."

"I'll try. Are you afraid of the dark, George?"

"Yeah, I am. And the dark is afraid of me."

Richard pondered the cryptic remark. "So, tell me, what was your dream last night?"

Maybrick narrated a second dream, recounting standing alone as a small child locked in a dark closet for hours, crying until no more tears would come.

Richard thought about the details. The dream made sense psychologically, no doubt the manifestation of repressed childhood memories. He wondered which family member might have locked Maybrick in a dark closet as a small boy. More importantly, why?

Little wonder the man was afraid of the dark and opted to sleep with the lights on.

Richard wondered what else might lurk in the shadows of Maybrick's subconscious and did he really want to find out?

CHAPTER SIXTEEN

New York City, two weeks later.

"Looks like we caught a break, Frank."

"What happened?" O'Meara asked, plopping an extra-large coffee and mounds of cream cheese wedged between two toasted halves of an onion bagel onto his desk.

"We got a call yesterday from a detective in Hightower, Missouri," Joe replied.

"Where the hell is Hightower?"

"About ninety miles south of St. Louis, an old town on the Mississippi that used to have a thriving towboat industry. Now, not so much. Looks like our warehouse perp showed up there and brutally murdered another female victim. Same MO, near as I can tell. He hacked her to pieces and left a bloody message on the wall. We received a report early this morning with what they have so far, but get this..."

"What?" O'Meara asked with a mouth full of bagel.

"This guy's confessed to several more murders."

"No way! Not possible some wack-job serial killer is running all over the goddam country brutally murdering women and this is the first we're hearing of it. The media would have been all over that."

"Yeah, exactly what I thought, but you've got to read the report." Joe handed him a copy of the case file. "If the killer's confession is legit, it's a goddam nightmare."

O'Meara cracked the file. "Let me take a look."

"There's something else. We got back the lab report on the cigarette butts we recovered from the crime scene. It's a type of cigarette called a *papirosa*. The brand is Belomorkanal, Russian, made with cheap tobacco and popular with the country's working and lower classes. Very high in tar and nicotine. Not for the faint-of-heart smoker. *Papirosas* are unfiltered and have a fairly long, hollow cardboard tube attached to the tobacco portion. Most people pinch the tube together before they light up. Belomorkanal is not an easy brand to find in the U.S. but they're online occasionally. You might want to try 'em, Frank. They're unfiltered just like your Lucky Strikes."

O'Meara was not amused. He gave Joe a disapproving glare and began reading the Hightower police report. He scanned page after page shaking his head, then tossed the report on his desk. "Damn. I'm catching the next flight out of LaGuardia to St. Louis. It's time to pay the Hightower PD a visit."

"Don't you think you should check with the chief first?"

"You're right. After I confirm my flight, send the report over to the chief and tell her I'm following up. If she says no, tell her I took a few days off to visit some long-lost relatives in Missouri."

"Right. I'm sure she's going to believe that. Have you seen what the weather is like in the Midwest right now? It's a real crap shoot. Snowstorms everywhere. Sure, you don't want to wait until it clears up a bit?"

"I'll take my chances. I'm gonna bring this sick son of a bitch back to New York City."

"Hey, slow down a minute. We don't know for sure if he's our guy. Don't you even want to talk to HPD first?"

"Who's the detective in charge of the case?" O'Meara asked.

"Chris Stanford. A veteran detective. From the looks of things, he appears to be a sharp cop. He's done some damn fine police work to catch this guy."

"Uh-huh. How many serial killers do you think he's dealt with in a pissant town like Hightower, Missouri?" O'Meara asked condescendingly. "Give him a call and tell him I'll be in his office first thing in the morning."

CHAPTER SEVENTEEN

When O'Meara parked his rental car in front of the police station, he scanned its exterior. Forty-plus years in New York City and he knew all too well the consequences of deferred maintenance when he saw it. Walking into the building, he judged that the functionality of Hightower's police station's eighties décor had exceeded its expiration date.

"What a dump," he muttered scornfully under his breath.

O'Meara cut an imposing figure. Meeting him once, even briefly, you were not likely to forget the Empire City detective. At six-three with a barrel-chested frame and shoulders beginning to stoop, he walked with a slight limp. Blessed with a perfectly straight nose, prominent cheekbones, a heavy brow, and chiseled chin, his face had once been alluring to women. But years of heavy drinking and a two-pack-a-day habit of unfiltered Lucky Strikes had left him with a wrinkled, bloated face and an abundance of spider veins on his nose and cheeks.

When the detective stared at you with his amber eyes your immediate reaction was to look away.

Despite his short fuse, incessant swearing and narcissistic tendencies his colleagues respected him deeply while giving him a wide berth. A partner of his for many years had observed, "When Frank O'Meara has an axe to grind stand clear of the sparks." Chris and Harry would learn the veracity of this statement before day's end.

Detective Stanford had not yet arrived, so the desk sergeant ushered O'Meara into Stanford's office and brought him a cup of coffee. O'Meara had read the report repeatedly on the flight from New York. As he gulped his coffee, he studied Stanford's office with the same meticulousness he would a crime scene. Nothing escaped his attention. He quickly surmised from the well-worn crime scene investigation books on the shelf and the numerous citations on the walls that Stanford was a more-than-competent detective, and wondered idly why he would hang out in a small town like Hightower. He then saw a framed photo of Stanford and his family propped alongside an old, fading Polaroid of a young boy standing next to a heavily decorated army officer. Kid of a Nam vet, he thought.

The detective's desk was a testimonial to order and efficiency with its neatly stacked piles of papers and carefully labeled folders arranged in alphabetical order in a holder on the corner of the desk. This guy was by the book. "Could be a pain in the ass to deal with," he mused under his breath.

The detective walked in a few minutes later, introducing himself with a firm handshake. "Detective O'Meara, Chris Stanford. Welcome to Hightower. We were expecting you two days ago."

"Yeah, the flight was rerouted four times because of the weather. Spent a whole day at O'Hare. Sat on a plane on the tarmac for four hours before the flight got cancelled. I didn't get into St. Louis until late last night, and they didn't clear the roads until early this morning."

Stanford cringed. "Yeah, terrible accident last night. An SUV slid off the road, down an embankment, and into the river about thirty miles north of here. All four passengers drowned, including two children."

O'Meara shook his head in sympathy. "Sorry to hear that."

"Anyway, sorry for your travel woes. Glad you got here safely."

"Right. Can I see the suspect, Detective Stanford?" O'Meara asked.

"Certainly. Would you like to talk about the case first?"

"I read your report. Damn good police work, Detective."

"Thanks. We got a couple of lucky breaks. The grand jury will start meeting in a couple of weeks."

"Great. Look, Detective Stanford—"

"Chris. Please call me Chris."

"Fair enough, Chris. And call me Frank," O'Meara replied. "About the case, I'm sure you can imagine I'm pretty anxious to talk to this Maybrick fellow."

"Absolutely. But Chief Monroe asked me to bring you by when you arrived so he could meet you and put a name with a face."

"Ah. Sure. But why don't we catch up with him after I've seen our guy?"

Chris shrugged. "Okay. Follow me."

"Why was he put in the basement?" O'Meara inquired as Chris led him down the stairs and along a dim and dingy hallway, a part of the station obviously not in regular use.

"Maybrick keeps everybody up at night."

"Huh? How so?"

"You'll see."

CHAPTER EIGHTEEN

Chris sensed an instant antipathy as soon as the serial killer and the New York detective locked eyes on each other. "Mr. Maybrick, this is Detective Frank O'Meara from the NYPD. He'd like to ask you a few questions."

"I told you all about New York already," Maybrick fired back, never taking his eyes off O'Meara.

"Yeah, I read his report, Maybrick. But I'm here doing my own investigation."

Chris handcuffed the prisoner and walked them to the interrogation room. Maybrick stayed mute and did not invoke his cigarette privileges. Chris wondered why. "I'll just sit over here, Detective O'Meara," he said, taking the chair by the wall.

"Your call," O'Meara said.

Chris watched and listened carefully. O'Meara worked methodically and efficiently with a laser-like focus. A very adept interrogator, the seasoned detective could teach him a thing or two. Chris chided himself when O'Meara asked Maybrick if he had killed anyone else in New York City. Why hadn't he thought to ask that? O'Meara never used a note, relying easily on his memory. Chris realized he must have had a very carefully thought-out set of questions in mind before even beginning the interview. By the time he finished his last question forty-five minutes later, Chris felt like a damn rookie.

"Well, what do you think?" he asked O'Meara as they sat in Chris's office, trying to ignore O'Meara's heavily scuffed cordovan wingtips planted firmly on his desk like they belonged there.

"I'm going to cut through the crap here and be frank, Chris. I believe you guys are in way over your heads on this case. Even with Maybrick's confession, it is going to be a tough prosecution. Interpol is going to want a piece of it. Two murders, two different states in the U.S., so the FBI, too. You can bet he's going to cop an insanity plea. When his goddam lawyers get cranking, they'll whine about not being able to get a fair trial and push for a change of venue. I don't know the judge here, but I'm guessing he will give it to them if only to take himself off the trial."

"What are you saying, Frank?"

"Let me take Maybrick back to New York City. NYPD spends more on paper clips in a year than your entire department budget. We need to make sure this guy either fries or gets put away for good."

Chris rocked back nervously in his chair. "You want me to release the suspect to you so you can take him back to stand trial in New York?"

"Exactly."

Admittedly, the prospect had its appeal, but a win in this case here in Missouri would make Chris's career. He could write his own ticket.

"Not sure that's possible. Like I told you before, the grand jury is going to start meeting in a couple of weeks." He waited for O'Meara's response, but the detective only rewarded his patience with silence and so he added, "Even if I thought it was a good idea, it's not my decision. I seriously doubt my chief and the county DA would go for it. Besides, the Percy County court has already been established as the court of record in the case. It's just not going to happen, Frank."

Frank looked unfazed. "Leave it to me, Chris. When I'm finished your people will be tripping all over themselves to put this sick bastard on a plane with me back to New York City."

"Sorry, Frank. Maybrick murdered a woman in Hightower, he was apprehended in Hightower, and he needs to stand trial here in Percy County."

"You're not being realistic. Do you have any idea what all of this is going to cost the county and this little town of yours if you keep this trial? Are you familiar with the Corona case in Yuba City, California, back in the early seventies? The first trial cost over three hundred fifty thousand dollars and damn near bankrupted the town. Do the math, Detective. That would be almost two-and-a-half million today. Even if this psycho's lawyers get a change of venue, Hightower could be on the hook for a huge chunk of change. From the look of things around here, I don't think you guys have those kinds of resources."

"Don't you think you're getting a little head of yourself, Frank?"

"I do my homework, Chris. We both know Hightower is dying. Your department has four old Crown Vics parked outside. I wouldn't be surprised if one of them is yours. I haven't seen one computer in this building with a with a flat-screen monitor. The place hasn't had a coat of paint for at least a decade. One of the lights in the interrogation room looks like it burned out years ago, and when my partner requested a copy of your report on Maybrick, someone actually faxed it to me. I can't tell you the last time I got a report faxed to me from another police department. And when your dispatcher offered me a cup of coffee when I got here this morning, I thought I was having a flashback. I haven't seen that Mr. Coffee model since the late nineties. You might be able to sell it as a collectible on eBay, and who knows, you might get enough money to buy a real computer."

O'Meara's brutal sarcasm aside, Chris knew the New York detective had sized up his hometown's economic plight accurately. Even without thinking about the long-term implications for himself, he found O'Meara's proposal unsettling. "I'm sorry, it's not my decision. But if anyone asks my opinion, I say Maybrick stays."

"You'd be making a big mistake, Stanford. I'm taking Maybrick back to New York City one way or another. It's where he murdered his first victim, and that's where he needs to stand trial. I know people who can make things happen. There are some big names who've taken an interest in this case. That's why I'm working it. Mark my words. Not for nothing, this son of a bitch's judgment day won't be in Hightower. I can promise you that," O'Meara said angrily. "We'll be in touch," he added as he threw on his overcoat and stalked out.

"No doubt," Chris retorted softly as his office door slammed. He replayed the whole conversation in his mind. This was the last thing he'd expected, but in his heart he knew O'Meara's argument made sense. Everyone's life would be easier here if they turned Maybrick over to the courts in New York. Things would get back to normal, and the town could put the whole mess behind it.

It only took Chris a minute on the phone with the Percy County DA to realize that he wasn't about to release Maybrick to the NYPD. "They can have him when we're finished here," the DA said irately. "I don't care how important this hotshot New York detective thinks he is. The suspect stays here, and I'll get a judge to make it stick!"

CHAPTER NINETEEN

The next morning, Richard returned to the police station and made his way to Chris's office.

"Back again, Dr. Crane?" Chris asked, swallowing the last bite of a baloney sandwich.

"Couldn't stay away. Our friend downstairs is a very compelling character."

"What do you have there?"

"Oh, just a sketch pad and some drawing pencils. Any reason I can't give them to our detainee? I think Maybrick might feel better if he could work on his art."

"How's that going to help you with your evaluation?" Chris asked.

"I'm not sure."

"When am I going to get your official psych eval?" Chris asked as he inspected Richard's bag. "The DA is expecting it soon. You know what an ass he can be when he doesn't get his way."

"I need a little more time."

"It's already been two weeks. What are you and Maybrick talking about?"

"Dreams, mostly. Pretty grim stuff."

After Richard and the detective escorted Maybrick outside for his ritual morning smoke Chris led him and the prisoner back downstairs to his cell. The heavy metal door made a loud creaking sound as it slammed closed, as if reminding Richard that Maybrick was a prisoner, not a regular client. Being down in the overflow holding area made him feel isolated and alone for their discussions, but probably made Maybrick open up more.

"What's in the bag?" Maybrick asked, pulling his chair close to the cell bars. "Christmas was three days ago."

"Not for Christmas, but a little gift." Richard noted the surprise on Maybrick's face. He handed the bag through the cell bars without revealing its contents.

"Thanks, Dr. Crane!" he exclaimed as he peered into the bag. "I can't tell you how wonderful this is! I've been wanting to do some drawing since I got here. I really appreciate it."

"You're welcome. So, you had another tough night, I understand."

"Never changes."

"Tell me about your dream."

"I haven't had this one in a while. It's similar to some of the others. Not nearly as gruesome, but just as scary."

"Tell me about it, Mr. Maybrick."

"Call me George, Dr. Crane. Please call me George from now on," he said.

"Okay, George. Now tell me about this dream of yours."

"It takes place a long, long time ago. I'm a priest and I'm on my deathbed. I'm suffering horribly with some kind of terrible illness. I'm burning up with fever and racked with pain. My body is covered with sores. There's nothing anybody can do for me."

"Are you afraid to die?" Richard asked.

"Yes, I'm terrified of dying because I'm in despair."

"Is your illness the cause of your despair?"

"No. I know that if I die in this state, I will burn in hell. I've done something horrible. I'm responsible for the torture and execution of a lot of innocent people. I tried to convince myself that I was doing right, but now I realize what I've done was wrong. It's not the illness but the guilt that is eating away at me. It is twice as bad as the physical pain I'm in. I've searched for forgiveness from God and found nothing."

"So, you don't know why you've done that is causing all this guilt?"

"Right. I just know I've destroyed many people. What scares me the most is that I'm going to my grave with all this remorse, and nothing will take it away. I can't think of anything worse," Maybrick said, his voice quivering.

"Go on."

"I'm dying in total, utter despair. Do you have any idea what that's like, Dr. Crane? I know it's just a dream, but it seems so real. I feel the despair at the very core of my being and it's devouring my soul."

Richard sat silently. He understood despair but could only try to imagine what it meant to be near death without any hope whatsoever.

"It's literally a person's worst nightmare."

"Fear of death is something all of us experience, George."

"Goddamit, Dr. Crane, you're not hearing me!"

Even though the dream had ended several hours ago Richard could see the terror on Maybrick's face as he revisited it in excruciating detail. "Tell me again."

"It's not death I'm afraid of in my dream, it's damnation. I'm supposed to be some kind of holy person serving God, but I've done unspeakable things and I know I'm going to burn in hell for all eternity."

"Try to remember what's happened to you to bring you to this place. What could you have done that would put you beyond the reach of forgiveness in your dream?"

"I can't remember. It's just not there. I wrack my goddam brain every time I have this dream, but it doesn't come to me. All I know is that I was responsible for something terrible and it's eating me up inside. I'm suspended between an overwhelming desire to die and put an end to my guilt and pain, and the worst kind of fear of spending eternity perpetually tormented by the fires of hell."

Richard knew a bit about torment and hell himself. Blessed with a brilliant mind, an eidetic memory, and good looks, he had graduated first in his class from one of the top med schools in the country. Poised to take the New York City medical world by storm, he'd quickly developed a thriving Manhattan practice. He'd won a highly coveted teaching appointment and enjoyed privileges at three of the best hospitals in the city. But then, after several years of unimaginable stress, he had turned to prescription drugs and alcohol to cope. His fall from grace came quickly and the ravages of addiction cost him his practice, his elevated status in the medical and academic communities, and, worst of all, his wife and two daughters.

Yeah, he'd suffered through years of personal hell.

But bad as it had been, it was nothing like the hell he now read on Maybrick's expression as he dropped his head into his hands and sobbed quietly.

In one of those rare moments in his career as a healer, Richard had absolutely no idea how to respond. So, he sat in silence, drenched in the terror and despair of a serial killer.

CHAPTER TWENTY

"I don't need this crap," Richard muttered to himself as he tried repeatedly to get his printer unjammed. Numerous books from his personal library were scattered haphazardly across his desk, mirroring the degree of his exasperation. To make matters worse, his computer had frozen up in the middle of a partially read clinical study on serial killers. He hated reading on an electronic screen, but his printer had a mind of its own, leaving him little choice. Adding to his frustration, an entire evening of research had yielded little insight into George Maybrick. From his vantage point, nothing about the confessed killer added up. He didn't easily fit any personality disorder profile in the clinical literature.

Richard stared at the nearly blank page in his notebook, then glanced at his watch. One-thirty in the morning. Time to take a break he told himself as he began massaging his tired eyes with the palms of his hands.

A cup of ginseng and honey green tea in hand, he sat restlessly in the chair usually reserved for his patients, trying to relax and put Maybrick out of his mind. He briefly considered calling it a night but decided to reboot his computer one more time and try another Internet search hoping something new would pop up. He began typing. Probably a waste of time, he thought but what the hell...one more search couldn't hurt.

Before he could even finish typing *treatment for chronic nightmares*, several options appeared on the screen. One result, *chronic nightmare disorder*, grabbed his attention. Clicking on it, more entries than he could read in a lifetime appeared. Tired but motivated, he began scrolling down the list. *Imagery rehearsal therapy, lucid dream treatment, desensitization therapy,* it went on and on. He clicked on the entry *regression therapy*, read a couple of paragraphs, and quickly dismissed it. Psycho mumbo jumbo. He scanned a study on the drug prazosin. The protocol had some promising results, so he made several notes as he scanned the study.

After an hour or so he caught himself dozing off. He drew in a deep breath, pushed away from his desk, got up, and walked around his office. He tried to take his mind off the problem, but it wouldn't let go. He knew the answer was out there somewhere. He just needed to find it. So he went back to the computer.

He had no idea why he added *hypnotherapy* to *chronic nightmare disorder therapy*. Must be because he was half asleep. Scrolling through several pages of results, nothing looked promising, until the summary from a regression therapist's blog site caught his attention.

A woman suffering from chronic nightmares finally finds healing in hypnotherapy after several months of past life regression work. www. *regressionhypnotherapy.com.*

Despite his skepticism, he clicked on the site. What he read left him dumbfounded. The blog told the story of a woman in her mid-thirties who had been suffering from a nightmare disorder since childhood. He cringed as it related in considerable detail a couple of the recurring horrific dreams the client experienced. Gradually, over a period of months using hypnosis, the therapist had taken her client back into her past lives where the young woman recounted some of the terrible things she had experienced in those previous lives. Many of the nightmares the client had experienced appeared to trace back to experiences from a past life.

Two months into regression therapy, under hypnosis the client went back to a previous life in Spain in the early seventeenth century, where she was caught up in a purge. The grand inquisitor, a Dominican priest sent by the Vatican to ferret out heretics, arrived in town following reports of witches in the area. In this past life, the client was a widow, a midwife and healer, who was named by one of her friends, a healer as well, who gave up her name during a confession. The widow was tortured, but bravely refused to confess, and resisted all efforts of the inquisitor to name other women as witches. In keeping with the custom of the time, she was given a final opportunity to recant while bound to a stake and atop a pile of wood about to be incinerated. Death by fire is one of the most painful ways to die, so as an act of mercy, if the accused recanted she was sometimes garroted instead, to spare them an excruciating death.

The client, as one of six women executed that day, refused to confess to witchcraft, and much to the inquisitor's anger and dismay, she announced to the crowd of townspeople who had gathered to witness the executions that God knew she had done nothing wrong and if anyone was going to hell it would be the inquisitor and his minions for killing innocent women. In the recurring dream, the client experienced the unimaginable pain of being burned alive.

Richard shook his head at the horrific tale, which he knew was historically accurate. But a past life? Seemed ridiculous and unscientific. Still, he wondered if the therapy had helped the client? It didn't have to be real, but if she believed it was, talking about the experience could possibly help.

He continued to read.

The blogging regression therapist told how curiosity had gotten the best of her, so with her client's permission she shared the details of the dream with a historian who had written extensively on the Inquisition. He referred her to several sources on an Inquisition Tribunal established in the area of Logrono in northern Spain between 1608 and 1610. He couldn't confirm some of the client's account, such as her comments regarding the condemnation of the inquisitor to eternal damnation for killing innocent women, but he did relate that many of the details fit the historical facts regarding the tribunal's work, including the trial and execution of six women.

Well, maybe the client had read about the Inquisition in school or something. Still, if the therapy had helped her get over her nightmares, it might be worth pursuing.

He typed *past life regression therapist* into the search bar, and numerous sites popped up. He rolled his eyes as he quickly scrolled past the so-called therapists who offered astrological counseling, herbology, energy balancing, crystal therapy, and a host of other new-age bullshit scams.

"Finally," he exclaimed, clicking on a directory of actual certified therapists. His search for someone local turned up nothing. A search of the St. Louis area revealed a substantial list of regression therapists. He began narrowing down the list by investigating each therapist's website. He tossed out those who were too woo-woo, not enough experience, too spiritual, sketchy credentials.

When he clicked on Dr. Shoshana Liebman's website, he knew he had found the right therapist. She was head of psychiatry at the University of St. Louis' teaching hospital, a distinguished chair in the behavioral sciences, editor of the *Clinical Psychiatry Review*, and the author of one of the leading scholarly texts on past life regression therapy. She was almost too good to be true. And she maintained a small private regression therapy practice just ninety miles away.

He bookmarked the website and jotted down her contact info on a post-it note. Then he closed his eyes and leaned back in his overstuffed office chair, and while thinking about how he would approach Dr. Shoshana Liebman with George Maybrick's case, he fell asleep.

A few hours later, a sharp knock on his office door startled Richard awake. He shut his eyes at the intense morning sun that shot like a laser through his office window.

"Come in," he said groggily.

"Dr. Crane. I'm so sorry. I woke you up." his confused secretary said, walking in hesitantly.

"It's all right. I was working till almost four this morning and must have crashed."

"Oh, dear. Coffee?"

"Thanks, Marta, that would be great."

"Would you like me to move your morning appointments back so you can go home for a while?"

"No. A cup of coffee and I'll be fine. I have a very important call I need to make."

Unaccustomed to being nervous, he sat anxiously at his desk counting down the minutes until nine when he could call the past life regression therapist's office. On the dot, he punched in her number.

"Dr. Shoshana Liebman's office, how may I help you?" the friendly voice on the other end asked.

"This is Dr. Richard Crane. Is Dr. Liebman in, please?"

Disappointment flooded him when the receptionist said a class lecture, rounds with the residents on the psych floor at the hospital, an entire afternoon of meetings, and a red-eye flight to San Francisco to keynote a conference the following day prevented the therapist from answering his call. It would probably be at least three days before Dr. Liebman could get back to him.

"Please explain to Dr. Liebman that I'm a psychiatrist who heads up the mental health services for a nearby county and I really need to talk to her."

"Is it an emergency, Dr. Crane?"

"No, but it's important enough that I'm willing to make myself available at any time of the day or night. I'll give you my cell number. If I can have just ten minutes of her time, I would greatly appreciate it."

He remained tethered to his cell the entire day, frustrated as the time slipped away. Maybe he should have said it was an emergency he chided himself, glancing at his watch one last time. It was late and he knew everyone but the hospital night staff had gone home.

He swiveled around to his credenza and retrieved an aged meerschaum pipe and a tobacco humidor from his bookshelf. He took a few seconds to admire his favorite pipe, which had transformed into a golden brown over the years. An infrequent ritual, the pipe was the last remnant of the only addiction he allowed himself. Once or twice a month, solitude permitting, he ignored county policy, wheeled his desk chair over to the old wooden window, pried it open, and lit his pipe. For a few brief moments, the winter air and toasted burley tobacco conspired to take his mind to a different place.

He thought about his daughters, as he often did, whom he had not seen in far too many years. The oldest would be twenty-five now, and his younger daughter in her first year of college. Birthday cards and gifts continued to go unacknowledged. All his years of sobriety had not brought them back.

And yet, slumped back in his chair slowly drawing on his pipe, despite his personal and professional exile to a place his former colleagues would have scoffed at—if they even knew where it was—he felt strangely at peace.

His cell phone started vibrating on his midcentury mahogany desk, forcing his attention back to the present. He quickly walked the short distance from the window to his desk. The name and number on the screen took him by surprise.

"Dr. Liebman! Thank you so much for returning my call. I didn't expect to—"

"I'm sorry to interrupt, Dr. Crane, but I'm boarding a plane in a half hour, so I've only got a few minutes. My assistant said you need to speak with me."

"Yes. Are you familiar with the brutal murder down here in Hightower in late November?"

"I seem to recall hearing something on the news."

"The police have the killer in custody. He confessed, and it appears he's responsible for several similar murders elsewhere, so a serial killer. I've been treating him, but I'm getting nowhere. Would you consider consulting with me on the case?"

"Symptomology?" Liebman inquired in a clinical tone.

"Chronic nightmares, for starters."

"Parasomnia?"

"Definitely."

"Do his dreams rise to the level of nightmare disorder?"

"He seems to fit the clinical profile for nightmare disorder, but I've treated many patients with the disorder and I've never seen anything as extreme as this case."

"How so?" Liebman asked.

"For starters, the onset of nightmares for children is typically three to six years. When I asked him how long he had been having nightmares he said he could never remember not experiencing the same horrible dreams over and over. But what completely baffles me is that some of his childhood nightmares included content not normally accessible to a child."

"That very interesting...and disturbing," Liebman observed. "Have you attempted any drug protocols?"

"Yes, but nothing works."

"Have you considered an anti-dopamine series? That has had some success in a number of patients."

"I've tried that, Dr. Liebman," he responded, trying to hide his exasperation.

"There's also been some promising research on prazosin. I'm sure you're familiar with it."

"I'm not sure he's a candidate for prazosin. I can't make a PTSD diagnosis at this point."

"What, exactly, is it that you think I can help you with, Dr. Crane?" Liebman asked, her patience clearly wearing thin.

"This guy doesn't fit any clearly defined disorder profile that I'm familiar with. I can't figure him out. I feel like the answer may lie within his dreams. I think he might be a candidate for regression therapy."

She paused for a moment. "Past life work?"

"Yes. I recently read where past life regression therapy proved successful in a similar case."

"Just how bad are his nightmares?"

He detected a hint of curiosity in her voice. "As I explained, I've never seen anything to this degree. And the dreams are...well, just awful."

"How do you think I can be helpful?"

"I'd like you to consider providing therapy for—"

"I'm sorry, Dr. Crane," she interrupted. "I'm not able to help you. My schedule is full, and you're quite a distance from St. Louis. I'm happy to refer you to another regression therapist. There are several excellent ones in the area."

He thought quickly. He knew he was losing her. "Have you ever regressed a serial killer, Dr. Liebman?"

"Are you trying to appeal to my sense of curiosity or the macabre, Dr. Crane?" she asked wryly.

"I can promise you this is unlike any other case you've ever had."

The silence on the other end of the phone told him she was thinking about it. But at length she said, "I'm sorry, Dr. Crane. I'm not able to help you. Give my assistant a call and she will be happy to refer you to several very fine therapists. They're starting to board my plane. Good luck with your case."

His heart sank. He tried to console himself with Dr. Liebman's offer of a referral to another therapist, but it didn't help. His gut told him that she was the right one.

CHAPTER TWENTY-ONE

"Dr. Crane?"

"Yes."

"Hello, this is Amanda, Dr. Shoshana Liebman's assistant. She told me to expect a call from you, but I fear I may have missed it."

In the two days since he had spoken to Dr. Liebman, Richard had begun questioning the wisdom of seeking a regression therapist. "My apologies. Are you calling with a list of therapists for me?"

"Actually, I'm not. Dr. Liebman is attending a conference in San Francisco this week, giving one of the keynote addresses. She asked me to call and let you know that she is willing to consult with you regarding the patient you discussed with her. She requested a copy of your case notes and any information the police will share. I'm working now to try to clear time for an appointment. It's going to be tough. She has a packed schedule, so if you can be flexible that will really help."

All his doubts about the wisdom of seeking a regression therapist flew out the window.

"Certainly. I can work with her schedule. I'll send a summary of my notes and the police report right away. Please thank Dr. Liebman for me."

"She'll be in touch in the next week to ten days, Dr. Crane."

Richard could not remember when he'd been so energized. He immediately began diving into Dr. Liebman's published work on past life regression in addition to reading books by Brian Weiss and other noted experts in the field.

One day his assistant knocked on his office door. "Dr. Crane," she said, "it's Detective Stanford from the Hightower police department on the phone again, asking to speak to you."

Richard glanced over at the stack of phone messages from the detective on the corner of his desk. With no real progress to report, he had been dodging the detective's calls.

"Please tell him I'll call him back this afternoon," he said and promptly returned to his reading.

A blog authored by a psychotherapist who specialized in regression therapy described a case that bore an uncanny resemblance to George Maybrick's. As Richard read the blog, the parallels astounded him. The case was of a woman in her early forties with a history of unexplained chronic nightmares dating back to early childhood. The quiet, unassuming, seemingly kind librarian had been arrested for a series of cruel murders. She had confessed to killing seven elderly people—a widower, two widows, and two couples. In each case, she had befriended her victims when they sought assistance at the local public library. After gaining their confidence, she had poisoned them and brutally disfigured their faces with an X-Acto knife. Shortly thereafter, she had resigned her library position under the guise of needing to return to her hometown to take care of an ailing parent. Her colleagues had never given it another thought. Once she had established herself in a new community, she allowed a reasonable amount of time to pass, then repeated the same MO.

She might never have been caught were it not for the only child of the final couple she killed. Following several months of grieving, the son of the two victims resolved to clean out their retirement home apartment. In one of his father's sports coats, he found a cell phone with a dead battery, which he promptly turned over to the police. A careful check of the call history identified the number of a woman who worked at the local library. However, she had already moved to another city nearly eight hundred miles away. The police traced her to a library there and brought her in as a suspect in the couple's murder. She confessed to poisoning the couple, and eventually told the police the whole story.

What intrigued Richard most in the blog was the woman's story of horrible nightmares and abuse as a child, and the description of the therapist's intervention using past life regression. In therapy, she recounted a past life as the child of a first-generation immigrant family, recalling in vivid detail living in the slums of Chicago in the late nineteenth century. At age four, her father died in a horrible accident in a meat packing plant. Her mother, who labored sixteen hours a day in a sweatshop, had to send the child and her younger brother to live with her late husband's parents. The grandfather abused her and her brother physically while the grandmother, too timid to interfere, looked on. In the dream, she died before her eleventh birthday from neglect.

After several sessions of regression therapy, the woman's nightmares began to abate. Within six months they ceased entirely. She received a life sentence without parole, pleading guilty to all seven murders. Still in prison now, she had apparently published several critically acclaimed volumes of poetry under a pseudonym.

As he finished the blog, Richard pushed back from his desk and sat quietly reflecting. Before this, he had never regarded past life regression therapy as legit. In fact, weighing in on the topic when it had first come into prominence with the publication of Brian Weiss's *Many Lives, Many Masters*, he'd written a scathing review of the book in one of the leading psychiatric journals, calling it "psychoscience fiction."

Now, he struggled to overcome the remaining mental prejudice against the therapy lurking in his psyche. But if regression therapy presented any chance of helping George Maybrick come to terms with the dark recesses of his soul, then Richard had a professional responsibility to explore the possibility.

He was deeply grateful for Dr. Shoshana Liebman willingness to shine a light into that darkness, but he also felt a sense of dread over what that darkness might unleash.

CHAPTER TWENTY-TWO

Richard drummed his fingers in place on Detective Stanford's desk. They were waiting for Dr. Liebman, who was due any minute for their first meeting.

Stanford, who was reading from a blue binder, ignored him.

"May I ask what you're reading?" Richard asked, tired of the silence.

"The St. Louis police blotter."

"Hmm. May I ask why?"

"Curiosity mostly, but I'm also looking for anything serious or dangerous that might somehow make its way into our little metropolis."

"But St. Louis is ninety miles away."

"Yeah, but when people commit serious crimes their first impulse is to go someplace where they can't be found."

Richard chuckled. "Surely you don't believe they would actually come to Hightower?"

"You'd be surprised. In the last five years we've arrested two people who committed serious crimes in St. Louis and fled to Hightower."

"Wow. What crimes?"

"Onc was about five years ago. One night we arrested a guy for hit and run. He'd blown through a stop sign going fifty in a thirty-five and killed an elderly man in the crosswalk. Someone witnessed the accident, but the street was so poorly lit all the witness could offer was that the vehicle was a late model dark-colored pickup truck. Not much to go on. The driver was smart enough to realize if your car gets damaged by a hit and run you don't take it to a local body shop."

"So, he drove to Hightower to get his truck repaired."

"When he showed up at one of the local body shops, he told a cockamamie story about being on vacation and his car being hit in a shopping center parking lot but he'd been unable to get the culprit's license plate number, of course."

"Sounds believable."

"Sure. But Fred, the body shop owner, called me and said he was a little suspicious. First, there was absolutely nothing in his pickup to suggest he was on vacation."

"He could have checked into a motel and put his suitcase, cooler, and whatever else he was traveling with in his room."

"Could have. And if that had been the only thing, I doubt Fred would have been suspicious. What really made him question the story was the fact that there was no evidence the truck had been hit by another car. There was plenty of damage all right, to the front bumper and left front fender, but no paint residue from the other car. Fred told me nobody gets hit by another car without leaving some paint on the damaged vehicle. To seal the deal, when Fred asked him if he'd filed a police report and contacted his insurance company, he hemmed and hawed. Fred figured the guy was trying to pull a fast one on his insurance company. He might have gotten away with it if I hadn't read about a hit and run involving a dark-colored pickup truck in the police blotter."

"Unbelievable." Richard glanced at his watch. Since Dr. Liebman hadn't yet arrived, he asked about the other arrest.

Stanford grimaced. "That one ranks up there as one of the saddest and most bizarre cases I've ever been involved in. Detective Caulfield and I arrested the suspect at the coffee shop right down the street. When we found her, she was reading about her own attempted murder case in the morning edition of the *Post-Dispatch* while she ate her breakfast. Go figure!"

"Damn, that takes stones," Richard said.

"She was a real head case. Her first child, a little girl, died at three years of age. Her five-year-old son was chronically ill. Just as he would start feeling better, he'd fall sick again. The doctors, her family, and friends all felt sorry for the boy. They were especially worried about the parents since they had already lost a child. The mother, an insulin-dependent diabetic who suffered from ocular migraines had her own health challenges. The husband worked two jobs to keep up with the medical bills. A family friend started a GoFundMe page and raised several thousand dollars to help the family. Then the last time the son was hospitalized, the floor staff noticed that his condition worsened whenever the mother visited him."

"Let me guess. The child went into a hypoglycemic coma and nearly died."

"How did you know?"

"It sounds like a case of Munchhausen Syndrome by Proxy—MSBP for short."

"Exactly right, Dr. Crane," Chris said. "I can't spell or pronounce it, but that's the mental disorder the mother had."

"You said the mother was an insulin-dependent diabetic. I'm guessing the mother was making her child sick by giving him insulin injections, among other things. If you're not diabetic and take insulin, depending on the dosage it can induce a hypoglycemic coma and can even kill you. Some people who don't suffer from diabetes have committed suicide by injecting themselves with insulin."

"When the medical staff became suspicious, they began watching the child's mother closely. He went into a coma and they moved him to the critical care unit and turned his hospital room upside down. In the medical waste container, they found a used five hundred-unit insulin syringe. The nurses put two and two together and figured the mother had tried to kill her son and called the police."

"But the mother figured out they were on to her and skipped town."

"Eventually she confessed to killing her daughter as well."

"What a pity," Richard reflected. "Munchausen Syndrome by Proxy is a fairly rare attention-seeking disease, extremely difficult to treat. It's also very difficult to prove."

"Speaking of difficult, how are things going with our friend downstairs?"

"I believe Maybrick is suffering from parasomnia."

"What the hell is that?"

"It can refer to a number of sleeping disorders. In Maybrick's case, I'm inclined to diagnose him with nightmare disorder."

Stanford looked incredulous. "Is that a real thing? I mean, are people who have lots of bad dreams actually diagnosed with a disorder? Is it serious?"

"Sometimes. George Maybrick appears to have an extreme case."

"Can you help him, Dr. Crane?"

"I'm not sure. I certainly hope so. It's why I've asked Dr. Liebman to consult with me on his evaluation."

Just then, there was a quiet knock. Chris jumped up and hurried over to open his office door.

"Good morning," the heavily bundled woman on the other side said. "I'm Dr. Shoshana Liebman. The desk sergeant said I could find Dr. Richard Crane here."

"You're in the right place, Dr Liebman. I'm Detective Chris Stanford. It's a pleasure to meet you. Welcome to Hightower."

"This is Dr. Richard Crane," the detective said pointing to Richard.

He stood, and they all sized up one another for a few awkward seconds.

"You look like you just came in from the cold," Richard said with a grin to break the ice.

"Probably because I just did," Dr. Liebman replied evenly.

Her response made Richard realize how frivolous his comment must have sounded to her. For a moment he found himself uncharacteristically fumbling for what to say next. "Where are my manners?" he muttered, jerking himself out of his fog. "My apologies, Dr. Liebman. Good to meet you."

He quickly walked over and extended his hand, and she took it, shaking it gently. "A pleasure Dr. Crane."

"May I help you with your coat?" he offered as she removed her tan kid gloves one finger at a time.

"Yes, thank you. I'm afraid I'm heavily layered this morning. The heater in my car is on the fritz."

She handed him her long cashmere muffler and he hung it on the coat rack, then held her heavy winter coat for her as she pulled her arms out to reveal a thick woolen sweater underneath.

"The sweater, too?"

"Think I'll leave it on for now, though I feel like I'm outfitted for an Artic expedition," she joked as she gingerly removed the scarf from around her carefully coiffed linen-blond hair.

"Indeed, you do, doctor," he said, making her smile.

Whoever it was he'd expected to meet at the Hightower police station that morning, the attractive and pleasant Dr. Shoshana Liebman was not it. Which pleased him immensely.

After shaking hands, Stanford said, "I'm sure the two of you want to chat before I take you to see the suspect. You're welcome to use my office. I have a few things to do. If you finish your conversation before I get back, feel free to bring Dr. Liebman down to meet Mr. Maybrick. We've set up a table and a couple of folding chairs outside his cell. If you prefer to meet in the interrogation room just let me know, and I'll have him brought there when I return."

"Shall we begin?" Liebman suggested as soon as Chris closed his office door.

"If I may, let me start by asking if you have any questions."

"Assuming today goes well and we all agree to move forward with past life regression work, is there a decent space for Mr. Maybrick and me to meet here at the police station?"

"Yes, Detective Stanford said there's an interrogation room he will make available."

"Regression therapy in a police interrogation room...that would be a first. Hardly ideal. The most important thing, however, is that wherever the two of us meet, it needs to be private, quiet, and the client needs to feel comfortable."

"Understood," Richard replied.

"What have you told Mr. Maybrick about me so far?"

He took a breath. "Nothing," he replied. "He doesn't know you're coming. I thought it best not to tell him."

"Because...?"

"I was afraid he would refuse to talk to you," Richard explained. "I would ask that you trust me on this one, Dr. Liebman."

"Of course, I trust your professional judgment, Dr. Crane, but you must admit that springing a PLR therapist on a client sitting in jail charged with murder is hardly following protocol. You've already spent time with Mr. Maybrick so I'm sure you have good reasons, but you should have extended the courtesy of letting me know."

"Well, when you put it like that..." He grimaced, his jaw tightening. Realizing that he had made a serious error in judgment, he opted to be completely honest at the risk of making the situation even more difficult. "Of course you're right, Dr. Liebman. My sincerest apologies. If I can be totally transparent... I was afraid if I told Maybrick he would refuse to see you, and if I told you he wasn't expecting you, you might refuse to come."

"And I might well have," she replied sharply. "But I'm here now, so let's try to move forward."

"I'd just like to say one more thing before we continue," he said.

Liebman leaned in. "Go on."

"I've had several conversations with Maybrick. I've been a psychiatrist for over three decades, but I've never encountered a patient like him before. There is something about him that both intrigues and scares me at the same time. I can't put my finger on it, and it baffles me to no end. I have a strong feeling… well, more a belief than a feeling, that you are the one person who can help unravel the mystery of who George Maybrick really is. Call it intuition, call it what you want, but that is a reason you're here."

She gazed at him in silence.

He said, "If you want to withdraw from the case, Dr. Liebman, I'd certainly understand. It was never my intention to mislead you."

"On the contrary, Dr. Crane, I'm even more interested. Thank you for your transparency and your confidence. I hope I don't let you down."

"Not likely, doctor. What other questions do you have?"

"It's my understanding that Mr. Maybrick doesn't even have a trial date set. How long do you think we'll have for any sort of therapeutic intervention if I conclude one is called for?"

"Good question. I'm not sure. This is unfamiliar territory for me. When I'm called in for cases involving serious criminal activity, I usually have three or four sessions with the inmate to determine if there's a mental disorder and any reason why the individual should not stand trial, and that's it."

"So, the difference here is that you called me in to consult on a case that may or may not morph into a therapeutic relationship. With past life regression therapy, the process is different for each person. Some find healing in just one or two sessions. Others can take months. Several factors are involved. There's the psychology of the individual. Are they disordered? If so, at what level? Functional impairment can be a consideration, although that doesn't seem to be an issue in Mr. Maybrick's case. Another critical factor is the person's openness to PLR therapy."

"Can you elaborate on that, Dr. Liebman?"

"The individual doesn't have to believe they have lived past lives, but they must be willing to consider the possibility. But living in great psychic pain can be a powerful motivating force. Many of the people I work with at the hospital and in my private practice have been living lives of quiet desperation. They are often aware that they may be significantly disordered, although they don't have a label or a diagnosis they can attach it to. To escape that kind of anguish many are willing to entertain just about any prospect, including reincarnation. Of course, some can't or won't acknowledge the possibility of past lives and seek relief in an alternative type of regression therapy, or not at all."

"How do you recommend we proceed?"

"Let's play it by ear," she suggested. "Let me meet with Mr. Maybrick and see what happens. It's possible this is the one and only trip I make to Hightower. He may be completely closed off to the whole idea. Still, I'm always hopeful. In my experience, there is an alchemy that occurs in the fusion of the conscious and subconscious that takes place during past life regression that is very powerful."

"Understood," Richard said, nodding in agreement.

"I know you were looking for something a little more definitive, but that's the best I can do at this point. Now, do you have any questions for me, Dr. Crane?"

"Just one observation, Dr. Liebman, and I hope you appreciate the spirit in which I pose it and won't be offended."

"Now I'm curious. I'm not easily offended, Dr. Crane, so I think you can assume you're on safe ground...for now," she offered, grinning.

"I know you do a lot of research and writing on PLR therapy. It's interesting that no psychiatric association has signed off on PLR as a therapeutic intervention."

"True. But as the head of psychiatry for a med school at a major university, I've been invited to give keynote addresses on past life regression therapy to the largest psychiatric conference in this country as well as in Europe," she reminded him, clearly put out by his comment. "Surely, you're familiar with the Department of Perceptual Studies project in the Department of Psychiatry and Neurobehavioral Sciences at the UVA med school, started by psychiatrist Dr. Ian Stevenson. He specialized in investigating cases of children who seemed to remember past lives, interviewed hundreds and hundreds of children from all over the world. He documented some of his findings in his book, *Children Who Remember Previous Lives*. You might want to take a look at it. Today his work continues with Dr. Jim Tucker, also a psychiatrist, who now heads DOPS. He and his colleagues continue to build on Stevenson's work. I recommend his work, *Life Before Life: Children's Memories of Previous Lives*, as well." She smiled. Besides, to the best of my knowledge, no psychiatric association has signed off on acetaminophen as a pain reliever, but that doesn't mean I won't take Tylenol for a headache."

Richard gave a nod. "Good point. One last thing. I need to be clear in my mind that your decision to consult on this case is primarily about George Maybrick and not the opportunity to study and perhaps publish about your therapeutic work with a confessed serial killer."

"Hmm. That's a very interesting concern coming from the person who dangled the prospect of regressing a serial killer to entice me to consult with him."

"Guilty as charged, but I was desperate."

"Desperation rarely makes for good medicine, Dr. Crane."

"I know," he acknowledged sheepishly.

"Nevertheless, I believe your desperation was born of a genuine desire to understand and help Mr. Maybrick. I won't fault you for that. Under similar circumstances I might have done the same."

Richard quietly breathed a sigh of relief. "Hearing you say that means a lot to me, Dr. Liebman."

"As for your question that goes to my motivation, I'm not the least bit offended. I respect the fact that you are trying to protect the well-being of Mr. Maybrick and make sure he doesn't become someone's research project. I can't fault you for that. In fact, it may sound strange, but it makes me feel better about working with you. I also know it was a difficult question for you to ask me. I admire and value people who are willing to pose hard questions." She nodded at his look of relief. "I inhabit several professional worlds. I'm a physician, a university administrator, an academic who does research, and a professor. All my roles are related to medicine in some way, often spilling over into one another. But I can assure you that first and foremost I am a doctor, a healer, and my patients and clients are always my very first priority," she said emphatically. "I would never compromise them or their treatment in the interest of research and publishing. I've taken an oath to do nothing less."

"As did I, which is why I asked you here, Dr. Liebman," Richard said.

"Please, call me Shoshana."

He gave her a pleased smile. "Thank you. And I'm Richard. May I take you downstairs to meet George Maybrick, Shoshana?"

CHAPTER TWENTY-THREE

When Shoshana followed Richard downstairs to the basement jail cell, they found George Maybrick rocking precariously on the back legs of his rusty metal chair, a distant expression on his face.

"George, I'd like you to meet Dr. Shoshana Liebman. She's come all the way from St. Louis to see you," Richard said.

"What for?" George asked curtly.

Shoshana stepped forward and answered, "My colleague, Dr. Crane, thought I might be able to help you."

"Help how?"

"He tells me you have chronic nightmares."

"Yeah."

"I have some experience treating patients with your condition," she replied.

"Ever treated a serial killer before?"

"Does it matter?"

"There's only one thing that can help me."

"And what is that, Mr. Maybrick?"

"Dying," he replied matter-of-factly.

"You want to die?"

"Yes, after the first death, there is no other," he muttered.

"I don't think that's what Dylan Thomas had in mind when he wrote that poem."

"You know Dylan Thomas?" George responded, clearly surprised and delighted.

"Some, but I'm not here to talk about poetry," she replied. Thomas was actually one of her favorites, too. She'd read in Richard's notes that Maybrick liked the poet so she'd reviewed some of his works in case they came up.

"Do not go gently into that good night," Maybrick recited. "Old age should burn and rave at close of day. Rage, rage against the dying of the light."

"And you, my father, there on the sad height, curse, bless me now with your fierce tears I pray. Do not go gentle into the good night. Rage, rage against the dying of the light," she added effortlessly.

"I'm impressed, but you skipped several stanzas."

"Intentionally. We have other things to talk about," she said.

"That's my cue. I'll leave the two of you to talk," Richard said excusing himself.

"Thank you, Dr. Crane," she responded.

After Richard disappeared down the hallway, for several moments a vacuum of silence formed between her and Maybrick, a silent dialogue taking place between them, a conversation every bit as real as if they were speaking aloud. The obvious connection emerging fascinated her and gave her hope.

"You like Dylan Thomas, don't you?" he declared, breaking the silence.

"A great deal. I wrote my undergraduate thesis on the imagery of death in his poetry. It was my introduction to psychology, which ultimately led me to med school and psychiatry."

He pulled his chair closer to the bars and immediately launched into another recitation of the poet's works on death. "And death shall have no dominion. Dead men naked they shall—"

"Ah, the opening stanza of *And Death Shall Have No Dominion*," she interrupted. "Do you know where the title of the poem comes from?"

"Of course," he replied confidently. "Paul's letter to the Romans: Chapter 6, verse 9, I believe."

"Quite right. Tell me, what do you make of the line *Though they go mad they shall be sane*?" she asked.

"I may have gone mad, Dr. Liebman, but I'm not insane," he assured her, sidestepping her question. "Now, here's one for you. Where does *Rising again from the sea* in the first and second stanzas come from?"

"That's a tough one. I seem to recall Thomas borrowed it from the Book of Revelations in the Christian scriptures. Chapter 20, verse 13: *The sea gave up the dead.*"

She was enthralled with the banter. She could tell Maybrick was enjoying it immensely. Despite being two of the most unlikely people to hit it off, a bond and level of mutual respect began to form between them in a remarkably short period of time.

"Well, Doc—do you mind if I call you Doc? It looks like we have something in common. I'm sensing a connection here."

Shoshana was unsure whether he was being serious or sarcastic but took it as a good sign anyway. "Doc is fine. But enough poetry, we have other things to talk about," she announced firmly.

Maybrick's expression stated clearly he was not pleased. Nevertheless, he said, "All right, we can get down to business, but we're not done with our dear Welsh friend."

"Thank you, Mr. Maybrick. I promise we can talk more about our favorite poet and his approach to death at another time."

"I'll hold you to that. And please, call me George."

"Okay, George. Thank you," she agreed with a smile. "Now, George, tell me about your chronic nightmares."

"Not much to tell. I'm sure Dr. Crane filled you in, otherwise you wouldn't be here."

"He thought I might be able to help you. Have you ever heard of regression therapy, George?"

"No."

"Are you interested in learning about it?"

"No."

"Do you always say no when someone offers to help you?'

"No."

She chuckled. "Right. Well, would you be interested if I said it could help you with your nightmares?"

He hesitated. "Maybe."

His tone of voice and body language signaled his interest, but for some reason it seemed important to him to appear indifferent. "I'm told you've had nightmares for as long as you could remember. Do you have any idea why you've experienced these horrible dreams most of your life?"

"Not a clue. Bad karma maybe."

"Do you believe in karma?"

"I don't know about karma, but I damn sure swear by fate."

"You believe you're here in jail because of fate?"

"No, not entirely. Fate didn't make me kill all those women. I made those choices, but something certainly pushed me along, kept hammering the idea into my head. I'm not a sociopath, Doc. I always felt some remorse afterwards. I know it sounds crazy, but when I was killing them, something made it feel right. Like I wasn't killing them, I was killing something inside me. I just don't know what. Not sure I ever will."

"I've spent a lot of time studying your case, and I think I may be able to help you, George."

"Why would you want to help someone like me? I've brutally murdered several women."

"I don't make judgments about my patients."

"Why not?" He seemed surprised by her response. "The qualities of mercy are not strained?"

"Yes, something like that. So, are you interested?"

"I guess so."

"How do you feel about hypnosis?"

"You're going to hypnotize me?"

"I'd like to try."

"And how is that going to help me?"

"Without getting too technical," she explained, "there are two states in which we are able to access levels of consciousness where our deepest selves are allowed to emerge. One is when we are dreaming, and the other is when we are in a hypnotic state. In a state of deep hypnosis, we let our defenses down. Sometimes we can get in touch with feelings...things that have happened that we can't remember. Sometimes things we aren't even aware of."

"How's that going to help me with my nightmares?"

"Quite often when we discover the cause of something, it loses its power over us."

"Dr. Crane said something like that. He and I have talked several times. He's got me on some drug to help me sleep but I'm still having bad dreams."

"I could explain a lot more about the subconscious and its relationship to dreaming, but for now I would just ask that you trust me, George."

"Still sounds like bullshit to me, Doc."

"Maybe, but what do you have to lose?" she asked.

He remained quiet for several moments as he pondered her request. She sat comfortably in the silence, sensing she had gotten his attention.

"I've never been hypnotized before," he announced finally.

"Most people haven't. I can assure you that it's perfectly safe when it's done by a trained professional."

"You're not going to make me do anything stupid are you, Doc?"

"No, George. You can't believe all that stuff you see on TV and the movies. No one can make you do anything under hypnosis that you don't want to do. I'll let you in on a little secret. All hypnosis is really self-hypnosis, the patient controls the process."

"Is that a fact?"

"Yes, it's a fact."

"Okay, I'm game. You're right, I guess. What do I have to lose? I trust Dr. Crane, so I guess I can trust you."

"Thank you, George. You'll also discover something amazing."

"What's that?"

"Our subconscious is not limited by our imposed boundaries of space, time, and logic. As I said before, hypnosis is nothing more than a deep state of relaxation that allows us to access parts of our mind that aren't easy to get to in our normal, everyday waking state. However, it's possible to access and dialogue with our subconscious, and often find that intuition and creativity break through into our conscious awareness."

"I haven't been relaxed more than a handful of times my entire life. Even when I'm painting, which is the closest thing I experience to tranquility, I'm not really relaxed."

"Well, let's give it a try. If at any time you feel scared or uncomfortable, just imagine you're looking at yourself from the outside."

"What do you think I'm going to find while I'm hypnotized, Doc?"

"I'm not sure. There are different types of regression therapies that take place in a state of hypnosis. I specialize in past life regression. Are you familiar with the concept of past lives?"

He started to laugh. "You mean reincarnation? You gotta be kidding me!"

She ignored his dismissive laughter. "Reincarnation is not just some New Age thing, George. It has a tradition dating back over three thousand years. I believe much of our present life has to do with our past lives. I can't prove that, but I've read hundreds of studies and countless books that make me think reincarnation is real. Full disclosure, I have a strong spiritual belief in reincarnation. Over the last thirty years, I've worked with well over a thousand patients and clients whom I have regressed under hypnosis."

"And did they get better?"

"Most of them did, some did not."

"So, you think my nightmares are some kind of punishment for something I did in a previous life?"

"Punishment, no. An explanation. There are a number of indicators that a person's current life is being impacted by something that occurred in a past life. Based on my research and work with clients, I believe that certain patterns of behavior can repeat themselves over several lifetimes."

"For example?"

"Well, for starters, your recurring dreams that contain things that are unknown to you in this life. The birthmark on your forehead is another."

"Gimme a break Doc! What's that got to do with anything?"

"Let me finish and then I'll explain. Other examples are unreasonable fears or phobias that a person can't account for, such as fear of the dark or claustrophobia. They suggest one's previous life experiences may be infiltrating one's current life. I suspect for you there are others in your personal situation, but I won't know for sure until you decide to explore your past lives."

"Now I'm really curious, Doc. What's the deal with the birthmark?"

"Dr. Ian Stevenson, a psychiatrist and one of the most famous researchers on past lives and reincarnation, wrote a book in which he shared two hundred recorded cases of children with birthmarks and birth defects. In his interviews with these children, they claimed to remember past lives in which they were wounded or injured. One child who recalled being shot had two birthmarks that approximated the entry and exit of the bullet. Several children with malformed fingers or without fingers recalled injuries to their hands in a past life where they lost fingers. In his notes, Dr. Crane recorded your dream in which you were beaten and robbed by three men, and you reported one of your attackers struck you on your forehead in the exact same spot where your birthmark appears."

"Which doesn't prove anything."

"Of course not. It's only a possible indicator. It may simply be coincidence and mean nothing at all. As a psychiatrist and a scientist, though, it makes me curious," she explained.

"I think I understand. So, what's the downside of this hypnosis? There's got to be one, right?" he suggested.

"An excellent question. I'm going to be as transparent with you as possible."

"So, I'll know what I'm getting myself into?"

"You might put it like that. First, there are many people in my profession who think past life regression is unethical because they believe it is not sufficiently evidenced based. There is also ample research that demonstrates that under hypnosis there is always the possibility of false memories, or cryptomnesia."

"Cryptomnesia?"

"When you believe you have an original memory or idea, that in reality you've already encountered previously but have forgotten all about it. This phenomenon has been well documented in past life regression, as well."

"Like…?"

"The most common examples are people who relate an experience from a certain historical period. Under hypnosis they are accessing their subconscious, but they may be accessing current memories and not realize it. They may talk about something they did or happened to them in a particular historical period, in a very convincing narrative. Later, the therapist really digs into the story and finds the person got the information from a book or movie, or even a television show. In one case, the person related her past life under hypnosis and when the therapist scrutinized her story, they found she'd repeated the same historical errors portrayed in a certain television program."

"I get the idea" George said with a frown.

"Another problem with hypnotherapy is that the therapist may ask leading questions or allow their personal beliefs to shape the narrative. Think of it like a lawyer leading a witness in a trial or deposition," she explained.

"Right. Anything else?"

"I firmly believe the fields of psychology, physiology and spirituality all offer compelling evidence of reincarnation. I can share them with you later if you're interested, but for now I want to wait and see what experiences unfold for you. Okay?"

"Hmm... I have to say the whole thing sounds a little sketchy to me, Doc."

"Well, it's important to understand that you don't have to believe in reincarnation and past life regression. You need only be open to the possibility. The decision is entirely yours. I never want a patient to enter into a therapeutic relationship with me unless there is a level of trust and they believe there is a real possibility they will experience some degree of healing as a result."

George still looked skeptical.

She asked, "What would you give to have just one night of being able to rest your head on a pillow and know with confidence that you didn't have to go to sleep afraid of being tortured by nightmares?"

He sat silently for several moments; jaw clenched in thought. "There's nothing I wouldn't do," he finally responded somberly.

"Then let's get started."

"Before we start, I have a question. I'm wondering what it's like when you experience your death from a previous life while you're under hypnosis?"

"That's a fascinating question. In thirty years of practice, only three or four people have ever posed that question to me. I'm curious, why do you ask?"

"I don't like surprises. If there's a terrible death in store for me, I want to be prepared."

"Understood. This might surprise you, but most people handle it very well. If a person is experiencing some negative reaction, one thing that that works very effectively is I invite them to imagine they are floating above and just watching. Some people choose not to experience their own death, and I always respect their wishes. Many others I've worked with lose their fear of death." She met his eyes. "Anything else?"

"No, I'm good, Doc."

"Before we get started, do you mind if I record our session? It might be helpful later, and I promise no one else will listen to it but me."

"Do you usually do that?"

"Yes, if the patient gives me permission."

"I'd rather not."

"I understand. I'll just have to take very good notes." She was disappointed but wouldn't go against his wishes. "Okay, shall we get started?"

"Sure."

CHAPTER TWENTY-FOUR

"George, I want you to think back to a pleasant childhood memory and share it with me in as much detail as you can. Tell me everything you can remember—what you felt, the smells, sounds, colors, textures, every sensory detail you can recall."

"Okay..." He squirmed nervously and thought.

She could tell he was really trying to come up with something. "Take your time."

He closed his eyes. "I remember one Christmas when I was nine years old. I got my first real set of oil paints and three canvases. I couldn't wait to use them. I literally wanted to attack the canvas with color, but my parents made me wait until the next day. My dad woke me up early the following morning, made me breakfast and then took me down to the river. It was cold, but I didn't care. I sat on a bench on the docks. I looked up and he handed me the wooden box and said, 'Okay son, paint,' and then he broke into a huge smile. My father was a man of few words and I've never forgotten the look of joy on his face, an expression of how happy he was for me. It is one of my enduring memories of my father."

"Can you describe him to me, George?"

"I'd rather talk about painting."

Without pausing for a response, he launched into a description of sitting for the rest of the morning and into the early afternoon painting the river and the landscape on the other side. He related in meticulous detail the blond wooden box with mortised corners and solid brass hinges that held the special gift. He described the sound of the taut ropes tethering the nearby towboats to the docks which creaked as they twisted and turned, and the loud caws of the crows perched in the trees at the river's edge. The eddies that formed around the docks, the scent of the linseed oil in the paints, the texture of the canvas, and his brush strokes—all of these things he related to her as if it was only yesterday.

She marveled at the detail, careful not to interrupt. After about twenty-five minutes, he abruptly stopped talking.

She wanted to ask him why he'd said little about his father, but that was not the purpose of the exercise. "How can you remember something almost three decades ago so vividly, George?"

"When you are happy, truly happy, only a hand full of times in your life, you don't forget it. I've tried to recapture the joy of that day many times with my art over the years, but never really succeeded. It's the only reason I still paint," he said wistfully. "I want to recapture that day with my father on the dock painting the river. If I could do that just one more time, I could die then and there with no regrets."

"Your painting may help you now, George."

"How?"

"I'm going to use a protocol developed by Dr. Brian Weiss, one of the foremost authorities and practitioners of past life regression. As you undergo hypnosis, I'm going to take you to a place that is safe, calm, and relaxing. When you hear my words, visualize them as if you were going to paint what I describe. Really focus on the image I create in a much detail as you can. It's important to process what you've experienced, so I'll give you a posthypnotic suggestion at the end of your regression inviting you to remember everything you've told me so we can discuss it. Are you ready?"

"As ever," he nodded.

"I'll count back from ten to one. By the time I reach one, you will be in a deep state of peace and relaxation." She began counting backward. When she finished, she asked him to imagine he was walking down a beautiful staircase. "Deeper and deeper. Down...down... Each step taking you to a deeper level."

She gave him a moment.

"Now imagine at the bottom of the stairs there is a beautiful garden, unlike any garden you have ever seen before. A garden of peace, calm, and tranquility. You are safe in this garden. It is filled with lovely flowers, plants in bloom, trees, and fountains with running water. Now, look around the garden and find a place to rest, perhaps on one of the many benches or on the fresh, green grass. As you find a place to rest, continue to let your body relax. You are now completely comfortable, relaxed, and calm."

She took a visual inventory of his vital signs and could see he was in a deep state of relaxation.

She told him to notice how relaxed he was, then said, "You have the ability to remember everything in this lifetime." She paused. "Now we can go further back in time if you wish."

He nodded. "Okay."

"I want you to imagine you are sitting in front of a large, beautiful mirror filled with light. As you look into the mirror, you see there are many mirrors. In each of these mirrors you are in a different time, a different place...perhaps in another lifetime. If you wish, you will be able to go back and remember. As I count from five to one, feel yourself being drawn into one of the mirrors. Five...four...three...going into the mirror...being drawn in...two...nearly there...one...you are there."

George sat arched back in his chair, his eyes moving. She could see he had transitioned into a deep hypnotic state. Despite having done hundreds of regressions, she felt a little anxious. Patients often went back to a very traumatic event their first time.

"George, I want you to look at yourself and describe what you look like. What are you wearing? What do your surroundings look like? Are there other people there? Try to let a date come into your mind."

He began to speak. "I'm with two other men. I'm dressed in religious garb, a priest. The other two men are accompanying me to assist in my work. We are on horseback traveling to a village in Germany. The village is outside of a larger town, but the name of the village or the town is not clear. I'm an inquisitor and demonologist, and I've been summoned by the bishop to set up a tribunal and investigate rumors that there are witches in the village. The local priest reported a woman who had healed a man near death. His physician had pronounced him incurable and said there was nothing he could do for the man and that he would die shortly. The family asked a woman known to be a healer in the village to try to cure him. She restored the man's health. The doctor reported to the local priest that it must be the work of the devil."

"Do you know what time period you are in?"

"No exact date comes to me. I think it's late sixteenth or early seventeenth century maybe. The next morning the two other priests accompany me to the house of the woman and we take her away. She has three small children. Her husband wants to fight us, but the woman tells him she's done nothing wrong and assures him everything will be fine. The three of us and the local priest take her to a place that is private where she can be questioned. She denies she is a witch. The two men blindfold the woman and place her in chains. One of the men strips her so that the pricker can search for the devil's mark."

"George, can you explain the pricker and the devil's mark?

"The pricker examines the body for the witch's teat. It could be a mold, a wart, or any kind of congenital deformity. If he finds one, he jabs it with a needle hidden in his hand. If the woman doesn't cry out in pain, then she's a witch. Then he shakes his head indicating the woman did not feel the pinprick so we begin to torture her for a confession and to find out if there are any other witches in the village. Around noon on the second day, after being tortured on the pulley she admits she is a witch but denies there are any other witches in the village. We know we are going to turn her over to the local authorities for punishment, but before we do, we continue to torture her for more information. Finally, around midafternoon she acknowledges that her cousin's wife might have supernatural powers. Since it's late in the day, we decide to wait until tomorrow to bring her in. The village priest agrees and departs to tell the family of the poor woman's fate." His words stopped.

"Is there more that you see?" Shoshana prompted.

"Yes, but it's difficult to talk about. For the next several days, our witch hunt continues. Under brutal torture using thumbscrews and the pear of anguish, the interrogated women admit to having accomplices. I wonder if it's getting out of hand, but a young woman near death from torture tells us she has a friend in a nearby village who is a witch, so the inquisition continues. It goes on for several more days. The impact on the local villages is horrendous. Even the local priest loses the stomach for it. We return to the villages many times. By the time we are finished with our work, only one woman remains alive in each of the two villages. All of the others have been burned alive, died from torture, or are imprisoned. The silence in the village is haunting. Even the local priest seems ashamed, suspecting he has betrayed his flock."

"What were you feeling during this time in the villages?"

"I felt some unease, but the bishop assured me that I was doing God's work. Witches are considered worse than heretics because they consort with the devil. Their souls belong to the Prince of Darkness, and therefore they must be destroyed. All of the witches we burned had confessed to *maleficia*."

"Do you feel any guilt?"

"Guilt...no. But I do wonder if we might have killed or imprisoned innocent women and children."

"Children?" she asked, trying to hide her surprise.

"Yes, children. Sometimes witches pass their dark arts on to their children, so they must also be identified and punished. In cases where a child is particularly precocious, it is permitted to torture that child to get to the truth."

"Have you executed children for witchcraft?"

"Only on rare occasions, when it is for their own good, to try and save their souls from the devil."

"Do you have a name?"

"No name comes to me, but I know I'm a priest."

"If you can, go to the end of your life. Take a few moments."

"I'm very ill and dying a slow, excruciatingly painful death. My body is covered in dark boils that ooze blood and pus. I have a burning fever and chills. I struggle to breathe. I'm coughing up blood, and my entire body is racked with pain. I have no peace. I wonder if it is punishment from God for torturing and burning people who might have been innocent. On the second day of my illness, a priest comes to me on my deathbed to administer the Last Rites of the Catholic Church. The rituals are administered in traditional Latin, the official language of the Church. When he performs *Extremae Unctionis* he refers to me by my Latin name, but I am unable to recall it. Petrus, maybe? The next day the priest returns to pray for me. '*Requiem aeternam dona ei, Dominae. Et lux perpetua luceat ei. Requiescat in pace. Amen*' are the last words I hear before I die. Despite receiving the sacraments, I die in a state completely devoid of hope or divine mercy. I know that my utter despair is a mortal sin. Unforgiven at the time of my death, I will be confined eternally to the very fires of hell from which I believed I was saving others."

"Are you ready to come back now, George?"

"Yes," he replied in a near whisper.

"I'm going to awaken you," she began, "by counting back from one to ten. When I reach ten you may open your eyes. One...two...three...you are beginning to awaken...four...five...six...more and more awake...seven... eight...nearly awake now... nine...ten. You're fully awake now, George."

CHAPTER TWENTY-FIVE

Shoshana had not spoken with George Maybrick since their first therapy session ten days earlier, but it was never far from her mind. A few hours of research at the university library confirmed his narrative under hypnosis. In a book entitled *Witchcraze: A New European History of the Witch Hunts,* a historian of the Inquisition narrated the account of the Jesuit Peter Binsfeld, a bishop, theologian, and demonologist. Between 1581 and 1593, the inquisitor conducted witch hunts in the German town of Trier and twenty surrounding villages. In two of those villages, only one woman from each village survived, just as Maybrick had described during his regression. The inquisitor demonologist had believed that torture was a perfectly acceptable means of obtaining confessions, in some cases even from children. He had subsequently died from the bubonic plague.

Most of the plague symptoms were accurate in Maybrick's description of his very painful death and echoed those of one of George's recurrent dreams. Shoshana realized that George's account of his past life as an inquisitor was the source of the dream Richard recorded in his notes that he sent her in which George describes himself as a priest on his deathbed suffering from the plague. In his dream he is dying in complete despair with the knowledge that he will be spending eternal life burning in the fires of hell.

Shoshana pondered whether there might be a connection between the misogynistic past life of a destroyer of witches and the serial killer in the present who preyed on women. But there were still many missing pieces. Rarely had she been so curious about what a client's next regression would bring.

When she approached Maybrick's cell for their session, she found him lying on his bed reading a book. "Sleep any better?" she asked after their greetings.

"Yeah, a little. Dr. Crane has me on a new med to see if it works better than the one I'd been taking. It's rare that I go gently into the good night. I slept through the night on Friday last week. But I'm still having nightmares."

"That's to be expected. You can't undo over three decades of nightmares overnight. No pun intended. Before we start, do you want to talk about our first session at all?"

"I thought a lot about what happened. I've never had a dream quite like that, but I did share with Dr. Crane a recurring nightmare where I die in great physical pain and despair."

"I know. I read it in his notes that he shared with me. I believe there is a connection with that recurring nightmare and the past life you connected with in our first session."

"But how do you know I wasn't just making up all that stuff about killing witches? I could just be messing with your mind, no pun intended," he said. "And even if I wasn't making it up, how could you ever prove that it actually happened in real life?"

"I can't, but our sessions are not about proving things, George. I've had enough experience with patients to convince me that we all have past previous lives, and for many of us these lives can be accessed, explored, and in some cases put to rest. That's what we're aiming for, not about proof."

"I understand."

"As we move forward, I do want to discuss something with you. The past life you accessed as a sixteenth-century inquisitor contained a lot of trauma. The anguish caused by the witch hunts and subsequent trials and executions, but also the existential or spiritual trauma you experienced at the time of your death. The bubonic plague presented its victims with an agonizing demise. On top of all that, you died in a state of despair. I learned from one of my Jesuit friends that in the Catholic faith, despair is the only unforgivable sin. As you said on your deathbed, it warrants a life of eternal damnation in the fires of hell. That is about as traumatic as things can get."

Maybrick grimaced. "I couldn't agree more."

"We know from our studies that about sixty percent of people who are regressed report suffering violent deaths. In children, it's even higher, around seventy percent. I didn't share that with you initially because I didn't want to predispose you to creating a false memory. Of course, violent death is only one source of trauma. People also report trauma from emotional or physical abuse, sexual violence, betrayal, sudden or unexpected loss of a loved one, and a host of other painful experiences."

"I see."

"But experiences from a previous life don't always have to be traumatic. People share happy times, as well. In fact, with some of my patients and clients, I deliberately try to get them to a place in a past life that brought them joy, peace, happiness, or some sense of well-being. Nevertheless, more often than not, the healing that needs to take place occurs when individuals get in touch with past life trauma. It can seep into a person's current life causing all sorts of complications, such as recurring nightmares or compulsive behaviors."

"Seems to make sense," he agreed. "And by the way, I wasn't making that stuff up."

"I understand. Anything else you want to talk about before we get started?"

"Let's say I really did go back to a past life…"

"Go on."

"How come I was able to go back so easily? I mean, I just kinda relaxed, imagined what you were saying, and I was suddenly there."

"We're not exactly sure why it happens, it seems to be a combination of factors."

"Like what?" He leaned forward.

"Well, some people seem naturally predisposed to hypnosis. People who are very creative or who practice meditation or other mind-focusing techniques often take to regression therapy quickly. Dr. Crane tells me you are quite an artist. I believe the hypnotic state comes easily to you, but your chronic dreams are the real key."

"How so?"

"Past lives aside, the fact that you have frequent and recurring nightmares tells me there is something buried deep in your subconscious trying to make its way to the surface. Sometimes our recurring dreams are accessing our past lives. Dreams are an attempt by our subconscious to get our attention. Our subconscious mind can repress trauma at an early age when the mind is incapable of processing it. In your case, we don't yet know exactly what your subconscious is trying to tell you. It's as if your dreams keep tapping you on the shoulder and saying pay attention!"

"I think my dreams are doing more than taping me on my shoulder," he joked. "More like a sledgehammer!"

She laughed, nodded in agreement and continued, "When we dream, the ordinary filters that keep us from accessing the subconscious are circumvented. If nightmares have some connection to something that happened to you in a past life, it just makes sense that you would be able to tap into your subconscious and your past lives more easily."

"Dr. Crane has shared my history of recurring nightmares. If some of these horrific dreams are manifestations of memories from a previous life, why would I want to be regressed and repeat the trauma of facing my nightmares all over again? A little emotionally masochistic, don't you think?"

"That's a very thoughtful question, George. I won't pretend that during past life regression, people don't experience uncomfortable or painful feelings. It's often impossible to bring those repressed memories up from our subconscious without negative emotions. But remember, you always have the option of declining or ending a past life experience if you find it too uncomfortable. Think about your first regression. You experienced a past life where you executed many women and perhaps some children and died a horrific death from the bubonic plague. But during that experience your mind always remained connected to the present. Under hypnosis, your everyday conscious awareness is still at work. It's why you can hear me and respond to my suggestions or questions. Finally, remember our goal is to bring your repressed memories, particularly those of traumatic events, to the surface so they lose their power over you."

"That all makes sense, Doc."

"We can do a little exercise if you'd like," she offered. "It might help answer your question. Sit back and try to roll your eyes upward as if to look at the top of your head." She paused for a few moments, giving him time to practice. "Now, slowly allow your eyelids to flutter down, but try to keep your eyes looking upward. Good, you can stop now."

"What was that all about?

"The ability to do what you just did is highly correlated with the potential for deep hypnosis. I watched your eyes. The more of the white part of your eyes that shows when they are rolled upward as far as they can go, the deeper a person can go into a hypnotic state. As your eyelids slowly closed, I watched how much of the whites of your eyes I could continue to see."

"How'd I do?" he asked, looking pleased with himself.

"Quite remarkably, really. It certainly helps explain why your first attempt at past life regression proved so successful." She smiled, and for a brief moment she forgot she was sitting in the same space with a brutal serial killer having an engaging, almost enjoyable conversation. The cognitive dissonance was a bit unsettling.

Shaking it off, she continued. "Your experience followed a very detailed narrative, but that isn't the case for everyone. One patient said his experience was like watching an old silent black-and-white movie. Other patients' encounters are less about imagery and more about experiencing a previous life through perceptions, emotions, or sensations."

"I think I get it."

"Then let's get started."

"I'm ready. And by the way, Doc, you can use the recorder if you want to. I'm okay with it now."

"Thank you, George. It might prove very helpful later."

Within five minutes of beginning the session she could see his eyelids fluttering, and knew he was scanning something deep in his subconscious.

"What do you see?" she asked.

"Nothing's happening. I'm trying, but nothing. I don't understand."

"Don't worry. It's perfectly normal. Just stay relaxed and be patient."

For the next half hour, he only recalled events from his current lifetime, though nothing about the murders. Each time he approached the mirrors, nothing happened.

She was about to give up and bring him out of the hypnotic trance when he began to cry.

"Can you describe what you see, George?" she asked.

"I'm a child, a little boy, all alone in the dark. I'm crying because I'm frightened. I've been locked in the closet to be kept away from something."

"Do you know who locked you in the closet?

"My stepmother. My father is away, fighting in a war, I think. His wife is sleeping with other men while he's gone. She doesn't want me to see what's going on, so she locks me in the closet in my room. I'm left alone for hours.

I caught her once. I woke up in the middle of the night and went to her bedroom. A man was on top of her. 'Mommy, what are you doing?' I asked. She became very angry and beat me. Now she locks me in the closet. Every time the doorbell rings I panic, thinking it might be one of her visitors. Finally, I cry myself to sleep. I hate the darkness and confined spaces. I feel scared, alone, claustrophobic."

"George, I want you to move forward in time and find out what happens to you."

He sat quietly for a few moments, and then began crying again.

"Tell me what you see."

"I'm sitting at the table having lunch. I live in a very nice Victorian home. I'm now about seven years old. My father has been gone again for several months. He's an officer in the British army serving in India. My stepmother is in the study reading."

"Do you know where you are living?"

"London."

"Is there anything around you that can help you determine a date? A newspaper or calendar maybe?"

"Around 1858. My father gave me a newly minted shiny half-sovereign before he left for India. He told me to keep it in my pocket for good luck. The date on the coin is 1857."

"Good. What is happening?"

"The doorbell rings. My stepmother tells me to answer it. I see a man in a uniform when I open the door. He looks very serious and asks to speak to my stepmother. She sends me away. I leave, but I stay close to the front door so I can hear what he's saying. He says, 'I have sad news, ma'am. There's been an accident. I'm afraid your husband has been killed outside of New Deli. His regiment was on maneuvers and there was an explosion in one of the munitions wagons. Several men were killed, including your husband.' 'No!' I cry out before my stepmother can even respond. I run back around the corner and grab the uniformed man and begin striking him, crying, and yelling that it can't be true. My stepmother grabs me. I intuitively know she doesn't care, but she's trying to pretend she does. 'That's no way to behave, child. Get hold of yourself. Your father would want you to be strong,' she says, devoid of emotion. I break away from her. 'I hate you!' I yell as I get to the bottom of the steps and begin running down the street as fast as I can." Maybrick sat sobbing for several minutes.

Shoshana debated continuing the session or stopping to process what had happened. She tried to separate her curiosity and desire to know what happened next with what was therapeutically best for her patient. She decided it was best to continue. "George, would you like to move forward?"

"No, I don't want to!"

"Can you try to move ahead one more time? Just a few years?"

"No!" The resistance in his voice took her aback. "Something terrible is going to happen and I don't want to see it."

"Okay. That's enough for today," she reassured him.

After counting him back, she gave him a few minutes to transition from deep hypnosis to an awakened state, then offered him a small box of tissues from her briefcase and asked, "What did you take away from today's session?"

"The light."

"What about the light, George?"

"I hate the dark. I always sleep with a light on. I don't like small spaces either. I've been claustrophobic for as long as I can remember. Even when I work on the ships I don't sleep in the regular quarters. I request a bunk near the deck, close to fresh air. If the weather is clear, I often throw out a bedroll and sleep on deck."

"You know, sometimes it's not the dark we fear most, but the light of day." He looked puzzled.

"Carl Jung once wrote, *The brighter the light, the greater the shadow.*"

"Which means?"

"Jung believed we all carry a shadow in our unconscious, and when we ignore or deny the existence of that shadow, we do so at our own peril. The shadow embodies our darkness—those thoughts, actions, feelings, and attitudes we want to hide. He referred to the shadow as the thing a person has no wish to be. Left unacknowledged, the shadow operates in our lives without us realizing it, and invariably gets us into trouble. Personal growth requires us to get in touch with our shadow side, shine a light on it, and incorporate it into our lives. Jung believed it's not about being good, it's about becoming whole. That said, many people, either consciously or unconsciously, fear the light for what it might expose in terms of how they live their everyday lives."

"Makes sense, I guess," he replied with a frown, clearly wondering what that meant for him personally.

"We can talk about it more later if you wish, but for now, do you see any connection between the life you just experienced and your nightmares?"

"I don't know, Doc. Do you think my fear of the dark and claustrophobia could be caused by my experience as a child in that previous life?"

"It's not really what I think, George. It's about whether *you* feel there might be a connection. I could give you countless examples of my clients over the years who discovered that the fears, phobias, likes, dislikes, dangerous behaviors, you name it, in their current lives could be traced back to something that happened in a previous life."

"Still sounds…far-fetched."

"Past life regression is not recommended for children, but several years ago, a couple brought their four-year-old daughter to see me. She was terribly afraid of water. The family vacationed every summer at a family home on a lake and they wanted her to learn how to swim. After a few sessions, she told me she remembered nearly drowning in a swimming pool when she was three years old. The parents said she'd never been to a pool, so I was pretty sure she was remembering a traumatic event from a past life. In a follow-up session we talked it through, and she was just fine after that. But you know what's really ironic?"

"What's that, Doc?"

"The last time I checked, she still holds the state high school record for the two hundred meter freestyle."

"That's unbelievable!"

"You've done healing work today, George. Let's start where we left off next session." She opened her briefcase, pulled up a book, and offered it to him.

He reached through the bars, retrieved the volume, and read the title. "*Witchcraze: A New History of the European Witch Hunts.*"

"Thought you might like to read it," she said. "Pay close attention to Peter Binsfeld, known by his Latin name, Petrus Binsfeldius. He's listed in the index. I believe the two of you might have something in common."

CHAPTER TWENTY-SIX

"Coffee?"

"No thanks, Harry," Chris replied grimly.

"What's wrong? You look like you just lost your mother."

"Worse," Chris said, sliding a folder in his partner's direction.

"How the hell did he pull this off?" Harry asked after reading the contents of the folder.

"Well, he said he had friends in high places."

"That's bullshit. They can't do this! Can they?" Harry asked in disbelief.

"They just did. Turns out our friend Detective O'Meara is a big-time local hero in New York City. He has the highest rate of solved murder cases of anybody in the entire NYPD. He's like a frikkin' demigod. This guy needs to get a life. He works cold cases in his free time. No wonder he's so damn good, it's all he does. When O'Meara flexes his influence, he gets his way. He even got the FBI to weigh in on it. He got a court order, and he's coming to pick up Maybrick next week."

"Maybe it is for the best, Chris. It's been two and a half months and our prisoner's been sitting downstairs with full room and board, doodling and bullshitting the shrinks. The DA has got his head up his ass and won't move forward because he's afraid he'll jeopardize the biggest case of his career, all while he's milking it for all it's worth. There's even a rumor going around he's got an offer in Kansas City, and he's stalling this case so he doesn't screw it up. Hell. I say turn Maybrick over to O'Meara and let's be done with him."

* * *

When Dr. Crane showed up the next day to visit Maybrick, Chris gave him the bad news.

"You're not going to let O'Meara get away with this are you?" Crane asked in obvious disappointment.

"I can't see that I have any choice, Dr. Crane. This New Yorker is holding all the cards."

"Dr. Liebman has only seen him four times, but she says that they're making significant progress. They've established a good relationship, and she believes he's made a turn for the better. She thinks she may really be able to help him. If Maybrick is taken away now, we'll have lost that possibility."

"Why the big interest in helping him, Dr. Crane?"

"I know he's a cold-blooded murderer, and I know what he's done, but there's something about him… I believe he's a tortured soul. If nothing else, aren't you at least curious to find out what makes this guy tick? Why he killed? Dr. Liebman is confident we'll be able to figure it out. We all know, including George, that he's probably on the fast track to death row, but I'd like to see him find a little peace before he goes."

"But you said in your preliminary report that you don't think he's mentally incompetent," Chris protested.

"He's not incompetent to stand trial, but that doesn't mean he's not in a lot of psychic pain. Don't forget, my report doesn't offer a diagnosis. The jury is still out on that."

"Does Dr. Liebman agree with all that?"

"Absolutely, and she's as curious as I am. George Lindfield Maybrick is unlike any case either of us has ever seen. He doesn't fit any known clinical psychological profile out there so far. He's an anomaly. If we can unravel his psyche, we may be able to help him. That's our job as doctors. We've taken an oath to act in the best interest of our patients, serial killers or not. Just as important, he may give us a better understanding of serial killers and help us catch them more easily in the future. Maybe even prevent some from becoming serial killers in the first place."

"Unfortunately, you've only got five days to do that. O'Meara is going to be here next Tuesday, and I'm betting he's going to show up bright and early."

Crane's eyes widened. "Sorry, I've got to run, Detective."

"What's the sudden rush?"

"I've got an idea. If it's any good, I'll see you first thing in the morning."

CHAPTER TWENTY-SEVEN

Chris arrived at the station earlier than usual the following day. He didn't expect to hear from Dr. Crane and was mentally preparing to transfer George Maybrick into the New York City detective's custody the following week. Much like Crane and Liebman, he had developed an unusual attachment to the confessed serial killer, and even felt some sympathy for him. Even so, he was over the whole drama and looked forward to returning to business as usual.

As he pulled out a report to work on, Dr. Crane surprised him with a knock at his office door. "I didn't think you were coming," he said after their greetings.

"Read this proposal, Detective Stanford, and tell me what you think. Dr. Liebman and I believe it just might work," Crane offered.

As Chris read through the pages, much of the psychological and medical jargon escaped him, but he understood enough to get the main idea. The two psychiatrists had laid out an argument that George Maybrick had entered into a therapeutic relationship and was technically in treatment. Both stated that it would be injurious to their patient to terminate his therapy at this time. Crane noted Maybrick's earlier comment to Liebman that he wanted to die, and that he evidenced suicidal tendencies, which added gravity to the report without saying directly that he was a threat to himself or others. Crane obviously knew the law since he cited Missouri statute 552.020, which clearly stated that a mental evaluation determining competency to stand trial must include an opinion as to whether the accused had a mental disease or defect. The proposal reasoned that the accused was still without a diagnosis, and while he was likely mentally competent from a legal perspective, a diagnosis still needed to be rendered to fulfill the medical responsibilities to the patient, the courts, and the Percy County DA who had originally requested the psychiatric evaluation. The proposal concluded with a request to withhold the transfer of George Maybrick until the current therapeutic intervention had been completed. They had conveniently left out a completion date in their final report.

"I don't know, Dr. Crane," Chris said after reading it over twice. "You have to know this proposal is a legal Hail Mary at best."

"Yeah. But what do we have to lose?"

"Absolutely nothing. I'll get it over to the judge. But even if he grants you a stay, he could be overruled the next day if O'Meara pushes it. The guy is connected like nobody's business."

CHAPTER TWENTY-EIGHT

"Morning, Detective Stanford."

"Good morning, Dr. Liebman. How are you?"

"Any word yet about O'Meara?"

"No, but no news is good news. Ready for your session with George?"

"Yes. Does he know?"

"Yeah. Dr. Crane felt we should tell him."

"How did he take it?"

"Let's put it this way. Detective O'Meara is not one of George's favorite people."

"He's not one of mine, either," Shoshana said. "Is he sleeping any better?"

"He's slept through the night four or five times since you were here last week. I don't know what you're doing, but it seems to be helping."

"The new meds might be helping, as well," she said, pleased with the progress George seemed to be making.

"How long do you think you'll need?"

She understood exactly what Stanford meant by his question. "I'm not sure, but the next two or three sessions could be critical."

"You'd better hurry. I'm afraid George is living here on borrowed time. Our friend in New York isn't going to take this delay lying down. Come on. I'll take you downstairs. We've already set up the table and chairs outside his cell."

* * *

Without the oppressive darkness, George now felt strangely at home in his cell. The small basement window left the space starved for natural light. His feet felt right at home with the hard stained concrete floors, having long grown accustomed to traversing the solid metal passageway floors of the freighters and tankers on which he had spent most of his adult life. He appreciated the anonymous maintenance man who decades ago had painted the three concrete cell walls a nice shade of green, long since faded, but green, nevertheless. As a painter with a keen understanding of chromatic theory, George knew green to be a healing color and the most relaxing color for the human eye to look at. All the cell furnishings were of a single piece fashioned from metal. "Is this the best you can do for a chair?" he had asked Stanford one day, pointing to the solid heavy metal chair next to his bed. "Every time I sit in it my ass hurts after a half hour," he'd protested.

"It's prison-issue furniture, George. Everything in a jail cell must be solid metal with no detachable pieces. Imagine what could happen if an inmate was able to unscrew or break off the leg of a chair or bed. He'd have one hell of a weapon."

"Got it. Makes sense," George had acknowledged.

A true introvert, George had begun to welcome the isolation of the basement jail cell. He had gotten used to the dank, musty smell and come to view the three walls and bars as a safe space where he only needed to interact with a handful of people. He routinely passed on breakfast, joking with Stanford, "I would rather have three cigarettes than three squares a day."

When the department retrofitted the locks on the upstairs cells with keyless electronic locks, it didn't bother with the cell downstairs, confident the criminal activity in Hightower would never again rise to a level necessitating the use of the basement cell. So, the sound of the heavy metal key as it rotated and clicked in the manual lock each morning was music to George's ears. It signaled the arrival of Detective Stanford on his errand of mercy to provide George with his clandestine cigarette break on the now-familiar back steps of the Hightower police station.

Boredom was not part of George's vocabulary nor in his psyche. His sister had gotten permission to bring him several books, including his tattered copy of *Collected Poems* by Dylan Thomas. Published after his death in 1953, the book included what the Welsh poet considered his best works. George thought of it as his most prized possession.

His two psychiatrists had also proved benevolent. Dr. Crane's gift of two sketch pads and a set of drawing and sketching pencils had vastly expanded George's ability to fill the unending hours in his cell with engaging activity. Dr. Liebman had gotten Detective Stanford's permission to let George borrow her small portable CD player and had gifted him with the *Dylan Thomas*

Caedmon Collection featuring the Welshman and other noted writers reading his poetry. Stanford and Crane had stood by as Dr. Liebman passed the CD player and recordings to him through the metal bars and looked on as his eyes glazed over with tears of joy and deep gratitude for her kind gesture.

From the first day George had taken up residence in the Hightower jail, he had dutifully counted the number of days he had spent there. One January morning during his ritual smoke break he announced to Stanford, "It's been forty-three days. Can you believe this is the longest time I've stayed in one place in my entire adult life, and I spent it in a jail cell?" He laughed. "Even when I came home to visit my mother, sister, and nephews I never stayed for more than a couple of weeks."

CHAPTER TWENTY-NINE

When Shoshana arrived at Maybrick's cell along with Detective Stanford, he pulled out the chair for her a safe distance from the cell and then departed.

"I understand you've been sleeping a little better, George," she said after Stanford was gone.

"Yeah. Since last week I've actually had several nights without any bad dreams. I can't remember when that's happened before."

"I know Detective Stanford has talked to you about being transferred to New York soon. We may not have much time left together, so I may push you a little. It's not ideal, but I think we're making progress."

He nodded. "It's all right, Doc. Detective O'Meara just won't give it a rest. Makes me wonder what went on in his past lives," he joked humorlessly. "Anyway, I really appreciate what you're trying to do. It can't be easy, helping me after what I've done. Most people would never understand that I may be a serial killer, but I'm not a monster."

George had taken well to the past life regression process, and within ten minutes he fell into a deep hypnotic trance.

"George, I want you to try to go back to your life in London from our second session." But when she invited him to move forward in that lifetime, he became agitated sensing something terrible in his future.

She suspected his reluctance to further explore that future held the key to something significant in his current life. As his eyelids fluttered, she knew he was scanning his subconscious for that time period. While no guarantee that he would venture back to this specific lifetime, his obvious intention to do so would greatly increase the possibility.

"Where are you, George?" she asked after a few moments.

"I'm in the East End of London. It's not my first time. I've been here many times before. It's a chilly, stormy evening. I walk by a church, St. Mary's. It's painted white, and...something unusual, there's a pulpit outside. People everywhere...mostly poor. The conditions people are living in are awful. The neighborhood has a very foul smell. Children, dirty and dressed in rags, are playing in the streets and alleys. A woman who looks frail and sickly is sitting against a fence outside a lodging house. She has an infant bundled in a threadbare blanket in her lap. I stop. Her baby, who can't be more than a few months old, is crying. I can see that they are both malnourished. Her eyes are sunken, her hair is matted, and several of her teeth are missing. The mother asks me for three pence for a night's lodging, and I give it to her. The streets are filthy, garbage everywhere. I pass an alley where the stench of urine is overpowering. A butcher shop fronting the street has blood and urine from the slaughtered animals running out of the front door into the street. I'm searching for somebody."

"Do you know who you're looking for?"

"No, not yet," he replied in a hushed tone.

"Do you know your name?"

"No. I wander the streets a bit and decide to have a drink. I round the corner and see a pub."

"Can you see the name of the pub?"

"Yes, it's the Ten Bells Pub. I go in for a drink. It's very crowded, with a heavy cloud of smoke—cigarettes, pipes, cigars...everyone is smoking. I have a couple of pints and head back out into the street. It's dark now. I can see a red glow in the sky. There must be a huge fire down by the docks. I can hear the sound of horse-drawn fire wagons off in the distance."

"Can you tell what year it is?"

"Uh... The eighteen eighties, I think. It's late summer."

"Do you know where you live?"

"Mostly on ships."

"What happens next on that evening?"

"I walk the streets for another couple of hours. Finally, I stop at another pub. There's a woman drinking. She looks drunk already. She's the one I'm looking for."

"Do you know why you're looking for her?"

"Yes. I'm going to kill her," he replied without hesitation.

Shoshana tried to hide her consternation. In all her years of regression therapy, she had only wanted to end a session a handful of times, but this was one of them. Her pulse quickened and her chest tightened. She felt the sweat gathering on her forehead and on the palms of her hands. She closed her eyes for a few moments, drew a deep breath, and made herself go on. "Please continue, George."

"The woman comes over and takes a seat next to me. She smells of gin and stale cheese."

"Can you describe her?"

"Short, a little more than five feet maybe, plump, brown graying hair, gray eyes, high cheekbones with delicate features. She looks to be in her early forties. She has a scar on her forehead and she's missing several of her front teeth. She's wearing an old black bonnet that looks out of place. Her clothes are ragged and worn, a brown ulster with brass buttons, brown skirt and jacket, a faded red cloak, and a handkerchief around her neck."

Shoshana marveled at the detail of his description. She could visualize the woman as he described her, which made her even feel more ill at ease.

"She introduces herself. 'My real name's Mary Ann, but everyone calls me Polly,' she says, and asks me to buy her a drink. I give her some change without saying a word and leave the bar. I don't want to be seen with her. I stand outside the pub and wait for her. When she leaves I follow her, but she's not alone for very long. She's a prostitute, but nobody is interested. Around two-thirty I follow her to a food stall at the corner of Whitechapel Rd. and Osborn St. She speaks to the owner for a few minutes, and he tells her she's drunk and to go away. I continue to stalk her. She seems to realize somebody is following her. When she turns around, she recognizes me even though she's very drunk. 'Well, I'll be blowed. It's the gentleman from the pub. Remember me? Polly? I've got to get my doss money or I'm on the street for the night. Fancy a go for four pence?' she asks. I say nothing. She takes me by the arm and leads me down the street. We walk several minutes, about three-quarters of a mile. She keeps muttering about her doss money. I'm trying not to be seen with her. We turn down a street—I see the street sign, Bucks Row—and there's a pub on the corner. The street is dark with warehouses on one side and run-down houses on the other. There's a stable. Without saying a word, she turns around, faces the stable gate, and lifts her skirt and dirty petticoat. I glance up and down the street. There's no one about. I grab her by the throat and begin choking her. She struggles, and I hit her with my fist on the side of the head. She falls to the pavement, nearly suffocated, and I pull out a knife and slit her throat. Something happens and I have to slash her throat a second time. The wound is so deep I can feel the knife hit her vertebrae. She looks up at me with dead, open eyes. I pull up her clothes and disembowel her. I remove her intestines and throw them over her left shoulder. I'm cutting away her reproductive organs when I hear a noise. In the distance, I see the silhouettes of two men coming down the street, but they haven't seen me yet. I wipe my bloody hands on her clothes and quickly walk away."

The killer's narrative left Shoshana shaken. She could feel the presence of a darkness that transcended the limits of time and space. She fumbled for a response, or a question, but her mind had locked up.

George began speaking again, but she interrupted him. She wanted to know how the killer escaped, but her curiosity was no match for her emotional exhaustion. She was relieved when she asked George if he was ready to return to a waking state and he nodded in agreement.

The irony of the revelation from George's past life was not lost on either of them. On the one hand, they had just experienced a gut-wrenching regression revealing a gruesome murder, but in that experience lay part of the explanation for Maybrick's current situation.

Still, she found herself fumbling in the dark. She could not bring herself to go through the session with him. Even George sat silently in his cell trying to come to grips with his ghastly revelation. She felt like she was performing psychic surgery without anesthesia, but understood that he was probably experiencing relief. His dark side, a fugitive of his subconscious for so long, had at last made its way to the surface. He surely must feel a huge burden had been lifted.

But not for her.

Finally, she spoke. "George, I don't think I can go any further today. But we'll have lots to talk about when we meet next week."

"I understand, Doc," he said in a hushed tone.

Without saying another word, she turned off her recorder, placed it and her notes in her briefcase, and left the station.

She felt racked by guilt on the long drive home. She felt she had penalized her client because of her own limitations. Maybrick had shared a long-hidden secret from a previous life that might well begin to explain his current impasse. But at the moment, she could not stand to be close to him. She felt ashamed professionally, and as a human being her quick exit from another person in need mortified her.

She needed to find a way to repair the damage.

CHAPTER THIRTY

"Good news, George. Dr. Liebman is coming to see you today."

"But it's Saturday, Detective Stanford."

"I know, but she called late yesterday afternoon and asked if it would be all right for her to come today. That's not a problem, is it?"

"No, not at all. Dr. Liebman and I have a lot to talk about."

"She asked me to check with you and see if you mind if Dr. Crane attends your session. She said she would explain when she got here."

"Kind of an unusual request, but it's fine with me."

* * *

Shoshana arrived at the Hightower police station earlier than Dr. Crane so she and Maybrick could talk privately first.

"George, I owe you an apology for the other day. I should never have left you like I did."

"I understand, Doc. I really do. It couldn't have been easy for you to listen to what I was remembering. I felt a lot better after our session even though we didn't get to talk about it. I'm afraid there's more, though. I'm beginning to believe you that some of my bad dreams may be related to a past life I'm only now coming to grips with."

"It's very likely," she said, glad he was starting to accept the process. "But remember, these experiences are in the past, and if you feel uncomfortable you can rise above them as if you were watching a movie, or we can simply stop the session. Since we may not have much more time, I'm going to keep gently pushing you."

"Okay. But why do you want Dr. Crane here?"

"I need someone else's perspective, George. I don't know what else we're going to uncover, but I think it would be better to have another person to help us process it all. It's not exactly protocol, but I hope we have your permission."

"It's fine, Doc," George said. "What difference does it make? I'm not going anywhere, and it's not like I'm going to be embarrassed."

"Have you given any thought to our session on Thursday?"

"It was so real, and I remember it clearly. I was right there reliving the entire thing. I felt the deep anger inside myself, and the experience of killing someone."

"Do you have any idea why you killed that woman?"

"Anger, rage. Hatred, revenge, maybe?"

"But you had never met her before. She was a complete stranger until she came up to you in the pub," she reminded him.

"True. I really don't know why."

She could see that while he was warming to the idea of a connection between his nightmares and past lives, he was still not making any connection between the prostitutes he had killed and his stepmother. She thought briefly about asking him if he saw any link between the two, but decided to bypass that question for the present.

"What about the murder in your past life and the murders now? Any connection?" she asked instead.

"You tell me. You're the one who is supposed to know how our past lives affect our current lifetime."

"I don't have an answer—yet. But I think we might get some clarity if you return to that life again. Are you willing to do that?"

"Yes," he replied.

She could see he was not looking forward to returning to this past lifetime in Victorian England, but that he sensed how crucial it could be.

They chatted for a bit while they waited for Richard, who arrived fifteen minutes later. After he and George exchanged greetings, Shoshana thought she detected some anxiety in George. Nevertheless, within ten minutes he had entered a deep, relaxing hypnotic state.

She invited him to return to his late nineteenth-century life again.

"I'm leaving a ship. We are in port for a few days. I'm sleeping on the ship at night and going to the East End during the day. I've decided to go to a pub for something to eat and a drink. There's a boy hawking newspapers. The masthead reads *The Penny Illustrated Newspaper*. He's yelling something about another murder. I buy a copy and see a picture of a murder victim on the front page. It immediately catches my interest."

"Why are you so interested?" she asked.

"Because I killed the woman."

She and Richard exchanged glances. "Can you see a date on the paper, George?" she asked.

"It says September, 1888. I take the paper with me to the Britannia, one of my favorite pubs. I order lunch—black pudding with cheese and stale bread—and begin reading the story. It tells how the woman, a local prostitute named Annie Chapman, must have been lured to a small yard behind a house on Hanbury Street. Her throat was cut and she was disemboweled, her organs thrown over both shoulders. The next day, the neighbors charged people money to see the murder scene. A costermonger even showed up selling refreshments. As I read the story, I replay the murder over in my mind."

"What are you feeling as you read?"

"The woman was a prostitute and deserved what she got," George shot back emphatically.

"Okay. Can you move ahead and see what happens next?"

"I'm back in port again. It's the same ship I worked on earlier coming from Germany."

"Can you see the name of the ship?"

"Yes, it's the *Sperber*, a steamship sailing from Bremen. We arrive on a Saturday in the morning and work until late afternoon. The weather is very poor, lots of rain. Everyone takes shore leave that evening. Most of the crew are German, but a couple of us are English. We're berthed at the London Docks, walking distance from the East End. There are pubs and prostitutes everywhere in the East End, servicing locals and all the merchant seamen from the cargo ships."

Shoshana wanted to ask him if he intended to murder again, but swallowed the words and said, "Go on."

"I start looking for a victim. I always know my victims as soon as I see them. I have a drink at the first pub I find, then head down to Flowers and Dean Street. I've been there before. It is one of the worst streets in the East End. I don't find the right woman, so I start making the rounds of the different pubs. Around eleven, it finally stops raining. I find my victim in the Bricklayer's Arms. She's having a drink with a man who's too nicely dressed to be from the East End. I'm trying to get as close to her as I can while remaining inconspicuous. A couple of her friends are teasing her about being with a fancy gentleman."

"Can you describe her, George?"

"Brown hair, blue eyes, with a kind of oval face. On the side of her mouth just above her lip she has a slight swelling or deformity. I'm drawn to the checkered silk scarf she's wearing around her neck. Her black, fur-trimmed jacket is well worn and she has red and white flowers pinned to her dress. The man keeps buying her drinks. After an hour and a half, he takes her by the arm and leads her out of the pub. She stumbles on the way out. The two of them walk for a few minutes, then turn down a street."

"Can you see the name of the street?"

"I can see the street sign but can't make it out clearly. It's something like Burns or Bern Street. It's very dark. I see a workers' club with a fair number of people inside singing and dancing, even though it's after midnight. I don't go down the street after them and remain at the corner, out of sight in the shadows. There's a man standing across the street from the couple smoking a white clay pipe and looking on. A night patrolman carrying a bullseye lamp comes by and turns down the street. I can see the woman take something out of her dress and offer it to the man, but he turns it down. I'm not able to see what it is. A few minutes later, the man and the woman get into an argument. I can't understand what they're saying, but I can tell he's very angry. Suddenly, he grabs her by her shoulders and throws her violently down onto the muddy street and walks off, muttering something to the man across the street who continues smoking his pipe while he follows the man from a distance. I look around. No one is nearby except for the people in the workers' club. This is my opportunity."

Shoshana nodded encouragingly when he hesitated.

"I approach the woman who's still lying on the ground in front of a large gate that opens to a narrow court. Even in the darkness, I can see she has mud and horse shit from the street all over her clothes. She's cursing the man who threw her to the ground. I notice she's holding a small packet of mints in her hand, and I think how strange it is that she is lying in the mud clutching a small bag of sweets. She looks up at me, still cursing. I bend down and she thinks I'm going to help her up. 'A proper gentleman,' she mutters between curses. I pull my knife from the inside of my coat and in an instant it's over. Suddenly, I hear a noise. I listen carefully as my mind filters out the singing and dancing at the club next door. It's a horse-drawn cart coming down the cobblestone street. Quickly, I wipe my knife off on her clothes and run the short distance to the end of the street. I don't know why, but I stop to watch and see what happens even though I'm putting myself at risk. The horse shies away from where the body is lying, which attracts the driver's attention. He gets down off his cart, and as soon as he realizes it's a body he runs into the club, coming out with two other men. Realizing the woman is dead, all three head in different directions to seek help. I know one of them will find a patrolman making his rounds in no time, so I run in the opposite direction."

"Then what happens?" she prompted.

"After a short distance, I sense I'm safely far enough away. I'm very frustrated. I realize I'm heading toward the city and away from the East End. I'm about to change directions when I see a woman ahead of me who is drunk and singing to herself as she walks. There's a sign on the corner that says Mitre Square. I follow her. She stops singing. I wonder if she hears me stalking her, but she's too drunk to know what's going on. I come up from behind and grab her by the throat and begin choking her until she passes out. Suddenly, I hear someone coming—two men. I prop the woman up against a wall and pretend that we are in an embrace. They walk by and say nothing. Then I drag her into a dark corner of the square. I'm now in a rage. It's the first time I've ever mutilated one of my victims in a blind fury. I slash her face repeatedly, cutting off part of an ear and the end of her nose, and make an incision under each eye. By the time I stop, she is completely disfigured. Then I cut her stomach open, taking part of her intestines and placing them between her body and left arm as I've done before. I throw the remainder over her right shoulder. When I remove one of her kidneys, I decide to take it with me. I don't know why. I've never taken a body part before. I look around to find something to put it in. I find an old newspaper, wrap the kidney in it, and set it aside. I see that my hands and my jacket have blood on them, so I cut a piece of the woman's apron and take it with me to wipe away the blood.

I know a bobbie will be making his rounds any moment so I'm anxious to get as far away as possible. Several minutes later when I'm safely back in the East End, I stop by a stairway and wipe off my hands and jacket with the piece of apron, then throw it on the stairs. I see something written on the stairwell wall in chalk, but I don't read it because I'm anxious to return to my ship. By the time I finally make my way back to the ship, it is nearly three in the morning."

CHAPTER THIRTY-ONE

"What do you think, Shoshana?"

"No idea."

"But you're the past life expert," Richard pointed out, sipping his coffee.

"Do you believe him?"

"Do you?"

"I do and intuition says George is telling the truth. I've just never had to deal with such a sustained level of violence. I've regressed clients who were cruel, sometimes brutally so, in past lives, as well as victims of violence, but nothing like this."

"There may be another explanation," Richard suggested.

"What's that?"

"Maybe George reads a lot."

"When you asked me for dinner, I didn't know we were going to be talking about work, Richard."

"I'm sorry. It's just that I can't stop thinking about Saturday's session. I keep replaying those murders over and over in my mind."

"And you think hc got all of that from books?"

"Maybe."

"What kind of books?"

"Please, Shoshana, we both know what we're thinking."

"I know...I know. It seems inconceivable that we're involved with a murderer whose past life evidences all the hallmarks of one of the most famous serial killers in modern history. There must be another explanation, right?"

"I think we do have to consider any and all other possibilities including that he has done a lot of reading."

"Maybe you think of a question I might ask George that wouldn't be accessible in a book on Jack the Ripper?" Shoshana suggested, convinced that George was relating real experiences from his past lives.

"Yeah, the Ripper's real name," Richard replied with a laugh. "Why do you think George keeps blocking his name in the past?"

"Very good question. Although I've seen it plenty of times with other patients but given George's capacity to remember with such vivid detail other aspects of his past life in Victorian England, it is a little surprising he can't recall his own name. Or his stepmother's name, either given what he shared about her in one of our sessions and the way she treated him before and after his father died."

"Or his father's, for that matter. Could it be some sort of dissociative amnesia? His regressions into that past lifetime have certainly yielded some terribly traumatic events."

"I considered that. Dissociative amnesia can sometimes target very specific memories, but it just doesn't ring true in George's case. I'm no expert in that aspect, but I'm unaware of any case study where a person suffering from dissociative amnesia has so much memory fluency around events but is unable to remember a name."

"Retrograde amnesia perhaps?"

"Sorry, doesn't really fit the profile here."

"Of course. I'm grasping at straws at this point."

"I appreciate your efforts, Richard."

"It's uncanny. At times, his level of recall and ability to relate details at such a granular level is reminiscent of hyperthymesia."

"I've thought the very same thing."

"Yet, he is unable to recall either his own name or his stepmother's."

"It's very possible we'll never know George's name from his past life as a serial killer. We can always hope he might relate something in a future regression that provides some clue to his identity. Although, to be perfectly honest, that rarely happens. In the end, it may not be all that important."

"Why not?"

"Weiss believes that when a memory a patient is trying to access isn't available to them it may be because they are trying too hard. He also suggests it may be that the information has no relevance to that lifetime's lesson. George remembering his name may be of more interest to us than to him because we're confronted with a mystery. And not just any mystery, one we very much want to solve."

"Makes sense. In the meantime, I'm busting my butt trying to learn as much as I can regarding the Victorian serial killer whose true identity remains a mystery to this day. I've been doing a lot of reading, and so far everything George related from his past life checks out. The double murder he described during his regression on Saturday squares exactly with accounts of the Ripper killings of Elizabeth Stride and Catherine Eddowes on the night of September 30, 1888. It's uncanny. Even his account of the writing on the stairwell wall checks out."

"What are you trying to say?"

"The night of the double murders, a bobbie on Goulston Street spied a piece of dirty apron on the stairwell of the Wentworth Dwellings, a tenement building inhabited mainly by Jews. The piece of apron had blood on it and proved to have been torn—possibly by the Ripper himself—from the apron that Catherine Eddowes was wearing when she was killed. George mentioned that exactly."

"You're right. He did, but what's relevant about the writing on the stairwell wall?"

"In Ripper lore, the graffiti found on the wall on Goulston Street the night of the double murder remains a very controversial topic for many reasons. As I noted earlier, most of those living in the Wentworth Dwellings were Jewish. Ripper scholars have offered all kinds of opinions regarding the wording of the graffiti. It doesn't help that each recorded slightly different versions of the chalk-written text. Nevertheless, there is general agreement that it went something like *The Juwes are not the men who will be blamed for nothing.*"

As he said it, Richard wrote the text on a piece of paper so she could read the message and note the unusual spelling of the word Jews.

He continued, "At the time, antisemitism was running high in the East End. In addition, rumors circulated that John Pizer, a Polish Jew with the nickname Leather Apron, was Jack the Ripper. That worried Police Commissioner Charles Warren, who feared riots breaking out if the graffiti remained on the wall at daybreak, giving the public an opportunity to see it."

"Quite the drama," Shoshana observed.

"It gets better," Richard assured her. "A photographer was supposed to come and take a photograph of the graffiti when sufficient light became available. In the meantime, the graffiti remained out of view as police covered it until the photographer arrived. But Commissioner Warren so feared a riot that he ordered the graffiti washed off before a photo could be taken. Today there are multiple theories on the actual text of the graffiti, who might have written it, and why. Jack the Ripper is still considered the culprit by some. If George's past life narrative is to be believed, he noticed the graffiti already on the stairwell wall."

"Which would mean the person who wrote it wasn't Jack the Ripper," she concluded. "If that's who George was in a past life."

"It's a shame we'll never be able to share any of this with the community of Ripper enthusiasts," Richard noted.

"Agreed."

"Jack the Ripper is considered the first modern serial killer, and 135 years later the case has yet to be solved. It makes him unique, translating into hundreds of books and mountains of gigabytes of information on the Internet. Ready for a fun fact?"

"Dare I say no?"

Richard immediately launched into an interesting and entertaining bit of trivia. "During the investigation of Catherine Eddowes' murder, the second victim on September 30, 1888, the police used optography on her to try to identify the killer. During the Victorian period, optography was all the rage—a pseudoscience resting on the theory that the eye retained the image of the last thing it saw at the moment of death. It was taken very seriously, and the police considered photographing the eyes of two other Ripper victims as well. The idea was so intriguing and compelling that optography was featured in some late nineteenth and early twentieth century novels and several movies."

"Just out of curiosity, who were those other two victims?"

"Annie Chapman and Mary Kelly. The fact that the police used optography as a crime detection protocol in three of the five Ripper murders shows how captivating the pseudoscience was…and how desperate they were."

She grinned. "That may be one of your most interesting and bizarre fun facts."

"I've also read several articles on the East End of London during the

Victorian period, and again George's past life description is spot on."

"How so?"

"I always understood there was a dark side to London during the Victorian period, but I had no idea of the level of abject poverty in the slums of the East End. Jack London, who lived in the Whitechapel area for several weeks to understand the life of the working-class poor called it the Abyss and wrote that the experience haunted him for years. Outsiders often referred to the East End as Darkest London."

"Survival must have been next to impossible," she said.

"It was. Children resorted to begging, stealing, even prostitution. Often, they were turned out at night so their mothers, reduced to sex workers, could service their clients in lodging houses. It was widely known that these children could be found sleeping under tarpaulins on the London docks. Despite being an affront to Victorian morality, for many women prostitution was a matter of economic survival. It's estimated that twelve hundred prostitutes plied their trade in Whitechapel. With the rapid growth of London, jobs for women were hard to come by. While some sixty brothels existed in the area, most sex workers walked the streets, making them vulnerable to physical violence, robbery, and sexual assault. To avoid arrest, prostitutes had to constantly be on the move, which put them at even greater risk. With two ports near the East End, thousands of sailors made their way to the area in search of alcohol and sex. There were a half dozen drinking establishments alone in the Whitechapel area where the Ripper murdered his victims, a few of which still exist today."

"Which prostitutes would frequent in search of clients," she added.

"And when they encountered a customer, they often turned around and hiked up their skirts in preparation for sex. Jack the Ripper scholars believe this was what happened with some of his victims. When they turned around, he seized them by their throats and strangled them until they passed out."

"Just as George described."

"Exactly. And he said he encountered his victims in the East End pubs."

They paused in an empathic silence, processing the brutal act.

"Slumming was invented by upper-class Victorian Londoners who used to take nocturnal tours of the East End. Sometimes they even dressed disguised as commoners so they could slum undetected."

"Curiosity?" she asked.

"Partly. But also, the desire to partake in the vices of slum dwellers. Slumming became so fashionable that the word was officially entered into the 1884 edition of the Oxford English Dictionary."

"That's certainly a bizarre twist on urban tourism," she remarked. "Your fun facts never fail to amaze me. Honestly, you should be on *Jeopardy*. I think you would do quite well."

He laughed. "Fun fact. I was on *Teen Jeopardy* in high school. I was a rabid Trivial Pursuit nerd. When *Jeopardy* came to New York and put out a call for contestant auditions, my friends encouraged me to sign up."

"How did you do?"

"That depends on one's perspective."

"Stop being cryptic, Richard. What happened?"

"Well, they tape a week's worth of shows in one day. I won the first three games. It was all on television. By game four I was feeling very confident."

"Confident or cocky?"

"Probably a bit of both, if I'm being perfectly honest."

"In the fourth game, I was in the lead, but it was hardly a slam dunk. A brilliant sophomore polymath from Seguin, Texas, of all places, was in second place. She had a chance of winning if she went all in and won Final Jeopardy, so I couldn't just play it safe. The category was island fauna. I felt really good about the category. If I bet fifteen hundred dollars and we both got the correct answer, I would win."

"Enough with the suspense, already. Did you get the right answer?"

"You mean the right question, don't you?"

"Whatever. Just tell me what happened."

Richard reveled in Shoshana's sense of anticipation and curiosity. "Care to guess the clue?" he teased.

"Please..."

"Two species of aves grounded by evolution that are found on a volcanic archipelago in the Pacific Ocean? Care to guess the question?"

"Absolutely no idea."

"Well, I was pretty sure the question referred to two species of birds on the Galapagos Islands. Running a mental checklist of birds found on the islands that couldn't fly, I only had thirty seconds to answer, and the music soundtrack was playing in the background, which kind of distracted me. Coming up with penguins was easy. The second species not so much. Then I remembered cormorants. There's a species of cormorants on the Galapagos that intrigued Charles Darwin because they couldn't fly."

"So, you won!"

"Not exactly. The guy in third place wasn't even in the ballpark. My nemesis in second place wagered everything and came up with the correct answer—what are penguins and cormorants? 'That is correct,' Alex Trabek announced. I knew I had the correct answer as well, and I was feeling ecstatic. Then my answer popped up on the screen. *The Galapagos penguin and cormorant*, followed by a collective sigh from the audience. I had committed the unforgivable sin in *Jeopardy*. Despite all of us being reminded twice to be sure to write our answers in the form of a question, I got so excited I blanked and simply answered the question. Of course, it cost me the game and twelve hundred and fifty dollars."

"You must have been crushed. Although, I must say the way it turned out makes for a far better story."

"Indeed. I did win some money, and for a brief time I was a rock star at school, until being replaced by the leading scorer in the regional boys' basketball playoffs."

"Very impressive, Dr. Crane! Remind me to make sure you're on my team if we ever play Trivial Pursuit."

"Of course, Dr. Liebman."

They finished their dinner, and for a while they talked about the horrible living conditions in Victorian London's East End. Then Richard dropped her off at her home. Regrettably, he declined her invitation to come in for coffee. Already late, he had an hour and a half drive back to Percyville. He found her just as personally engaging as he did professionally. Barely down the front walkway, he already wondered when he might see her again. Had she enjoyed the evening as much as he did? He really hoped she had.

CHAPTER THIRTY-TWO

"Where did all this goddamn snow come from? I've never seen anything like it. Eighteen inches in thirty-six hours! The weatherman this morning said it's the heaviest snowfall on record in Hightower since 1953."

"We've got bigger problems than the weather, Harry," Chris replied.

"What's up?"

"Our friend in New York is still at it. I knew that son of a bitch wouldn't give up."

"What's the prick up to now? We've got the judge's ruling on our side. Maybrick stays here until the shrinks are done with him."

"Check this out," Chris said, tossing a large envelope on his partner's desk.

Harry took out the folded pages from the envelope and began reading. "It's a subpoena for Maybrick's psych files! I thought they're supposed to be confidential."

"They are. O'Meara knows that. He's fishing, and the judge will never go for it," Chris said.

"He can take his subpoena and shove it!"

"Amen to that."

"What are we going to do, Chris?"

"Sit on it for a couple of days and then give it to the judge. I'll ask him to wait as long as he can before he rules on it. You never know what O'Meara will come up with next."

"Are you going to tell our friend downstairs?"

"No. What's the point? No reason to upset George unless we have to respond to the subpoena," Chris replied.

"How's he doing?"

"Pretty good. He's sleeping a lot better. Dr. Liebman was supposed to be here on Tuesday, but with the weather, she hasn't been able to make the drive from St. Louis. She called and said she'd be here tomorrow if the roads are clear."

"Any idea what's going on in the therapy?"

"No clue. George is her patient, so she is bound by doctor-patient confidentiality. She hasn't said much, and I haven't asked."

"Come on, aren't you a little curious about what they're talking about? I see Crane is in on it now. That should make an interesting little trio," Harry said dryly. "If that bastard cops an insanity plea, I'm going to really be pissed at those two."

"He won't," Chris assured his partner.

"How do you know?"

"I just do."

"You'll have to forgive me, Chris, if I seem skeptical."

CHAPTER THIRTY-THREE

The following morning, the two psychiatrists arrived at the police station within ten minutes of one another. They chatted briefly in Chris's office before he escorted them down to Maybrick's basement cell. As they walked down the hallway, Richard handed his colleague an envelope.

"What's this?" she asked.

"I'll tell you later."

Maybrick was sitting on his bunk sketching and working on his third cup of coffee when they approached his cell.

"I understand you're sleeping better, George," Dr. Liebman said.

"Much better. Thank you."

"Are you comfortable with Dr. Crane joining us again?"

"Sure. How about a smoke first?"

Chris cuffed Maybrick and led him outside for his ritual cigarette break whenever the detective worked the morning shift. He had actually come to enjoy the few minutes each morning with Maybrick on the department's back steps.

"Just one more, please, detective. It's Friday and I won't get another smoke till Monday unless you're coming in over the weekend," Maybrick pleaded. Before Chris could reply, he quickly lit another cigarette with the remnant of the one he had just finished.

"Enjoy it, George. I'm taking Julia and the kids to St. Louis this weekend to see the zoo and planetarium, so I won't be here."

After Chris escorted Maybrick back to his cell he removed the restraints, he excused himself and returned to his office.

* * *

"We've got a lot to do today, George. Are you ready?" Shoshana asked.

"Sure, but can we maybe go someplace else today, Doc?"

She understood the question. She glanced over at her colleague. He had grasped its meaning, as well. "We really need to bring closure to that lifetime. I know it's not easy, but it's important that you do it. I believe it holds the key to understanding much of what you're experiencing in your present. Are you ready?"

"Okay."

"Do you know where you are, George?" she asked as soon as he fell into a hypnotic state.

"I'm back in the East End. I'm sitting in a pub having a beer, watching and waiting."

"What are you waiting for, George?" she asked.

"A victim," he answered calmly.

"Can you see the name of the pub and where it's located?"

"The Britannia again. It's at the corner of Commercial Street and Dorset Street. Dorset is one of the most dangerous streets in the entire East End. The locals just call it the Street because it is so dangerous and filled with doss houses. Around eleven, an attractive woman comes into the pub. I know immediately she's the one. People seem to know her by name. Some of the patrons call her Mary and others refer to her as Marie. Everyone seems to know her, so she must live close by."

"Can you describe her?"

"She's in her mid to late twenties, red, maybe blond hair, with blue eyes and a fair complexion. She is pretty. Kind of stout. She's already been drinking and starts flirting with some of the patrons. After a half hour, one of them purchases a pail of beer and follows her out of the pub. I leave and follow them, but not too closely. They walk a short distance down the street and disappear through a narrow passageway. A sign says *Miller's Court*. There is a gaslight close to the entrance. I stand across the street and wait. About a half hour later the man comes out carrying his pail. I cross the street and head down the passage to the courtyard, a cul de sac surrounded by several houses with whitewashed fronts. It has started raining. I can hear someone singing and I look in a window. It's the woman from the pub. I start to knock on the door but decide to wait in case she's expecting someone else. I return to the street and resume my vigil. The rain continues and it's getting colder. Several minutes later, she emerges from the courtyard, and I begin to follow her up the street. She stops someone she knows and asks to borrow sixpence, but the woman has no money. 'I must go and look for some money,' she tells the woman. She walks a couple more blocks and begins to throw up. I seize the opportunity to approach her and ask if she is all right. 'I had a glass of beer earlier and I've brought it up again,' she says. I ask, 'What are you doing out here in the cold and rain?' She says, 'I need some money.' Gazing at her up close, even in the darkness I can see she is much prettier than the others. 'I've got to pay rent in the morning,' she explains, 'or old man McCarthy will throw me out on the streets.' I say nothing, but she says, 'It's cold and your clothes are damp. I live just 'round the corner. I've a fireplace where we can warm ourselves and you can dry your clothes.' I nod in agreement. 'All right my dear. Come along. You will be comfortable,' she tells me and takes me by the arm and leads me back to her room. She pulls a rag out of a broken windowpane next to the door, pushes back the curtain, reaches in, and opens it from the inside. 'Lost the key months ago,' she tells me." George frowned.

"Did you go in?" Shoshana asked.

"Yes. As soon as she lights the lone candle in the room, I can see she lives in a very small space. Her bed is next to the door with a small nightstand, and there is a cupboard in the corner with some pottery, a couple of ginger beer bottles, and a scrap of bread on a plate. I walk over to look at an engraving hanging over the fireplace. It's hard to see in the dim light, but I can make out the title *The Fisherman's Widow*. There's clothing lying about. She removes my jacket and places it on the back of a chair near the fireplace. I panic that she's going to find the knife on the inside of my jacket, but she doesn't notice. There's one small piece of wood near the fireplace which she throws on the embers, and it catches quickly. She invites me to sit on the bed while she takes off her clothes and puts on some sort of chemise or nightgown. I think it's strange that she carefully folds her clothes and places them on the other chair in the room. I realize that she has no idea who I am."

"Can you see what happens next, George?"

"While she's trying to coax me into bed, I walk over to my jacket and carefully remove the knife from the inside pocket. As I approach her bed, she sees the knife and screams, 'Oh murder!' I grab her around the throat and begin choking her until she loses consciousness. Then I pull a corner of the bed sheet over her face and cut her throat. I'm sure someone must have heard her, so I listen carefully, but no one upstairs in the house stirs. This is the most brutal of all the murders because I'm safely inside the victim's room and have all the time I want. I lose all track of time and spend at least two or three hours mutilating and disemboweling the body. At one point I throw some of her clothing on the fire for more light."

He then laid out in excruciating detail how he cut his victim to pieces, carefully placing parts of the body in different places around the corpse and on the nightstand. After he removed the victim's heart, he wrapped it in a piece of cloth and placed it in his jacket.

Shoshana found herself becoming physically ill.

Richard appeared less shocked. She figured he must already have known from his research exactly what Jack the Ripper did that night.

"After I finish, I clean myself up and let myself out locking the door behind me," George concluded.

"Was that the last person you killed, George?" she asked.

"Yes. I also believe that I met my end several days later while returning to my ship docked on the Thames."

Richard glanced over at her, then leaned forward and asked him, "George, did you ever write a letter about the murders?"

"Yes, in the fall, maybe in October. I can't remember exactly. I sent a letter to a gentleman in the East End."

"Do you remember who?"

"I believe his name was Lusk. George Lusk. He was the head of a vigilance committee trying to protect the neighborhood and solve the murders. The penny press carried stories about him and his group quite frequently."

"What did the letter say, George?"

"I can't recall the entire letter, but the return address was *From Hell*. I sent part of a kidney I had removed from one of the victims a couple of weeks earlier. I wrote that I had eaten the other half, which of course I hadn't, and that I might send the knife I'd used to remove the kidney later on."

"How did you sign the letter, George?" Richard asked.

"Catch me when you can, Mr. Lusk," he replied.

"Is that the only letter you sent?"

"Yes."

"George, has your name come to you yet?" Shoshana asked.

After a moment of silence, he responded, "Yes. They call me Jack. Jack the Ripper."

She knew she and Richard were thinking the same thing. A grisly reality held prisoner for 135 years shackled in George Lindfield Maybrick's subconscious had finally escaped.

Shoshana struggled to collect herself. Richard reached over and laid his palm over her shaking hands. She knew she had to continue, so she ignored the sound of her heart pounding in her chest. Not even the unexpected news of the tragic loss of her husband in a terrible accident had taxed her nerves like the words Jack the Ripper emerging from a deep and dark place in George Maybrick's subconscious mind.

"George does your birth name come to you?" she asked.

"No," he responded.

She had originally planned to wrap up the regression of George's life in Victorian England during this session, but she couldn't bring herself to do it. Closure would have to come later. She didn't even ask him if he was willing or ready to terminate the session. She simply returned him to a normal waking state as quickly as possible.

For a long moment, they all sat in utter silence. No one knew what to say. George's description of Mary Kelly's brutal murder had created an atmosphere of horror. A malevolent shroud hung over the jail cell, as if she and Richard had witnessed the murder itself. For the first time she understood the expression make your skin crawl.

Ironically, George appeared to be feeling much better. "I feel a lightness I've rarely felt before in my life," he said, breaking the silence. "The closest to what I'm feeling was when I created beautiful things with color on canvas. Though, too often my demons highjacked my creative energies, producing sketches from my dark side."

She knew that once therapy brought issue-causing past events percolating to the surface of a patient's consciousness, those events lost their power. George's subconscious had now shed its burden. The unspeakable had been spoken.

"And… Now I understand."

"What do you understand, George?" she asked.

"Why I killed all those people."

"Why?" Richard asked.

"My stepmother. I was trying to kill my stepmother. I hated her for what she did to me and my father. He was a good man, and she rewarded him by sleeping with all those men while he served his country in the army." He scowled. "It's so ironic."

"What is?" Shoshana asked.

"I've been trying to kill someone who's been dead for over a century."

"Can you tell me what you're feeling now, George?"

"On one level, I feel revulsion for the way I brutally murdered those women in my past and present life. It was wrong, cruel, unforgivable. I see that now. But I also feel a tremendous burden has been lifted."

Once brought to light, the darkness cannot stand.

She thought back to an earlier comment, "The greater the light, the stronger the shadow." The contrast impressed her and told her that a powerful transformation was in process within him.

"What about your father? How do you feel about him?" Richard asked.

"Ambivalent. I had only a few memories. At some level, I felt he had abandoned me. He was very much absent because of his military duties, and I didn't really think about him much. The hatred I felt for my stepmother may have driven out any strong feelings of love I might have had for my father."

"Well done, George. But I think that's enough for one day," Shoshana suggested.

George and Richard both nodded in agreement.

CHAPTER THIRTY-FOUR

"What a day!" Shoshana exclaimed as she and Richard exited the Hightower police station.

"You look tired," he said.

"Exhausted would be more like it. I'd already done a whole day's work and then some before I got in the car and drove here."

"Let me buy you a cup of coffee before you get on the road." He glanced at his watch. "If you wait another forty minutes, you'll miss the rush hour traffic when you get near the city."

She noted the time, mentally checking his traffic calculations. "You're right. And a cup of coffee sounds good."

"Great. There's a nice place right over there." He pointed to a diner across the street, looking pleased she had accepted his offer.

"Hello, Dr. Crane," the waitress said in greeting as they entered the diner. "Your regular booth is free."

"Thanks, Sally. This is my colleague, Dr. Shoshana Liebman from St. Louis. We're going to have some coffee before she makes the drive home."

"What a beautiful name, Doctor." Sally smiled. "Grab a seat and I'll be right over with your coffee."

"So, you're a regular here, I see," Shoshana remarked when she and Richard were seated.

"I always stop in for a coffee, sometimes lunch, when I come to Hightower once or twice a month. The coffee is always fresh, the food's pretty good, and the service is excellent. I'm sure by this time you've figured out Hightower can use all the business it can get. Sally has been here as long as I can remember. She's sharp as a tack, just never had the encouragement or resources to leave Hightower. I helped her get her GED and tried to encourage her to go to community college. She gave at up after a semester."

"Here you go, folks. Two black coffees." Sally set down the mugs with a smile and headed for another customer who was calling her.

"May I ask what brought you to Percy County?" Shoshana asked Richard.

"You're a long way from New York City." She could see the confusion on his face at her question. "I read your bio on the Percy County Mental Health website," she explained.

"Ah. Hmm...that's a very long story. And you know what they say about long stories. They take a long time to get to the end."

"Maybe you'll share your story when we have more time?"

"Perhaps," Richard replied dryly. "Did you want to talk about this afternoon's session with George?" he asked.

She was unsure what to make of his ambivalent reply and obvious change of subject. She took a sip of coffee. "I believe we reached a tipping point this afternoon, and I know we need to talk about it, but I would prefer to wait until tomorrow. I don't think I have the emotional energy to process it all right now."

"I get it. We can talk by phone in the next day or two. I agree the session was a turning point for George. And, if I haven't said this before, I should have. You are absolutely brilliant at what you do."

"Thank you for your kind words, Richard. It means a lot coming from such a respected colleague."

Richard winced. "Stop. We're beginning to sound like a mutual admiration society."

They both broke out laughing.

"I agree," she said with a grin.

"I was wondering, do you have any interest in bonsai?" he asked.

"Can't say I know that much about it. Several years ago, I visited the bonsai museum in D.C. The collection was amazing. It's a beautiful art form. Why do you ask?"

"I'm coming to St. Louis for the Bonsai Festival this weekend. It only takes place every four years so it's a special event with exhibits and displays. It's held at the Jewel Box in Forest Park and the convention center. Would like to join me?"

"I'd love to, Richard, but unfortunately I have a book review to write and I'm preparing a paper that I'm delivering at a conference next month. I'll be at my desk writing all weekend."

"That's too bad," Richard replied, not hiding his disappointment. "What's the topic of your paper?"

"I'm exploring whether PLR therapy might be used to treat patients with moderate to severe thanatophobia. I haven't pursued using regression therapy as a treatment, but I'm trying to create a theoretical model that addresses the ethical implications as well as the possibilities of past life regression as a therapeutic intervention."

"Whoa. Existential death anxiety and reincarnation. Fascinating marriage of ideas, but way above my pay grade. Whatever possessed you to put those two concepts together?"

'Another long story, and I have a long drive ahead of me."

"Maybe you can share it with me at some point?" he asked, his eyes brimming with curiosity.

"Perhaps," she replied with a wink.

"Touché," he said. "Why the grin?"

"Am I?" she asked coyly.

"You are."

"I'm pretty sure I was smiling."

"No, you were grinning," he insisted.

"Smiling, grinning, really what's the difference?"

"Well..." For the next five minutes he explained the nuances between smiling and grinning. "Different facial expressions communicate different emotions. A grin can express insincerity, amusement as well as pleasure. A grinning person often feels playful, lighthearted. A smile communicates happiness or pleasure. When one grins, the mouth is typically open, teeth visible. As an expression of happiness and pleasure a smile always signals a positive emotion. In terms of smiling, everyone is different, depending on their facial movements. Some people smile, lips open, teeth showing, but many people smile simply by raising the corners of their lips. A smile tends to be more open than a grin. Grinning tends to be more subtle. Smiling always expresses positive emotion. A grin can sometimes be a negative expression of emotion indicating disappointment or dissatisfaction."

"Richard, you're being pedantic," she finally interrupted. "Still, I'm impressed."

"That certainly wasn't my intention."

"Good thing I didn't smirk!"

"Indeed. A smirk warrants a whole other discussion," he joked.

"How did you come to know so much about the distinctions between smiling and grinning?"

"Facial expressions are an aspect of body language. When I talk with a patient, I want to learn everything I possibly can that might give me some insight into who they are and what they're thinking. A smile is a facial expression that tells me a person is experiencing pleasure and joy—something I would want to know. Equally important is when a patient or client is signaling insincerity, amusement, perhaps dissatisfaction. I knew you were grinning because you turned my own words against me. The amusing gotcha moment was reflected in your grin. By the way, you are smiling right now, and if you don't mind me saying, you have a beautiful smile."

She suddenly felt self-conscious. Nonetheless, she felt happy. Here was a person who, far from being a pedant, had gone to considerable lengths to study facial expressions so he could better understand and help his patients. Being around him made her happy.

As she looked up and took another sip of coffee, she noticed the smile on his face, as well.

CHAPTER THIRTY-FIVE

Three days later, Richard was unable to contain his enthusiasm when his vintage analog Silvertone radio alarm awakened him at six-thirty a.m. He immediately threw off his covers and jumped out of bed. His dark roast coffee, already ground and resting in the bottom of his French press, waited patiently for hot water. Coffee, shave, shower, more coffee for the road, and he was off.

An hour and forty-five minutes later, he was waiting in line to present his American Bonsai Society membership card for his all-inclusive weekend pass to the festival. Standing in line, he gazed in awe at the Art Deco greenhouse built in 1936 as a WPA project, part of the New Deal to provide jobs during the Great Depression. Although he had visited the Jewel Box countless times, he never ceased to marvel at the greenhouse's cantilevered vertical glass walls rising five stories, creating an extraordinary feeling of open space. Although a fraction of the size of the convention center, some of the most extraordinary examples of the art of bonsai could be seen in the Jewel Box during the quadrennial festival.

As he did each festival, he began with a careful exploration, making mental notes of the different offerings so he could plan what he most wanted to see. Several years earlier he had spent nearly two hours studying one tree, a hundred-year-old black pine bonsai, the most challenging species to sculpt into a bonsai.

Four hours later wandering through an area devoted to Chinese junipers, his cell phone rang. Ordinarily, he put his phone on silent in public venues, but he was the backup emergency on-call for the weekend and didn't want to miss a call from the hospital.

"Dammit," he muttered under his breath, not bothering to look at the screen. "This is Dr. Crane."

"It's Shoshana," the voice on the other end responded. "You're supposed to be having fun, Richard. You sound so businesslike."

"My apologies. I thought it was the hospital trying to get me. I'm on backup this weekend."

"So, how are the bonsai?"

"I'll confess, being at the festival is the closest thing to dying and going to heaven. Each bonsai is more beautiful than the last. Right now, I'm standing in a sea of Chinese junipers. Earlier, I saw a giant sequoia bonsai forest that's over one hundred and twenty-five years old. Absolutely breathtaking!"

"It sounds amazing. The reason I'm calling is my writing has gone really well this morning, better than I expected, and I thought I might take a break and join you for a couple of hours at the festival."

"Really?" He was unable to hide his excitement. "That would be wonderful. I'm at the Jewel Box in Forest Park. I'll go to the convention center tomorrow. Let me come and pick you up."

"No need. I only live a few miles from Forest Park. I'll Lyft over."

"Perfect. I'll meet you, say, around two o'clock at the entrance of the Jewel Box?" He smiled as he turned off his cell.

With a passion for bonsai and a deep attraction to Shoshana Liebman, spending the rest of the afternoon with both promised more joy and happiness than Richard could ever remember.

And the promise was delightfully fulfilled. Rarely had he enjoyed his time with anyone more than the afternoon they spent together at the Bonsai Festival. Was it a date? Or just two friends spending time together? In the following days, he found himself constantly thinking about when he would have a chance to see her again. And not at a police station.

The opportunity presented itself sooner than he expected.

CHAPTER THIRTY-SIX

Shoshana had completely forgotten about the envelope Richard had passed to her at the Hightower police station before George's last session. She'd discovered it a few days later going through the documents in her valise and immediately opened it and read its contents.

She'd been spellbound by her colleague's notes. He had predicted with tremendous accuracy Maybrick's account of the murder during his last session. The victim's name, where she lived, the descriptions of the victim and her room, even her final cry for help, as well as the grisly details of the murder and subsequent mutilation of the victim. His notes had left her with lots of questions. They would have much to talk about the next time they met.

She was very attracted to her new colleague. She knew little about him, but there was a vulnerability there and an aura of kindness that appealed to her. She sensed he was a wounded soul with a good heart.

She had thoroughly enjoyed their bonsai experience the previous weekend and found his passion for the ancient Japanese art form inspiring.

On Wednesday morning after addressing a group of hospital administrators and physicians at the university in Cape Girardeau, Richard surprised her by walking up to her after her presentation.

"Ever had Canjun food?" he asked.

"Can't say that I have."

"Well, there's a great Cajun restaurant right on the river. What do you say to lunch? Broussard's has the best gumbo and crawfish etouffee I've ever eaten."

"I'd like that a lot. We have much to discuss regarding your predictions and George's last regression."

Driving to the restaurant, she felt excited over another opportunity to spend time with Richard. But at the same time a little guilty knowing they should be concentrating on their patient and not themselves. So, she opened their conversation by focusing on the case.

"How did you know?" she asked as she sipped a glass of pinot noir and gazed out at the river. A train of barges slowly churned upriver, pushed by a massive towboat.

"I've been doing a lot of reading on Jack the Ripper. There are countless theories about who he was and how many victims there were, but all of Maybrick's murder recollections are generally thought to be Ripper victims. I guessed that in his next session he would regress to the murder of Mary Jane Kelly, the fifth and final Ripper victim. All of the murders he remembers from his past life have been explored and written about extensively. The notes I gave you predicting George's account of the Mary Kelly murder came right out of Paul Begg's books, which I have studied in great detail."

"So, you don't believe George is sharing actual past life experiences."

"I'm a medical doctor, but I'm also a scientist. As I doctor, I believe the experiences he shares during his past life regressions are real, but as a scientist I'm still skeptical. You read how much I was able to glean from reading accounts of the Kelly murder, and how close I was to predicting what he would share. He filled in a few gaps and changed the story a bit and *viola*. His descriptions of the murders are uncanny, but there's really nothing truly revelatory in any of his accounts. Doesn't it least make you wonder a little, Shoshana? Could he just be gaslighting us?"

"Oh, it's possible he's drawing from things he's read or seen in his current life, but I think it's highly unlikely. I've regressed well over a thousand patients and never had anybody even approach the level of deception you're suggesting. Besides, what does George have to gain from faking accounts of murders that occurred over a century ago?"

"I don't know. I've thought a lot about that too, and I don't have an answer. He's not claiming insanity, something he could have if he wanted to be clever. He's clearly smart enough to fake it. Instead, he's taken full responsibility for all his murders even though he's looking at death row."

"And how do you explain the reduction of his chronic nightmares? Think all of that is an act too?"

"Not at all. And I can't argue with the fact that he seems to be doing much better," Richard conceded. "Although the medication could also be working," he added.

"I'll admit it's nearly impossible to believe we have stumbled on a serial killer who was Jack the Ripper in a previous life. The odds of winning the lottery are probably a lot better. But I believe him. And I think you do, too, Richard. You just won't allow yourself to accept something so preposterous, so implausible, so beyond the pale of imagination. And yet...the impossible has happened."

"You're probably right," he said. But she could see by his expression that he was not entirely convinced.

"Sometimes I feel like a character in a gothic horror novel, with no idea how the plot ends."

"You are, Shoshana, but it's not fiction. I want to believe George, and I truly do want him to find peace," he said, "but I just can't be sure about these regressions. I still have doubts."

"I swear Richard Crane," she said wryly, "you must have the word doubt tattooed on your soul."

"Very likely...if I have one," he replied in an attempt at humor.

She was not amused. His persistent skepticism pissed her off.

He tried to explain. "I didn't mean to imply any criticism of your amazing work, Shoshana. You've helped hundreds and hundreds of patients to find healing. I deeply respect and admire the work you do, and I feel terrible that I may have given you a different impression. Please accept my sincerest apology."

"Thank you, Richard. We both took an oath to help people when we finished med school, and I've always tried to live up to that oath."

"Of course," he replied sounding sincere.

He wasn't off the hook yet by any means. She continued, "I'm an observant Jew in the Reform tradition. I believe in God, and if pressed, I could give you a whole host of reasons why I believe the divine exists. I can't say, however, I know that with absolute certainty. It's why they call it faith. In some respects, the existence of God and reincarnation are cut from the same cloth. You can't prove they exist, but you can't prove they don't exist."

"True enough."

"In fact, in the Jewish faith there is a rich tradition of *gilgul*, the Hebrew word for wheel or cycle, used to refer to reincarnation. In Kabbala, the Jewish mystical tradition, there are many references to reincarnation. Celebrating the merits of *gilgul*, one Jewish rabbinic scholar said it can rectify the damage from a previous life and help the soul evolve towards perfection in this current life."

"Interesting. I'll have to look into *gilgul*."

"Anyway. I feel there is considerable evidence that George Maybrick was a serial killer in a past life as well as in this one, some quite empirical I would argue, but we'll never be able to prove it beyond all doubt. The difference between us is that I don't need absolute certainty about things, I just need a reasonable amount of evidence. When I act on that belief, I give my patients the real possibility of healing themselves. What I do know with near certainty is their lives nearly always get better. That's all the certainty I need."

"Point taken, Shoshana. When you put it that way, it makes sense. The possibility that the soul has multiple lifetimes to perfect itself beats the idea that you only get one shot, and if you really screw up your consequences are eternal damnation," Richard mused.

"That's certainly one way to put it."

"So, which came first, your belief in reincarnation as a spiritual practice or as a psychotherapeutic intervention?"

"The latter," she said. "I attended a session on past life regression at a mental health conference. The whole idea fascinated me and I did a ton of research. Reincarnation made so much sense to me that I ended up enrolling in a certification program to become a past life regression therapist, eventually incorporating it into my psychiatric practice. As I continued my study, I discovered that several faith traditions besides Judaism embrace the idea of reincarnation."

"I think Christianity missed that memo," he said.

"You think? You enjoy sharing fun facts. Here's one for you. At one time you could find references to reincarnation in both the Hebrew and Christian scriptures. In 325 A.D., the Roman Emperor Constantine and his mother, Helena, had those references in the Bible deleted. Constantine argued that if Christians believed in reincarnation it would give them license to behave badly, knowing they always had opportunity in the next life to make amends."

"The good emperor sounds pretty cynical."

"Agreed, but despite Constantine's effort to eliminate the belief, several early Christian theologians believed in reincarnation, and it wasn't until the sixth century that reincarnation was declared a heresy by the Catholic church."

"Wow. Interesting."

"I know you're not Jewish, but do you come from any particular faith tradition?"

"Barely. My father was an atheist who never thought much about religion. Magical thinking, he called it. My mother was raised a Methodist, but had become a borderline agnostic by the time I was born. She made a serious study of the world's major religions, practiced meditation daily, and landed on secular Buddhism. For reasons I'll never understand, she made no effort to encourage me to explore my own spiritual path. Left to my own devices, I came to believe that all religious practices are suspect."

"How so?"

"When people are occupied with eternity, they often forget that we live in the present."

"That's one plug for agnosticism I haven't heard before."

"Please don't take offense, Shoshana, but I generally find science and reason to be more reliable than God."

"No offense taken." she said.

"I do find your comments on early Christianity and reincarnation very intriguing, though. I'll have to the do some reading on it."

"I hope you will, Richard. Circling back to our previous discussion… I don't want to beat a dead horse, but may I ask you one more question?"

"Absolutely."

"How many things in your life have you been certain of?"

He sat nervously sipping his lime and club soda. "Not many," he admitted. He cleared his throat. "Shall we move on?"

"Good idea," she said with a laugh. "I'm very curious about something else. May I ask you one more question? This will be the last, I promise."

"Of course," he replied immediately.

"I was intrigued by the letter you mentioned in the last session. Why did you ask George about it?"

"Great question." Richard responded enthusiastically.

She could see he was glad she had asked, no doubt for the opportunity to answer.

"Let me guess," she drawled. "You read about it."

"Yes. There is an entire book dedicated to the Ripper letters entitled, *Jack the Ripper: Letters from Hell*. It's a fascinating and at times entertaining read."

"I might have known," she said, rolling her eyes.

"It's interesting stuff. The Whitechapel murders generated several hundred letters, a thousand by one estimate, to the police, journalists, news agencies, and involved citizens like George Lusk. Over time, most of the letters were lost, destroyed, even stolen. Only about two hundred and sixty survive today. All kinds of theories regarding the murders and identity of Jack the Ripper have been based on these letters. The killer got his moniker from someone who signed a letter and postcard as Jack the Ripper. Some of the letters advised, even chastised, the police regarding their investigation. We know now that most of the letters were fakes or pranks. In some cases, enterprising journalists are strongly suspected of having penned some of the more famous letters to keep the murders foremost in readers' minds to sell newspapers. Today, some writers still believe that several of the Jack the Ripper letters were written by the real killer. Serious scholars believe most, if not all the letters, did not come from the Ripper's hand."

"That makes sense. During the regression George said he only wrote one letter, and that he'd enclosed a portion of a kidney from one of the victims."

"It's generally referred to as the From Hell or the Lusk letter. It's one of the letters that's disappeared, unfortunately. What we have today is a copy of a copy. Both the original letter and the official police photograph of the letter are no longer extant. The person who wrote the letter included it in a three-and-a-half-inch square carboard box that also contained a portion of a kidney. The package was postmarked on October 15, 1888, and George Lusk received it on the following day. Lusk headed up the Whitechapel Vigilance Committee, a group trying to protect the neighborhood and to help the police find the killer. A pathologist examined the kidney and determined it was a portion of a left human kidney that had been preserved in spirits. He stated that the person from whom the kidney had been taken suffered from Bright's disease and was a sickly alcoholic woman who had died within the past three weeks."

"Bright's disease. Hmm...that's an archaic term for acute nephritis, isn't it?" she asked.

"Good memory, Shoshana. I had to look it up in an old medical dictionary. We know excessive alcohol use is linked to acute nephritis, or Bright's disease as it was referred to during the Victorian period. We also know that Elizabeth Eddowes, one of the victims George recalled killing in September of 1888, was an alcoholic, and he distinctly remembered removing one of her kidneys. Coincidence? Maybe. It's interesting that George said he wrote only one letter, and he chose to include a part of the victim's kidney with the letter. I'm also intrigued by the fact that the one letter he claims to have written is one of the only two letters that serious Ripperologist believe are likely to have been written by the actual killer."

"Maybe Jack the Ripper was a necrophiliac," she suggested, and they both burst out laughing.

"That's one for the medical books. You've got a great sense of humor," he complemented her.

"Thank you, Richard. I have to ask. I'm amazed by your recall. How do you possibly remember all these details? You're like a walking Jack the Ripper encyclopedia."

"I have an eidetic memory. I read something once and it's in there forever," he replied, tapping his temple. "But there's actually no need for me to be a walking Ripper encyclopedia. There already is one. *The Ultimate Jack the Ripper Companion: An Illustrated Encyclopedia.* It's a whopping seven hundred and fifty pages."

"And you have a copy, no doubt."

"Yep."

"Richard Crane, you're impossible!"

"Which explains why I have so few friends."

"Shifting gears..." Shoshana said. "We haven't brought closure to this past life of George's yet. Let's keep thinking about a question we might ask him that only the real Jack the Ripper would be able to answer. One that's not in any of the books. Would that convince you, Richard?"

"The only problem is it doesn't matter what question we come up with.

There's no way of verifying whether his answer is true or not."

"How's that?"

"It's a Catch-22, Shoshana. If we ask a question that we can verify through some current source, then George might have access to the same source and that proves nothing. If we ask a question that we are unable to verify then there is always the possibility that's he simply lying or confabulating and we have no way of knowing for sure."

"Ugh. You're being impossible again!" she said in frustration.

"Maybe, but I'm right."

"Yes, I suppose so. Still, there must be something we could ask that would give us a good clue."

"I'm sure there is, but I don't know what."

"Well, I'm going to let you solve the mystery of whether or not our patient is really Jack the Ripper. I'm a therapist not a cold case detective, and I'm going to try to help George find some closure."

"Agreed. Why don't you regress our friend one more time and see if he can tell us how and when he died. In the meantime, I'll try to come up with a question that only the actual Jack the Ripper could answer, Catch-22 or not."

"Sounds like a plan. For now, let's enjoy some good Cajun food and talk about anything that has nothing to do with Victorian serial killers or past life regression," she suggested.

"Great idea. I'd be interested to hear your thoughts about our bonsai visit."

CHAPTER THIRTY-SEVEN

"George Maybrick is such an enigma," Chris mused.

"That's an understatement," Harry agreed.

"I just wish I could get a better sense of what makes him tick."

"Why don't you reach out to his sister, Heidi Carson," Harry suggested.

"Hmm. I'll give it some thought. I wouldn't be compromising the case in any way."

"Whaddya have to lose?"

Less than twenty-four hours later, Chris was knocking on George's sister's front door. "Good afternoon Mrs. Carson. Thank you so much for agreeing to speak to me. How is your mother doing?"

"It's kind of you to ask, but not well, Detective Stanford. She's dying. My mother has cancer and has declined all treatment. Do you believe in God, Detective?"

Still standing on the front stoop, the question took Chris by surprise. "I guess so. Can't say I've given it much thought. Why do you ask?"

"If there is a God, I pray he will take my mother before George's trial. We are trying to keep all of this from her. She doesn't deserve to go to her death knowing her son is a serial killer."

"I'm so sorry, ma'am. I noticed your mother's frailty when my partner and I visited her at Riverview Assisted Living."

"Thank you, Detective Stanford. I sense you genuinely mean it," Mrs. Carson replied. "What do you want to talk to me about? My brother? If so, there really isn't much to say."

"Honestly, I'm just trying to get a better understanding of who your brother really is."

"I'm very aware of the appalling things George has done. When Detective Caulfield found those horrible drawings under George's mattress, it made me sick. How could my brother do that? He's not evil. I believe that with my whole heart."

"What can you tell me about him that would lead you to say that?"

"I would really prefer not to talk about George."

Chris realized he was not going to be invited inside. "I know this ordeal must be very painful for you. I'm sorry to have troubled you. Good afternoon, Mrs. Carson. I wish you and your mother well," he said, turned, and started down the front walkway. He had gone about ten yards when he heard Mrs. Carson call out, "Detective Stanford, please come back. I'll speak with you."

He turned around and headed back to the front door. "Thank you. I appreciate it."

"Please come in," she said. "I was just about to make a cup of coffee. Would you like one, Detective?"

"I'd love a cup. May I ask what made you change your mind about talking?"

She paused for a few moments. "I think you're a decent man, Detective Stanford. I've visited George a couple of times in jail, and he tells me you have been very kind to him, taking him outside several mornings a week to smoke. Even though you could get into hot water with your chief."

Chris laughed. "Yes, your brother loves his tobacco. I've never met anyone who derived as much pleasure from a cigarette as George. Every time he takes a drag it's like a religious experience."

She laughed. "For sure!" Then she became serious. "I think we both know where all this is headed. My brother will most certainly be convicted. This is Missouri, so I fully expect he will receive the death penalty." Chris started to interrupt her, but she stopped him. "I've spoken to someone who understands these things, and she was very frank with me about what to expect."

"I see."

"But the reason I agreed to speak to you? I want at least one other person to know the George Maybrick that I know."

"Please, tell me," he replied, nodding his head slightly.

"George and I were born here in Hightower," she began. "My father married my mother, sold the family farm in Kansas, and came here to work on the towboats. Only a few months away from retirement, he died a slow, painful death in a towboat fire because of a poorly serviced diesel engine. Senseless."

"I'm sure it was devastating for you and your mother,"

"My father was my mother's rock. She never stopped grieving my father's death. When I helped her move to Riverside, in her closet I discovered she had kept my father's only suit, two dress shirts with ties, and his black wing tips. She had never been able to part with them."

"She must really have loved him."

"My brother is nine years younger than me. My mother was forty-three and my father almost forty-nine when he was born."

"I take it the pregnancy came as a surprise."

"That would be an understatement! The doctors had told my mother she couldn't have children. I was an unexpected but happy surprise. My mother's pregnancy with George was inconceivable."

They both laughed at the pun. "I can imagine."

"She didn't work outside of the home and my father earned a very modest salary. This house is not much, but my parents made it a home. We had the essentials, and that was about it. Do you have children, Detective?"

"I do. A five-year-old daughter and a son who is about to turn eight."

"Then you know the financial responsibilities children bring. I remember overhearing my parents talk about how another child would be a financial challenge. My mother cried, but my father assured her everything would work out. He would pick up extra hours on the docks. Despite the struggles, they both loved George. My father never really understood him, but he truly loved him," she assured Chris.

"Can you tell me anything special you remember about George growing up?"

"Special? How do you mean?"

He smiled. "Well, for example, he seems to be a gifted artist despite having no formal training."

"You know what they used to say about Picasso?"

"I don't."

"That he could draw before he could talk. I'm not saying my brother is another Picasso, but from an early age he demonstrated an amazing talent. As soon as he could hold a crayon, he started making pictures. By middle school he could draw just about anything you set in front of him. Art became George's passion."

"Your mother told me about his scholarship to an art school in New York and how it didn't work out."

After my father's funeral he returned to New York to finish the semester. When he came home for Christmas, he never returned to art school. Shortly after his twenty-first birthday, he decided to become a merchant seaman."

"What can you tell me about his nightmares?" Chris asked.

"You know about the nightmares?" Mrs. Carson asked somewhat surprised.

"Everyone at the police station knows about George's nightmares, Mrs. Carson. He scared the hell out of the officers on the late shift his first few nights in jail."

"Of course. What was I thinking?" She paused for a moment and then continued. "While you're aware of my brother's nightmares, there's more you should know."

"What's that, Mrs. Carson?"

"Almost from the day he was born, my brother was a strange, or I should say an unusual child. As an infant, he seemed agitated most of the time. He cried a lot, day and night. He was never at peace. It worried my parents. The pediatrician told them they had an unusually colicky baby. My mother tried everything to get George to stop crying. After his first birthday he went to the hospital to have some tests run, but the doctors couldn't find anything wrong with him."

"When did the crying finally stop?"

"It never did," she answered somberly. "When he was two, it actually became worse. He woke up in the middle of the night crying several nights a week. But it was not the normal crying of a baby. I can't describe what it was like, but I sensed he was experiencing great fear or discomfort. Again, my mother took him back to the pediatrician, who explained that George was having nightmares or night terrors. All perfectly normal, he assured her, and that he would outgrow them."

Chris had a doubtful expression on his face. "How could a two-year-old have nightmares?"

"My question exactly. What experience would cause a baby growing up in a normal household where he is clearly loved and cared for, to have nightmares? Finally, the pediatrician suggested my parents take George to see a psychologist. My mother drove George to Percyville for therapy every week for several months, but he didn't get any better. The psychologist suggested that perhaps my parents might have done something to traumatize my brother. Someone even came to the house from Family Services to investigate. My father, who had a bad heart and rarely got angry, hit the roof."

Chris nodded. "Dr. Crane said George told him he could never remember not having nightmares."

"It's true."

'Obviously, he never outgrew having them."

"No. It deeply saddens me to say this, but I truly believe my brother came into this world a tortured soul. There is a heavy darkness that has overshadowed his entire life. The only things that seem to bring him some respite are his painting and reading, especially poetry."

'Yes, I've heard him quote Dylan Thomas several times."

"His absolute favorite," she replied with a faint smile. "In some respects, the two are kindred spirits."

"How so?"

"One a poet, the other a painter, they both had remarkable talent yet very little peace or happiness. Thomas battled terrible alcoholism and drank himself to death at thirty-nine."

"It had to be very difficult on you growing up with all this," Chris said.

"Yes, but even harder on my parents. By the time George turned seven, they were at their wits' end. It devastated them to see their child in a constant state of fear, agitation, unhappiness, whatever you want to call it, and nothing seemed to help. He never had a normal life. He couldn't have sleepovers with friends because of his nightmares. Which also meant I couldn't have friends over, either. For my thirteenth birthday, I wanted to have a slumber party with several of my friends. My mother said no because George might have one of his nightmares and scare everyone. For a while I became very angry. Our whole family life seemed to revolve around my brother and his dreams. When he turned sixteen, my father converted the garage into a cottage and George moved out there. My brother welcomed it, but so did I and my parents."

Chris shook his head. "None of this seems fair, Mrs. Carson."

"You're right, it hasn't been easy. And to make matters worse, as my brother got older he was better able to articulate his dreams, and they were horrific. I couldn't handle it emotionally. It was like experiencing severe PTSD, and I don't make that comparison lightly."

"I understand."

"No offense, Detective, but I don't think you do. You can't imagine what it's like to go to bed every night dreading that a child will wake up sobbing, or worse, screaming, because he's had another horrific nightmare. It's like being in hell."

"I don't know what to say other than I'm truly sorry for you and your family, Mrs. Carson."

"There were two other things George was very afraid of—the dark and small, closed spaces. As he got older and could articulate his nightmares, he shared a recurring dream where he found himself locked in a dark closet for hours, sobbing uncontrollably. I have no idea if the nightmare caused his fears, or if the fears created his nightmare, but they were both very much a source of great anxiety for my brother."

"I can see your brother has had more than his share of psychological issues."

"None of which are his fault. For his sake and mine, I have tried to understand George. When I was in nursing school, I did some research on nightmares."

"Where there any insights you discovered in your research regarding George and his nightmares?"

I learned a couple of unusual things about my brother's dreams that didn't fit the research. He had an uncanny recall of his dreams. Most of us can remember a portion of a dream but we forget quickly. But invariably, my brother could remember the entirety of most of his dreams."

"That does seem highly unusual."

"Also, sometimes he dreamed with his senses. He claimed he could smell, taste, even feel things in his dreams. Not all the time, but often."

"Strange. Could you give me an example?"

"He had a recurring nightmare where a group of thugs threw him into an icy cold river during wintertime. He could say in excruciating detail how the freezing water felt, stabbing him all over his body as he drowned and died. Another time, when he was only four years old, he told us about a dream that took place in China. In the dream he was eating some sort of fowl on a bun covered in a very dark thick sauce that tasted very salty and a little sweet all at the same time. We had no idea what he was describing and guessed it must have been Peking duck. Having never eaten it, we didn't have a clue how it's served. Years later, I ordered Peking duck in a Chinese restaurant in St. Louis. My date passed me the hoisin sauce. It looked and tasted exactly as my brother had described it. Tell me, how does a four-year-old so accurately describe the taste of a dish that he has never seen, let alone tasted, in his life?"

"A fascinating question, and way above my pay grade, Mrs. Carson," Chris answered. "Could you give me another example of a dream that was beyond his realm of experience?"

"George had a recurring dream about war. He was in the French army. He didn't know which war, but he gave a very accurate account of the abysmal conditions of trench warfare in World War I, including sharing the trenches with hordes of rats. As he got older, elements of the dream sometimes changed, but the circumstances never wavered. Eventually, what was an interesting historical dream became a nightmare."

"How so?"

"George is shot in the head by a German sniper."

"Is it possible your brother read about World War I in a book, or saw something on TV that might have influenced his dream?"

"Doubtful, the first time he shared the dream, he was five. My father, who was mildly amused and not all that curious, asked him where he had read a book about the war. He looked at my father and said with a straight face, 'Daddy you're so silly. You know I can't read chapter books yet.'"

"Still, it's possible he might have seen a war movie or documentary on television."

"You don't really believe that do you?"

"I'm a detective. I must consider all the possibilities."

"Of course. I'd ask you for one favor. I'd like my mother to be able to see George one last time."

"I don't think—"

"Please, can you take George to see my mother at Riverview?"

"That would be pretty hard to pull off, Mrs. Carson."

"I get it. But my mother has cancer. The doctors say she only has three to four months."

"Does George know?"

"He doesn't, and I don't want him to," she said emphatically.

"Even if I could get George out of jail, how do you think your mother would react seeing her son in handcuffs, foot shackles, and a waist restraint? She would be devastated."

"No doubt. She knows nothing about George's upcoming trial and the charges against him. She is so frail; it would probably kill her. Is there any way…"

"You're asking for no restraints? I'm sorry, impossible," he assured her.

"Please? It's the last opportunity for a dying woman to see her son. I'm begging you, please, please try."

"Chief Monroe would never go for it, and the judge would throw me out of his chambers for even asking. He denied your brother bail, so he's not going to release him from jail to visit his family. What you're asking me to do would take a miracle, and I don't believe in miracles."

"You don't have to believe in miracles to make one happen," she said. "I'm only asking you to try, Detective Stanford. What harm could that possibly do?"

He could think of several. Nevertheless, he said, "Okay, Mrs. Carson. I'll make a request, but please don't get your hopes up."

CHAPTER THIRTY-EIGHT

"Judge Stevens will see you now, Detective Stanford. A heads-up—he's a little grumpy this morning."

"Just my luck," Chris muttered as he entered the judge's chambers.

"Good morning, Detective Stanford. What can I do for you?" the judge asked in a very businesslike tone.

"I have a very unusual request, Your Honor," Chris replied nervously. "It's regarding the Maybrick case."

"And...?" The judge stared at him as several moments ticked by. "Well, out with it, Detective. What is your request?"

"Your Honor, I would like permission to allow George Maybrick to visit his very ill mother."

"Detective Stanford, you don't need my permission for that. Why are you wasting my time?"

Chris sensed the judge's displeasure but pressed on. "Your Honor, I would like to take the defendant to the nursing home where his mother is living."

"I'm sure you're aware of the circumstances in which a defendant can be held without bail."

"Yes, Your Honor."

"Then what would possibly make you think I'd give you permission to take him out of jail for any reason?"

Chris could see his request had angered the judge. So, he felt he had nothing to lose. "There are extenuating circumstances, Your Honor. His mother is dying. It's the last opportunity Mrs. Maybrick will have to see her son. Because of her age and terminal cancer, she has not been told about the trial and the charges her son is facing."

"I'm truly saddened to hear about Mrs. Maybrick's illness. This is clearly an unfortunate situation."

"Yes, Your Honor," he replied, nodding in agreement.

"But even if I allowed the defendant to visit her, what do you suppose her reaction would be when she sees him in handcuffs? It seems to me, that would cause more harm than good."

"Well, Your Honor..." Chris replied hesitantly.

"Detective, you're not about to ask me—"

"Yes, Your Honor," Chris interrupted the judge midsentence. "I would take every precaution. Maybrick would wear an EM bracelet and he would never be out of my sight."

"Absolutely not!" the judge roared. "If anything went wrong, you'd lose your job and I'd find myself riding the bench in night court in St. Louis for the remainder of my career. At my age, that would be like a prison sentence."

"I'm not asking for the defendant, Your Honor. It's for his mother."

"The answer should still be no. But...I appreciate your compassion, so I'll think it over this evening. Be back in the morning at eight-thirty sharp and I'll give you my final verdict."

The next morning Chris found himself once again sitting outside of the judge's chambers. He had spent most of the night wide awake, wondering whether he had made a huge mistake. The judge intimidated him, and he felt like a child in serious trouble with an unrelenting parent.

"Judge Stevens will see you now, Detective Stanford," the administrative assistant informed him as she opened the door to his chambers.

"Good morning, Your Honor," Chris said, walking through the doorway.

"Morning, Detective. Well, I'm sure you are anxious to hear my decision."

"Yes, Your Honor."

"I've decided to grant your request. The defendant may visit his mother wearing only an electronic ankle bracelet. But Maybrick may never be out of your sight, not even for one second. If he has to take a pee, you better be standing right behind him. Have I made myself clear, Detective Stanford?"

"Yes, Your Honor. Thank you, Your Honor. You're very kind, and I promise there will be no surprises." He hesitated. "May I ask, what made you change your mind?"

The judge pondered the question, then said, "Someone once observed that the shortest distance between a human being and truth is a story. So, I'll share a quick story with you. There once was a very driven, ambitious prosecutor who had dreams of becoming a judge one day. He decided to prosecute a case that no one thought he could win, including his DA. The hard-charging prosecutor spent months preparing for the trial. Three weeks before the trial began, his father was diagnosed with stage four pancreatic cancer. The doctors told his family the father probably had two or three months to live, but given the advanced state of the cancer he might die at any time. The prosecutor, who lived some distance from his father, called him regularly while he worked nonstop once the trial began. He told himself that as soon as the trial concluded he would catch a flight and be at his father's bedside. By all accounts he tried the case brilliantly, and against all odds, he won. Sadly, only a few hours after the jury returned a guilty verdict, he received the news that his father had passed away. Later, he received an appointment to the bench, in part because of his reputation from that case. He had accomplished his goal to become a judge, but at what cost? To this day, he deeply regrets not finding a way to see his father before he died."

It didn't take a psychic to know the judge was speaking of himself.

"I understand, Your Honor," Chris said.

"Good luck, Detective Stanford. Don't mess up."

CHAPTER THIRTY-NINE

"Here, put these on," Chris told George as he handed him a brown grocery bag.

George emptied the contents onto his cell bunk. "Where did you get these, a thrift store?" he asked, holding up a pair of scuffed black chukka boots.

"Yeah, and everything else, too," the detective answered. "On my own dime. You should be more grateful."

"I'm just giving you a hard time, Detective Stanford. What's with the civvies? Are we going somewhere?"

"Yeah, I'll explain in the car. Now lift your foot onto the chair so I can put this EM bracelet on you."

During the twenty-minute ride over to Riverview, Chris explained to the shocked prisoner that he was taking him to see his mother and explained the agreement he had made with the judge.

"No funny business. I will shoot you if you try anything."

Chris wasn't serious, of course, but Maybrick didn't have to know that.

"I promise. I can't tell you how grateful I am. I really wanted to see my mother before...Detective, why are you doing this for me?" George asked.

"Your sister pleaded with me. In case you didn't know, she can be quite persuasive."

"That's Heidi for you. Life has not been easy for her, but she's still always thinking of others, especially our mother. I don't know what I would have done if she hadn't been around to take care of Mom after our father passed away."

"She told me how much help you've given her over the years. She wishes you had spent more time closer to home, but she truly loves you and is very grateful for all you've done for her and the boys." He glanced over at George. "There's one other thing you should know."

"What's that?"

"Your mother has cancer. She's dying and only has a few months to live. She didn't want you to worry, so she asked your sister not to tell you."

"So ironic," George murmured. "I gave my mother a lifetime of worry. Now she's dying, and it's me she doesn't want to be worried. She is one remarkable woman. Thank you for telling me, Detective Stanford. It means a lot."

When they arrived at the nursing home, the staff had already taken Mrs. Maybrick out onto the lawn. She sat in a wheelchair bundled up, sunning herself and enjoying the unusually warm February weather.

Chris decided to remain inside the building out of sight, but he never took his eyes off George, as he had promised the judge. He had no idea what mother and son were talking about, nor did it matter. Several times he saw them break into laughter, which brought him joy. Thirty minutes passed, then an hour, then another half hour, but the time passed quickly for Chris. Perhaps too quickly, considering the circumstances.

After about two hours, George bent down and embraced his mother with a delicate but loving hug. It was clear neither mother nor son wanted the embrace to end, nor did either of them have the emotional resolve to let the other go. It was both painful and beautiful at the same time. Chris wanted to look away, but he knew he couldn't.

Finally, after several minutes Mrs. Maybrick released George and kissed him goodbye.

On the drive back to the police station, Chris allowed Maybrick to be alone with his thoughts. He welcomed the silence. Deeply impacted by the encounter between George and his mother, Chris pondered the irony that neither mother nor son understood what the other knew—that it would be the last time the two of them would ever see each other.

CHAPTER FORTY

"Dr. Crane, nice to see you," Chris said, looking up when he heard the knock at his office door. "What can I do for you this morning?"

"I've brought an article I want to share with you. Do you have a few minutes to look at it?"

"Sure, I'd be happy to, but I warn you, I'm a slow reader."

"Let me begin with a question," Crane said. "Have you noticed everyone involved with the murder investigations in both Hightower and New York all seem to repeat the same refrain, that they've never witnessed anything like it before?"

"Well, Dr. Crane, that was definitely my reaction."

"I called Detective O'Meara last week and asked him for a copy of the full police report, including all the photos."

"And...?"

"O'Meara definitely has some anger management issues and could do with some therapy."

"No doubt you shared that with him," Chris replied dryly.

They both immediately broke out in laughter.

"Actually, I did share with the detective that it isn't unusual for cops who have witnessed horrible murder scenes to experience real trauma, and I encouraged him to talk to someone."

"I'm sure that went over well."

"Our friend told me he didn't need to talk to any—I believe the term he used was goddam shrink."

"No surprise there," Chris replied. "Did you remind him you're a goddam shrink?"

"No." Richard laughed. "The good detective immediately launched into a tirade about how George Maybrick needs to be extradited back to New York and stand trial where he committed the first murder. I tried not to engage on that one, but then he said something that really got my attention. I'll never forget it."

"Don't keep me in suspense," Chris said, leaning across his desk and looking the psychiatrist directly in the eyes.

"He said—and this is pretty much verbatim—'I've been in law enforcement for damn near forty years. I work in the largest police department in the goddamn country with over thirty-six thousand officers. I'm telling you, Crane, I've seen more than my share of godawful crime scenes, but neither I nor any other officer in this whole goddamn department has ever seen anything like what I witnessed in that abandoned warehouse on the waterfront. This merchant seaman bastard is some sort of shapeshifting psychopath who turns into a serial killer when his feet hit dry land. So let me make this clear. I'm gonna make it my life's work to bring that goddamn son of a bitch back to this city so he can stand trial for what he's done.' When he finished his rant, there was this dead silence on the phone for about thirty seconds, then he hung up."

"What do you make of that, for crissake?"

"Well, he gets points for creative language. I've never heard any killer described as a shapeshifting psychopath. These are two words not typically seen together in the English language," Crane said laughing.

"Doesn't reflect well on merchant seamen as a profession, either," Chris added, prompting more laughter.

"All joking aside, I have to say it was a rather disconcerting conversation, but two things really struck me. The first thing that stood out was his comment that it was a crime scene unlike anything he or the department had ever seen before. This is exactly what you, Detective Caulfield, and all the other investigating officers here in Hightower have said, too. Dr. Anjali, the ME, said the same thing at both the crime scene and in Donna Strickland's autopsy report."

"Obviously, we don't see this kind of thing in a nothing town like Hightower. But New York City with eight million people and thousands of police officers? That's saying something."

"No kidding. But there's something else," Crane said. "Something in O'Meara's voice."

"What are you getting at, Dr. Crane?"

"Underneath all that bluster, anger, and goddamn this and goddamn that,

I sensed real fear in his voice. He sounded very afraid. Believe me when I tell you this. Our favorite New York City detective has stared into the dark abyss and is now being held captive by it. I worry he has no earthly idea how to break free."

Crane's revelation rattled Chris. The psychiatrist's phone call with Frank O'Meara had clearly been as powerful as it had been disturbing. How to unravel the implications of Crane's haunting narrative? Chris decided to stow it away to process later.

"What about the article you mentioned when you first came into my office?" he asked.

Crane took a folder from his worn leather satchel and slid it across Chris's desk. "The article is from an academic journal, not always easy to follow, but I think you'll find it fascinating reading."

Chris looked at the name of the journal. *The Journal of Investigative Psychology and Offender Profiling.* "You've got to be kidding me, Dr. Crane. What is this?"

"An academic publication that focuses on criminal profiling."

"I'm a detective. I know what criminal profiling is."

"I meant no offense. Check out the article," Crane urged.

Chris opened the folder and read, "*The Jack the Ripper Murders: A Modus Operandi and Signature Analysis of the 1888-1891 Whitechapel Murders.*" He looked up. "Jack the Ripper? Are you saying George Maybrick is copying the Ripper murders?"

CHAPTER FORTY-ONE

Richard understood from the detective's brusque response that he had annoyed Stanford. He needed to shift the focus of the conversation.

"I hope you'll read the article, Detective Stanford. I'd like your opinion. It is an in-depth analysis of Jack the Ripper's MO and provides some fascinating insights. What I'd like to point out for now, however, speaks to how our whole conversation began."

"You mean everyone involved in this case commenting that it's not like anything they've ever seen before?"

"Exactly. The findings of this study may well explain why that is."

Richard removed another copy of the article from his satchel and began thumbing through it. "Read where it says *Discussion* near the bottom of page eighteen and continue reading until the *Conclusion* on page twenty," he said. "You'll need to read the complete study to get the full context, but from these few pages I believe you'll get an understanding of one of the more important findings, the one that relates to our current discussion."

Richard sat reviewing the margin notes on his personal copy while Stanford read to himself. He saw that the detective immediately became engrossed in the article. A good sign.

At one point Stanford stopped, looked up, and asked, "What's picquerism?"

Ignoring his mispronunciation, Richard replied, "The short version is, getting off on the sadistic penetration of someone else's skin with a sharp object like a pin, knife, or razor, usually in the groin, breasts, or buttocks."

"Very sick," Chris said matter-of-factly and resumed his reading. Several minutes later, after a second reading, he laid the article on his desk.

"What do you think?"

"I think you may be on to something, Dr. Crane. I got a C-minus in my criminology stats course, but I know enough to figure out what these guys are getting at. The Ripper MO they created seems spot on. We need to talk about the relevance of the study to George Maybrick, but first, what I really find intriguing is how they created the Ripper's MO and identified his signature characteristics by doing a granular analysis of his murders. Then comparing their findings with a database of over thirty-three hundred murders from the nineteen eighties and nineties was pure genius...very solid research. Their conclusion that experience and confidence will modify an offender's MO over time, but signature characteristics will remain stable was really interesting."

"Agreed, Detective."

"What's especially unbelievable is that in all that data there wasn't a single other case with the same MO and signature characteristics as the Ripper. That's damn significant," Stanford concluded. "Not one!" he repeated, shaking his head in disbelief.

"That is, until now," Richard corrected. "When you compare the signature characteristics of Jack the Ripper's MO with the murders George Maybrick confessed to, they are eerily similar."

Stanford met his eyes. "I wouldn't say similar, Dr. Crane. I'd say nearly identical. I'm willing to bet if you gave the people who conducted this study a copy of the police reports from New York City and Hightower and didn't tell them when or where the murders took place, they would tell you they were committed by Jack the Ripper."

Crane nodded. "Dr. Liebman and I came to the very same conclusion."

"So, you're suggesting that Maybrick is a copycat killer inspired by Jack the Ripper."

"Well, possibly. At any rate, it might be worth your time to read up on Jack the Ripper. It might give you some insight into our friend downstairs, and how and why he's driven to do the specific things he does."

CHAPTER FORTY-TWO

"For me?"

"Yes."

"Whatever could it be?" Shoshana mused.

"A book and a case abstract from a classic textbook that you and I both read when we were undergraduates."

"Oka-ay."

Richard detected a look of confusion on her face. "I'll explain. When you were wrapping up your session with George last week he mentioned that he was killed as he returned to his ship docked on the Thames. That prompted a kind of *déjà vu* moment. In his past life, George brutally murdered women and then returned to his ship, essentially avoiding capture. I kept turning that scenario over in my mind, and then I remembered."

"What did you remember?"

"Decades ago, I read an account of a psychopath who killed his wife and then signed on to be a merchant seaman. He went on to murder women while he was in other ports and then shipped out, again avoiding capture. I couldn't remember the source or details, so I started going through some of the books in my library."

"You're killing me with suspense," she said dryly.

"Sorry. As I thumbed through a chapter on character disorders in Coleman's *Abnormal Psychology in Modern Life*, there it was!" He handed her some copied pages.

She read the summary of the case, then announced, "This is very interesting."

"My thoughts exactly."

"Checks a lot of the boxes," she said. "Thirty-five-year-old psychopath with sadistic impulses in a contentious marriage. Starts drinking. Gets in an argument with his wife who tells him she's pregnant. Strangles her and then mutilates her by slicing her open to see if she's really pregnant."

"Then he becomes a merchant seaman. Two years later he finds himself on a ship docked at the port of San Francisco. Meets a woman, takes her to a hotel, chats for an hour, and then strangles and mutilates her by cutting off one of her breasts."

"He commits another murder in the same city, but it's five years later."

Richard nodded. "We don't know what, if anything, happened during the five-year interim between murders. Then similar MO. Picks up a woman in a bar, they both get intoxicated, go to a hotel, get undressed, and she passes out before they have sex. The killer strangles and mutilates her, cutting out a portion of her sexual organs."

"Clearly this guy was no Jack the Ripper," Shoshana observed. "There are significant differences. There's no evidence the Ripper had any interest in having sex with his victims. While they both strangled their victims, the Ripper also cut every one of his victims' throats."

"Yes. Similar MOs with notable differences," Richard agreed. "My point is, here's a real-life example of a merchant seaman who kills women while he's in port and then avoids capture by returning to his ship and travelling to another destination far away."

"Not that we needed any corroboration. George Maybrick confessed, remember?"

"True." He handed her a book. "Here's where it gets interesting."

She glanced at the title. "Hmm, *Jack the Ripper: The 21st Century Investigation* by Trevor Marriott. Another theory on the identity of the Ripper I'm guessing?"

Richard nodded. "Trevor Marriott is a retired British homicide detective, and his book posits a novel theory about the identity of Jack the Ripper. Fun Fact: To date there are over a hundred people identified as Ripper suspects, and still counting."

She glanced at her watch. "I have a class to teach in an hour. Maybe you could just give me the Cliff Notes?"

"Of course. My apologies. I'm pretty captivated by the whole Ripper mystery and get carried away."

"Oh really? I hadn't noticed," she replied with a laugh.

"Anyway. Marriott makes a compelling case for Jack the Ripper being a merchant seaman who worked cargo ships. There are several takeaways from his book worth noting. First, he expands the number of possible victims. He suggests the killer may have been responsible for several brutal murders of prostitutes in Nicaragua in 1889, as well as a victim in a German port and another prostitute killed in Whitechapel eight months later."

"All the murders had the Ripper's MO?"

"Many of the hallmarks. Marriott revisited the Whitechapel murders with the discerning eye of a veteran detective and challenged some of the assumptions of the original Victorian-era investigators. Some of those beliefs continue to the present day."

"For example?"

"Marriott questions that the Ripper possessed some medical knowledge and used a knife with the precision of a surgeon. He points out that only two of the Ripper victims evidenced organs being expertly removed. He reintroduces the theory that the victims might have had their organs removed at the mortuary before the police surgeon conducted the postmortem examination. There's another book written by an historian who makes the case that Jack the Ripper was Robert Mann, a mortuary assistant, but that's a different story."

"Anything else?" she asked.

"Another thing Marriott challenged is that Jack the Ripper lived and worked in Whitechapel. Because five of the murders took place in Whitechapel within a mile of each other, some of the strongest Ripper candidates resided there. Investigators back then argued that he eluded capture because he was a resident able to freely negotiate the labyrinth of streets and alleyways of Whitechapel in the dark."

"Do you think Marriott makes his case?"

"I'm no expert, but I've done a pretty deep dive into the Ripper literature over the last six weeks, and I think he makes some pretty compelling arguments."

"He said there were more victims, right?"

"Well, I'm not entirely convinced. Maybe Martha Tabram was. She was killed nearly three weeks before Polly Nichols, who's considered the first of the Ripper's five victims. I believe Tabram may eventually emerge as a legitimate Ripper victim. There is some very good research to support that.

Either way, I'm very impressed with Marriott's thorough investigation. I'm betting he was a very successful homicide detective. In the book he took a very granular look at the available maritime records in terms of the cargo ships moving in and out of London as well as Germany and Central America. He crosschecked the arrivals and departures of cargo ships against the times and places of the murders. He focused especially on ships that put in at the London Docks and St. Katharine's Dock."

"Why those two?"

"They're the two docks within closest walking distance of Whitechapel. Correlating the arrival and departures of cargo ships with the dates of the murders, Marriott created various scenarios around the dates of the Ripper murders. Despite his best efforts, there is simply not enough information from the crew records to be able to identify and crosscheck potential suspects. Several ships from the German ports of Bremen and Hamburg regularly transported cargo to London, unloading and loading at the London Docks and St. Katharine's Dock. While the crews were primarily German, they also included a small number of British merchant seamen. Typically, a seaman signed on for one voyage at a time. When they reached a destination, the crewmen had the option of signing on for the return voyage or opting to work on another vessel."

"So, what is all of this telling us?"

"Well, Marriot writes that if we just focus on the two docks in proximity to where the murders occurred, on any given day there were approximately forty ships near the East End with crews of roughly twenty-five sailors each. That potentially puts a thousand merchant seamen there each day. If you include ships at the six other docks farther from Whitechapel, that number grows to two hundred ships and five thousand merchant seamen in London on any given day. Marriot hit a dead end in terms of identifying a Ripper suspect using crew records. However, he is surprised the police never focused on that possibility. I think he makes a compelling argument that the Ripper might have been a merchant seaman."

"Such as?"

"All the murders occurred on weekends when there were fewer people around the docks whose suspicions might have been aroused. Marriot notes that some of the original witnesses interviewed by the police at the time described the suspect as shabbily dressed and looked like a sailor. The number of East End drinking establishments and prostitutes were a major draw for seamen. All the canonical murders took place within a mile of one another. Sailors who worked the ships that docked within easy walking distance from Whitechapel would have been very familiar with the labyrinth of streets and alleyways in the Whitechapel district where the murders took place."

"Which would allow him to escape quickly and remain undetected by the police street patrols," she agreed.

"Exactly. Marriot points out the job of merchant seamen was difficult and required them to be rough and tough in the harsh environment of ocean-going vessels. Many had joined up one step ahead of the law and were prone to violence. Perhaps some were even murderers."

"Seems like a bit of speculation to me."

"Point taken. I think there is a fair amount of conjecture on the author's part, but I don't think Marriot is far off the mark. While he couldn't successfully determine the identity of Jack the Ripper, I think he provides considerable circumstantial evidence and makes a very compelling case that he probably came from a merchant seaman background. I also find it interesting that Coleman presents a similar modern case in his abnormal psych text."

"Similar, yes, but very different scenarios on many levels."

"Agreed. I was only suggesting a similar dynamic."

"So. We have a case study from a classic psych text, a well-developed theory from a veteran homicide detective, and the past lives of a serial killer that all point to the Ripper being a merchant seaman who used his profession to remain undetected and literally get away with murder. You've made a believer out of me, Richard," she declared.

CHAPTER FORTY-THREE

"Any word from Detective O'Meara?" Shoshana asked as she and Richard walked into Detective Stanford's office.

"*Nada*, but you can bet he's working on something. Here to see George?" the detective asked.

"Yes. How's he doing?"

"Pretty good, Dr. Liebman. We're even considering moving him upstairs. He's still having a few nightmares, but most nights he sleeps like a baby. It's the darndest thing. I don't know what you guys are doing, but it's working. Meanwhile, I expect the DA to ask for a trial date any day now. Once he makes a request, it could go on the docket at any time. We could be sitting in a courtroom in three or four weeks."

"That soon," Richard murmured. "Does George know?"

"Hasn't asked, and I haven't told him. Come on, I'll take you downstairs. He's had his morning cigarette break so he's in a pretty good frame of mind."

For a second time, Richard passed her an envelope on the walk down to the basement cell.

"What's this?" she asked with a smile. "Another prediction?"

"Could be. Or maybe bedtime reading for later," he teased.

When they reached the end of the hallway, they found George in his cell listening to Dylan Thomas reading *Fern Hill* while he sketched feverishly with an unlit cigarette—illicit contraband conveniently overlooked by Detective Stanford—dangling from his lips. He quickly set aside his sketchpad and pencil. "Got a match?" he asked, smiling without fumbling his unlit cigarette.

"Good morning, George," she greeted him. "Nice try."

"Morning, Doc," he replied.

She immediately noticed a transformation in the cell. He had taped some of his drawings on the faded-green cinderblock walls. She still found it uncanny, his capacity for remembering places he had visited from around the world as well as his ability to recreate them so accurately. His attention to detail was so fine that his pencil drawings looked almost like photographs.

"Nice. Who's your decorator?" Richard joked.

"Do you like it?" George asked when he saw her admiring one of the drawings.

"Very much. St. Petersburg. The Winter Palace?" she asked.

"Yes," he replied. "Been there?"

"A long time ago," she said. "It was beautiful, but it was January and fifteen degrees below zero!"

"Here, Doc, I would like you to have it," George said as he carefully removed it from the wall and handed it to her.

"It's beautiful, George. I'm going to have it framed and hang it in my favorite room in my house."

"Which would be...?

"My study, of course."

"I'm honored, Dr. Liebman," he said in a reverential tone. It was the first time he had ever used her professional title. She heard the respect and affection in his voice.

After admiring the drawing, she said, "So. Any thoughts about our last session?" She was anxious to get to work.

He grimaced. "It was rough. The murder of that woman was painful to relive, but I'm kind of ambivalent. I have a terrible sense of guilt that will forever stick with me, but I'm also relieved that I'm coming to grips with what's driving my actions."

"You still haven't remembered your name in that lifetime?" she asked.

He shook his head. "No."

"But you said you were called Jack the Ripper," Richard said.

"Yeah, Dr. Crane. I've thought a lot about that. I don't know what to tell you. Some of the dreams I've had for so many years are very much like his murders. Could I have been the actual Jack the Ripper? Who knows? That's a very surreal and disturbing thing to wrap my head around."

"Indeed," she agreed. "Shall we get started, then?"

As soon as he had fallen into a deep state of relaxation she said, "George, I want you to go back to your time in Victorian England and try to remember when you were a child."

She and Richard sat patiently waiting for him to access his subconscious.

After a couple of minutes, he began to speak. "It's wintertime, December I think, a few days before Christmas. I'm leaving my house to meet a friend. As I'm walking to the front door, my stepmother calls me into the study where she is having her afternoon tea and reading a book. She tells me that in a few weeks it will be my tenth birthday. She explains that my father had set aside a trust for my education, and it was his wish that I attend boarding school when I finished primary school. 'When the new school year begins, you will be attending Cheltenham College in Gloucestershire, the same school your father attended. It's where he completed his first military studies. It's a fine school she assures me. I can tell she resents spending the money, but there is nothing she can do about it because the trust is in my name."

"Can you describe your stepmother's appearance?"

"She's a very attractive woman with a slim build, dark hair, black I think, and brown eyes. Her hair is parted down the middle and drawn into a bun with a silver and pearl hairpin my father gave her. She wears the slightest hint of makeup so it looks completely natural. It's clear why my father was attracted to her. She is always well-dressed, even on casual days when she's not going out or isn't expecting guests. She prefers to pair a dark-colored bodice with a high neckline with a light-colored dress. She typically wears bustles but hates them and frequently complains when she sits down 'Leave it to a man to create something that would cause a woman so much discomfort.'"

"Can you recall her name?"

"No, but my father sometimes referred to her as his angel or dearest."

"How did you feel about being sent away to boarding school?"

"Quite happy, but I didn't let her know that. My stepmother hates me, and she knows that I loathe her as well."

"What kind of person is she?"

"She's a cruel woman," he said. "I told you about her locking me in a closet for hours. My real mother died when I was born, but I never understood why. My stepmother would always tell me it was my fault she died. My father didn't speak of my real mother very often, but I do remember him talking about how gifted she was with needlework and sewing. During her confinement, she made me a beautiful quilt for the nursery. My father always said how excited she was to be a mother, and she spent hours making a special quilt just for me. I grew up with that quilt. I treasured it because it was the only memory of my mother that I had. One day I returned home from school and the quilt was gone. 'I threw that ugly, shabby thing away. I wasn't going to have it in my house anymore,' my stepmother told me when I asked her what happened to it. 'I hate you,' I screamed at her. She slapped me hard across the face. The pain was terrible, but I refused to let her see me cry. My face was swollen and discolored so badly that she kept me home from school for a week so no one would know what happened."

"Do you remember how old you were?"

"Around seven or eight. I remember that displayed proudly on the piano in the study was a large photo of my father in his military uniform with all his ribbons and metals. The day after his funeral, she removed it."

"She does sound cruel. Are you able to move forward and see what happened to her?"

After a few moments, he nodded. "It's December and my final term at boarding school has ended. I'm very excited. I've enrolled at university for the first term which begins in the new year."

"How old are you?"

"Sixteen. When the hansom drops me off at my house, I knock on the door, but no one answers. When I try to use my key, it doesn't work. Finally, I realize the locks have been changed. I go next door to see if the neighbor can tell me what's going on. When she opens the door, she seems taken aback to see me. When I tell her I can't get into the house she responds, 'You don't know?' I said 'I'm sorry but I have no idea what you're talking about,' She said my stepmother sold the house and moved away two months ago. 'Do you know where she moved?' I asked. She said 'I have no idea. It was all so sudden. Your stepmother didn't even say goodbye, she just left. This must be so upsetting for you. We just assumed she told you where she was going. You poor child, you're welcome to stay with us for a few days until you can get things sorted out.'"

"Hmm," Shoshana responded. "Then what happened?"

"The following day I go to the office of the barrister who advised my father and assisted him with his will and estate plans. We know each other because he helped transfer the funds from my education trust to pay for boarding school. He is angry at my stepmother for what she has done, but he isn't surprised. When I ask him why, he explains that my stepmother had tried to contest the will so she could access my education trust and take that money as well. When I asked what recourse I had, he explained that even if my stepmother could be located nothing could be done to her legally because my father left everything to her apart from my trust."

"So, what did you do?"

"The barrister assures me the trust still contains sufficient funds to enable me to attend university and to pay my living expenses while I focus on my studies. I attend university for two terms and then drop out. I don't really have any goals or anybody to guide me, so I decide to join the Royal Navy, which is the best in the world at the time. When I turn twenty, I receive a commission as a lieutenant because of my education and my father's military service. I love being on the ocean, so when I leave the navy a few years later, I become a merchant seaman."

"Did you ever encounter your stepmother after she sold the house and moved away?"

"No, never again," George said.

Shoshana decided to progress to closure. "George, I want you to move forward to the end of your life and try to remember your death."

CHAPTER FORTY-FOUR

Richard sat attentively listening to the details of George's final minutes of life in Victorian England. As soon as George described walking down the docks in search of his ship and seeing three men in the distance, Richard immediately recognized the scenario. George's regression unfolded just as he had described weeks earlier when he'd shared the recurring nightmare about his death. He was accosted by three men on the docks on a foggy night as he returned to his ship. Even the dialogue between him and his killers was the same, as well as the beating and being struck on his forehead with a leather truncheon. George concluded with the haunting description of his final moments of life when his killers threw him off the dock, leaving him to drown in a horrible death.

"I'm sinking. It's very cold and I'm enveloped by the darkness. Within seconds, the faint light from the dock lamp is extinguished by the depths of the Thames. I remember my last gasp for air and the cold water filling my lungs as the strong current carries me rapidly away."

Richard found the drowning man's unemotional description disconcerting. Unlike the time before when he gave a terrified account of his dream, now his demeanor was tranquil, almost serene. Richard didn't understand the difference.

"George, do you know what year it is?" Shoshana asked.

"I'm not sure. I'm still in my thirties, so it must be the late eighteen eighties or early eighteen nineties."

"Has your birth name come to you yet, George?" she asked.

Richard knew she was just as curious as he was to find out who the real Jack the Ripper might be.

"Sorry. No."

"Try a little harder, George," she pushed.

After a few minutes he responded. "It doesn't come to me. For some reason I'm blocking it."

"Can you remember the name of the ship you are trying to reach?"

"The *Sylph*. It's a British ship that has been in dock for several months undergoing repairs. The ship is headed to Barbados, so I signed on for a turnaround because it means more pay, and the Caribbean weather is warmer."

"Can you recall what happened to the knife you used for the murders? Was it with you when you drowned?" Richard asked.

"No. We aren't permitted to bring weapons on the ship. I wrap it in a piece of canvas soaked in whale oil and put it in an old box I bought in a secondhand shop on Spitalfields Street. Then I bury it.

"What does the box look like?"

"A thick brass box long enough to hold the knife. There were someone's initials deeply inscribed on the lid in English Roundhand script."

"Can you see the initials?"

"They aren't completely clear to me. LPB or LBP, maybe PLB. Something like that."

"Excellent, George. Can you describe the knife?" she asked.

"Yes, it's a post-mortem knife. Long blade about six inches in length, and a special notch on the handle for the thumb. It's very sharp."

"Can you remember where you buried it?"

"In a cemetery, under a small grave marker."

"Can you remember the cemetery or the grave marker, George?" she asked.

"No, I can't," he responded. "I buried the knife several days after I killed my last victim. I tried not to carry it around unless I intended to use it. I was never able to retrieve it because I drowned a few days after I buried it."

Shoshana shook her head slightly, grimaced, and glanced at her watch. She realized that any more questions would probably yield similar answers. She was disappointed that he could not remember his birth name. After such definitive closure, this would no doubt be the last time he'd regress back to that lifetime. Still, in the course of less than an hour, George had given an account of his birth and death in his relatively short but eventful Victorian life. It would be a lot to process, so she invited him to end the session.

"What are you thinking, George?" Shoshana asked as soon as he had readjusted to a waking state and seemed comfortable.

"Everything is now very clear," he answered.

"How so?"

"I could feel the deep hatred for my stepmother. So much so that I wanted to kill her. I think I might have if I'd been able to find her again. She cheated on my father and told me it was my fault my mother died. I didn't know what to do with my loathing. That's why I killed all those women, and why they were mostly whores...like my stepmother. I had to exact my revenge somehow."

Everything he said made perfect sense. She was glad he had come to the revelation all on his own. He had transferred all the loathing and hatred he felt for his stepmother onto the unsuspecting prostitutes who worked the streets of Victorian London's East Side, brutally murdering at least five of them before his own untimely death.

"George, do you see any connection between that lifetime and this one?" she asked.

"There must be a connection. I wish I could recall more about my other lives between then and now. I know I was a French soldier in World War I who died fairly young, but not what my life was like. And who was I between then and now? I must have been someone."

"We may find out at some point if we have more time. Typically, people don't recall all their past lives, only those that contain important information or life lessons."

Richard asked, "Do you see any pattern in what you have experienced thus far in your present and past lives?"

George sat in his cell, pensive, searching for an answer to the question before he eventually responded, "Death has not come easily to me. I always seem to die in a violent or frightening manner. The only time I had to really think about my dying was when I was an inquisitor hunting for witches. I died a priest, supposedly a holy man of faith, in total doubt about the meaning of my life, and in complete despair, an unforgivable sin. It was every bit as painful as being sucked into the cold darkness of the Thames."

"You think violence and fear are the pattern?"

"No, more like hatred. I suppose," George mused, "murdering all those women over the last seven or eight years was an effort to alleviate the hatred from my past lives lying deep in my subconscious. It wasn't right what I did. Something inside compelled me to kill, but I made a choice. Despite the compulsion, I could have acted differently, but I didn't. It's as if I've been living every day suspended between two dark places—my unconscious shadow side and the desolation of death."

"When, like a running grave, time tracks you down," Shoshana offered. "The opening line from the Dylan Thomas poem *When, Like a Running Grave*," she explained for Richard's benefit.

George immediately understood the reference and recited the remainder of the stanza. "Your calm and cuddled is a scythe of hairs, Love in her gear is slowly through the house, Up naked stairs, a turtle in a hearse, Hauled to the dome."

They all sat back and contemplated the meaning of the poet's words. Finally, Shoshana broke the silence. "Dylan Thomas's poetry is replete with both death and images of the dead, some rather bizarre and eerie. I think his message here is one of equanimity. None of us escapes the running grave. Time invariably and successfully tracks down all of us. Some have more time than others, but in the end, we are all found."

"Agreed," George responded with a wry smile.

"We never did have that conversation I promised you regarding the image of death in his work. In my study of Thomas, I discovered that he accepted death as part of the life cycle. His poetry is meant to encourage his readers to confront death."

George nodded. "He was quite sickly as a child, with terrible asthma and bronchitis. As a result, his fear of dying began at an early age."

"And he took full advantage. His mother overindulged him as a child, which created a lifelong pattern in his adult life of seeking attention and sympathy. Apparently he was quite good at it and frequently took advantage of his friends, who invariably forgave him or overlooked his transgressions."

"Surely you're aware, Doc, that he was greatly influenced by the psychoanalyst Sigmund Freud. You know better than me how Freud felt about death."

"As well as many others. You're an artist, so I'm sure you can appreciate surrealism's influence on Thomas's poetry."

"Right, although he disavowed it. I think he was more disturbed by death than you give him credit for, Doc. He was absolutely horrified by the death and destruction of World War II. So much so, that he hardly wrote anything during the war."

"Good point. I still believe that hidden behind death in Dylan Thomas's writing is the reality of rebirth. Life and death are like partners in this cosmic dance of ours. One cannot exist without the other, and so Thomas celebrates both."

"Beautifully put. Dr. Shoshana Liebman. I'm sure Dylan Thomas would agree."

"Thank you, George. It's possible you may never fully understand the thread running between your past lives and today, but perhaps it doesn't matter," she said.

"Kind of like why I love to paint. I have this creative gift, but I can't explain it. The why doesn't matter. It is what it is, even though I don't comprehend it."

His insight impressed and touched Richard. George's inner logic had propelled him to a level of understanding that had brought him to a state of relative calm. Nothing else really mattered. Richard suspected the serial killer would rarely have nightmares ever again.

"Speaking of art. George, I have one last request," Richard said. "Under hypnosis you described the kind of knife you used to kill your victims. Would you sketch me a picture of the knife? As detailed as you can?"

"Do you want it to scale?"

"Yes, if it's not too much trouble?"

George picked up a large sketch pad, a graphite pencil, and began to draw. While he had seen several of George's pencil drawings, he had never seen him actually sketching. Whenever they'd found him at work, he always put his pencil and sketchpad aside as soon as they arrived. Now, he rolled his eyes upward to the left visualizing the weapon, paused for a few seconds, then began to draw. His left hand moved quickly, confidently pausing to make a small correction.

Richard looked on with Shoshana, mesmerized as George worked. "It's like watching a photographic image appear in a darkroom," he whispered to her.

Within a half hour George had created a drawing that from several feet away could easily have been mistaken for a photograph. "I prefer an impressionist style, but I can do photorealism pretty well when I want to," he announced proudly as he held the drawing up for them to see.

"Your work is exquisite," Shoshana said. "It was truly a privilege to watch you draw, George."

"I agree," Richard said, realizing they were quite possibly staring at an image of the actual knife used by Jack the Ripper. The contrast between the beauty of the drawing and the subject's use in real life was not lost on him. Dare I ask if I may have the drawing, George?"

"Of course, Dr. Crane," George replied. He penciled his initials and the date with tiny characters in the corner of the drawing and handed it to Richard. "My pleasure."

CHAPTER FORTY-FIVE

Richard could hardly contain himself. In his wildest dreams he never imagined what his own detective work would turn up. On the one hand, today's discovery was exhilarating, but on the other, it was a horror beyond anything he thought possible.

He desperately wanted to share what he had uncovered with someone. Initially, he thought of Detective Stanford. But no. While Richard trusted him completely, the detective knew nothing about the regression therapy George had been going through over the last few months. He decided to reach out to Shoshana instead. He would share the email response he'd received from the FBI but hold back the photographs until he was sure she was prepared to see them.

He picked up his phone and nervously called her number. "Good morning, Shoshana. Do you have a minute?

"Sure. What's going on?"

"Do you have time to meet to talk about George Maybrick? I've uncovered a couple of things I believe you will find very interesting."

"Can't you tell me over the phone?"

"Not really. They're documents and photos. Any chance you're free this weekend? Maybe we could meet over dinner?"

"I'd love to, Richard, but this weekend is busy for me."

"I see."

She must have heard the disappointment in his voice, and said, "But I'll be in my office all day Saturday preparing a report. Could you meet me there? I know it's a long drive..."

"Sure, that would be great," he readily agreed. "Should we meet around noon?"

"Perfect. I'll certainly be ready for a break by then."

"How about I pick up some sandwiches and show you what I've uncovered over lunch."

"Perfect," she replied. "I'll text you directions to my university office and see you Saturday at noon.

Two days later as he made the drive to her office in St. Louis, he wondered how to share what he had uncovered. He was comfortable sharing the communication from the FBI analyst, but the photographs he was unsure of. The graphic photographs he carried in his satchel were now indelibly seared into his visual cortex. And those images rendered every theory, assumption, or belief about derangement and murder that he ever entertained moot. Would it be fair to inflict those images on Shoshana?

CHAPTER FORTY-SIX

"Corn beef on rye or pastrami on whole wheat?"

"How about a half of each?"

"You got it. How's the report coming along?"

"Vision statements, measurable outcomes, accountability, key performance indicators...sometimes I ask myself what's the point. But enough of that. Let's eat. And I'm curious what brings you here today."

"As I mentioned, I have some things I want to share with you. Before I start, maybe can you tell me what you're thinking about George?"

"I think he has found a level of peace through the past life regression therapy. I really believe he's coming to terms with what he has done and learned some important life lessons. Of course, he will never be able to escape the tremendous guilt he feels over killing those women."

"May I ask you a personal question, Shoshana?"

"Of course."

"Are you sure there's no countertransference going on?"

"Yes, I'm sure." She seemed surprised by his question. "I'm acutely aware of that possibility. I have a little bell that goes off in my head when I or the patient dip our toes into transference and countertransference waters."

He knew she understood his inquiry came from a place of care and concern. "Do you think George is a candidate for additional therapy?"

"Probably, but I believe he has come to terms with his greatest demons."

"I think you're right. There are many questions left unanswered, though that may be for the best," he observed. "But I do have one you may be able to answer."

"What's that?"

"What do you make of George's fascination with Dylan Thomas? Seems odd."

"Interesting question. I suspect the answer may lie with something Dylan Thomas once noted when asked about his work. He said his poetry was the record of his individual struggles from darkness to some measure of light.

I suspect that despite a lifetime haunted by darkness, George holds out the possibility of finding light, and that's why Thomas's poetry resonates so profoundly with him. But probably at an unconscious level, so he doesn't realize the connection."

"Makes sense," Richard mused.

"Do you now believe one of George's past lives really was as Jack the Ripper?"

"Probably, but it never hurts to have a little more evidence. Which is something I've been working on."

"Really?" she said in an exasperated tone.

"Come on, Shoshana. You're a scientist. You know you can never have too much data. So, I asked Heidi Carson for permission to search the cottage again. I spent three hours going through all his many books. She told me that for the past sixteen years he would always come home with his seaman's bag full of books, then stack them against the wall with the others. When he left, he would load the bag up with other books and take them with him. I don't know if he read them all, though his sister insisted he did. Either way, George was an eclectic reader... books on dreams, poetry, art, especially impressionism. And a lot of history books, especially on World War I and Victorian England. He could have gotten some of his description from them. But there was nothing in his collection of books that would have provided the immense detail he shared about Jack the Ripper."

"He could have books elsewhere, or read them and discarded them," she suggested, playing devil's advocate.

"Perhaps, but I don't believe he did. I guess we'll never know for sure."

"Not enough to finally convince you, though?"

"I told you I'd welcome any additional evidence we could find outside of George's subconscious. You've been more than patient with my persistent skepticism, but it's proving beneficial. Let me show you what I've discovered."

He pulled a folder out of his satchel, opened it, and gave her a handful of documents.

"What is it?"

"Detective Stanford gave me a copy of the police and medical examiner's reports from the murder in New York City. As you know, the Whitechapel murders remain one of the greatest detective mysteries of all time. Many experts agree there were more than five victims, and I think that's a real possibility. There are countless books filled with photos, documents, police reports, coroner reports, and inquests on his suspected victims. When I compared the police and coroner's reports for George's last two murders side by side with the final two East End murders in 1888, the similarities were uncanny."

"What are you getting at?"

"Look for yourself. It's hard for me to believe, but very possible that George read in granular detail about the Ripper's victims and then painstakingly recreated them over a century later. That's a lot of work, and if he went to that much trouble, don't you think he would want somebody to know about it?"

"Okay. Admittedly, you may be on to something," she said, clearly intrigued by his theory. She scanned through the reports and compared them with the copies he had made of several Ripper texts.

"There's more," he said. "Remember I told you about the hundreds of letters from individuals claiming to be Jack the Ripper? Here's a copy of one of the letters that Ripper scholars believe the killer might have written. It's referred to as the From Hell or Lusk letter."

"Okay…"

"And remember I asked George if he'd written any letters?"

She nodded. "Of course."

He removed several photographs from the folder on the table. "I sent a digital photo of the letter to a friend of mine who is an accomplished photographer. He blew up the words *From Hell* and *Catch me when you can* from the Lusk letter and digitally sharpened the resolution. Here they are." Richard handed her the two enlarged photos. "The crime scene in New York City had *From Hell* scrawled on the wall in blood. In Hightower the murderer wrote *Catch me when you can*. Now, look at these," he said, unable to hide the excitement in his voice. "I also asked my friend to enlarge and enhance the police photos of the writing on the walls from both of George's crime scenes."

She appeared stunned. "I can't believe the similarities in the handwriting. There are differences, to be sure. Writing large letters in blood on a wall isn't the same as with pen and paper, but the words in the letter bear an uncanny resemblance."

"I agree."

"Did you show these to Detective Stanford?"

"Not yet, but I did get the name of a handwriting analyst from him, a forensic document examiner at the FBI. I emailed her copies of all the images, contemporary and historical, and asked her three questions: Are the similarities a coincidence? Could the texts all be written by the same person? Would it be possible for someone to intentionally copy the handwriting from the letters onto the walls of the crime scenes?"

"Did you hear back from her?"

"I did. See for yourself." He handed her a copy of the FBI examiner's response.

"Unbelievable," Shoshana muttered as she read the email.

"What do you think?" he asked.

She laid the email on the desk. "Fun fact, Richard. In Hebrew there is no word for coincidence."

"Fascinating. Is that your take-away from the email?"

"It's interesting that the examiner says coincidence is always possible. And she warns that she would need a lot more information to render a conclusive opinion. But despite those limitations, she believes the writing at both modern crime scenes were written by the same killer, and more important, there is a very high probability the writing in the letter from 1888 came from the same hand. It's possible an individual working from the letter could copy the writing on the walls of the crime scenes, but she doesn't believe that's the case. Just replicating the texts on paper would require considerable practice even if the person possessed considerable forgery skills. And it would be even harder to replicate the handwriting on a wall with blood."

"What do you think of her conclusion?"

"It makes perfect sense. When you factor everything together, the odds that the killer went to all the trouble to basically forge those words is a very long shot. I think her conclusion that there is a very high probability they came from the same hand is very credible...and disturbing at the same time."

"I agree."

"I'm beginning to believe you were a detective in a previous life," she teased.

"Given what I've shown you this morning, are you aware of any articles that explore similarities between handwriting in a previous and current lifetime?

"It's not an aspect of reincarnation I've studied. However, there's evidence that some people have talents and abilities they've exhibited in previous lifetimes. I'll look around and get back to you."

"That would be great. I wonder if George was an artist in a previous life?"

"I'd bet on it," she replied without hesitation. "I would have liked to help him identify and explore a previous life that speaks to his brilliant artistic gift. Sadly, given his situation, there are things we will be unable to explore."

"Not enough time," he agreed.

"I also wish we could have spent more time exploring the people that he incarnated with over his lifetimes."

"I'm sorry, I'm not sure what you're referring to?"

"This may be a bit out there for you, but it's thought that we incarnate with a core group of the same people. The relationships change over the different lifetimes, but the souls are the same."

"Maybe you and I knew each other in a past life," he suggested, only half in jest.

"It's too early to tell," she responded smiling. "But it wouldn't at all surprise me."

He smiled back.

"Don't tell me... Is the Dr. Richard Crane I know becoming a believer in reincarnation?"

"I still entertain a bit of skepticism—an occupational hazard I'm afraid—but I'm close to becoming a believer."

Her smile widened. "I'm delighted to hear you say that."

"For good reason, and here's why," he began. "I haven't shown this to anyone else, in part because it is very macabre and visually disturbing. I want you to see it, but I don't want to burden your memory with the visual images. They are photographs of Jack the Ripper's and George's final victims. I'm taken aback every time I see them, though they are very compelling."

"You have my attention, Richard. But how could you possibly have a legitimate photo of the Mary Kelly murder scene?"

"It was the custom at the time to take photographs of the deceased. There are extant mortuary photographs of Jack the Ripper's first four victims. Because the murders took place on the streets, the bodies were taken to the mortuary where a doctor conducted a postmortem examination. The bodies were cleaned, and in Catherine Eddowes case, sewn back together." As he talked, Richard took out his phone and pulled the images up on the Internet for her to see.

She grimaced when she saw the photo of Eddowes' mutilated body literally stitched back together. "My God, this is awful!"

"I know. Maybe I shouldn't show you the rest?"

"No, please continue, Richard."

"Very well." He collected his thoughts. "Unlike the previous four victims, Mary Kelly's murder took place in her room at Miller's Court. It proved to be the most brutal of all the murders because the killer had the luxury of time to mutilate the victim after he killed her. Upon entering the room and seeing the mangled corpse her landlord said, it looked more like the work of the devil than a man."

She swallowed. "Go on."

"Because the murder occurred indoors, it gave the police their first real opportunity to photograph a Ripper victim *in situ*. Copies of the police photo can be found on the Internet. You can even view a very realistic digital 3-D projection scan of the crime scene, which is even more eerie. And all gruesome, to say the least. I've studied the photographic evidence of Mary Kelly's murder carefully and read the results of the postmortem examination multiple times."

"I don't have a good feeling about what's coming…"

"With good reason. It chilled me to the bone."

"What did?"

"I asked Detective Stanford for a copy of the photos from the Strickland murder crime scene. There were a lot, from every angle imaginable. He said he knew it was overkill, but he wanted to be sure he didn't miss anything.'"

"What did you find?"

"Are you prepared? I warn you; this is nothing like dissecting a cadaver in med school. I get visual PTSD every time I look at the photos. I want you to know how deeply disturbing these images are. You may not want to see them."

"You wouldn't be showing them to me if you didn't think it was important. So yes," she replied with some reluctance. "I do."

He pulled another folder from his satchel, removed a sepia-toned photograph, and passed it to her. "This is a copy of the photo the police took of Mary Kelly in her room when her body was discovered." He gave her time to process the image. "And here is a 3-D camera projection of Mary Kelly's death bed." He played a short YouTube video with haunting background music.

"A little difficult to see much detail," she said, "but the image is horrific."

"The medical examiner's report helps fill in some of the visual details, and you get a much better understanding of exactly what you're looking at. The photo shows very clearly that Mary Kelly's face is disfigured beyond all recognition. Beginning with Elizabeth Stride, his third victim, and each victim thereafter, the Ripper progressively disfigured his victim's faces until with Mary Kelly, she was impossible to identify. There are all kinds of theories of why Jack the Ripper did this but that's a discussion for another time."

"This is very gruesome and morbid stuff, Richard. I don't need to read the postmortem report. The images tell me everything I need to know." She gazed intently at the vintage photograph.

"By the time I asked Detective Stanford for copies of the crime scene photos of George's last victim, I had studied both this photograph and Mary Kelly's postmortem medical examiner's report very carefully. Nothing, however, could have prepared me for this." He handed her a second photograph from the folder. "As I was looking though the stack of police photographs of the Strickland murder, this one caught my eye. At first, I couldn't believe what I was seeing. I stared at the image for a long time, trying to take it all in. Never in my life have I ever gotten such an existential feeling of dread."

He carefully watched Shoshana's response.

A look of terror slowly appeared on her face as her gaze shifted back and forth between the two images. "Oh my God!" she cried.

CHAPTER FORTY-SEVEN

"A Saturday morning call, Richard? To what do I owe the pleasure?"

He took a deep breath. "A couple of reasons. Mainly, I wanted to see how you're doing. After I showed you those horrible police photographs, I began to regret it. I know seeing them had to be very difficult, and I want to say I'm truly sorry."

"No need. I won't pretend I wasn't deeply disturbed by what they revealed. But I'm glad you shared them with me. If I ever needed confirmation that George Linfield Maybrick was Jack the Ripper in a previous life, those images confirmed it. That being said, I don't believe I need to see or discuss them ever again."

"Agreed. I may share them with Detective Stanford at some point if it seems appropriate, but you and I certainly don't need to revisit them in the future."

"You said a couple of reasons. What else is on your mind?"

"Wondering if you've found anything interesting on handwriting and reincarnation?"

"As a matter of fact, I did. My notes are in the study and I'm on my way out the door. Can I call you later?"

"How about if I drive to St. Louis this evening and take you to dinner, and we can discuss it then?"

"Dinner, hmm...sounds great. Tell you what. I'll let you take me to dinner this evening if you let me make you breakfast in the morning?"

After a moment of shock, he said as calmly as he could muster, "How can I refuse an amazing offer like that? Does Italian sound good?"

"Perfect," she said. "I haven't had a good veal ala Milanese in ages."

"I'll make a reservation at Charlie Gitto's On the Hill and pick you up around six. Okay?"

"Looking forward to it."

CHAPTER FORTY-EIGHT

Richard could not remember when he'd anticipated anything as much as the prospect of having dinner with Shoshana Liebman that evening…and breakfast in the morning. Surely, she couldn't possibly mean… No doubt she had a guest room.

When he arrived promptly at six, she answered the door, greeted him, and immediately excused herself. "Please, make yourself at home, Richard. There's club soda and fresh cut limes on the bar. I'm finishing up a call with my daughter. I'll only be a few more minutes."

He poured himself a club soda and wandered into the living room. Off to the left was Shoshanna's study. Floor to ceiling shelves filled with books and art pottery surrounded a comfortable room with a beautiful Oriental rug, an oversized distressed leather recliner, and a vintage Mission Arts and Crafts desk with matching chair. A signed baseball caught his attention. It was signed by Carl Yastrzemski. How on earth had that found a home on her study bookshelf? A wooden plaque with two brief lines of Hebrew stood on the shelf next to the baseball. Maybe a biblical quote?

On the wall over the desk hung a powerful abstract expressionist-style painting. Black, multiple shades of grey, unbleached titanium, white, and various intensities of cadmium red filled a large canvas in an unadorned black frame. Quite taken by the canvas, he studied it intensely for several minutes.

In the corner was a large reproduction of an eighteenth-century Giovanni Maria Cassini terrestrial globe. He rotated it slowly, noting the countries that did not exist over two centuries earlier. He spun it, and gently stopped with it his index finger to see where it would land. *Virreinato de Nueva Espana*, the Viceroyalty of New Spain, a large area of the Spanish empire that was now the southwestern United States.

The geography lesson on impermanence caused him to pause and reflect on the many changes in his own life. Much like the grand Spanish empire, his world had become considerably smaller since his exile to Percyville,

Missouri.

However, things were looking up. The sound of footsteps bounding down the stairs caught his attention.

"I'm starved. Can't wait for dinner," Shoshana announced enthusiastically. Framed by the doorway and wearing a black kaftan dress, she looked like a life-sized portrait of a beautiful woman in a Whistler painting. Her fragrance was lovely.

"You're wearing Shalimar."

"How could you possibly know that?"

"It's an exquisite and very popular perfume with women who have impeccable taste. Rita Hayworth and Brigit Bardot loved Shalimar. The fragrance is unmistakable. Fun fact, in the movie *See No Evil, Hear No Evil*, Richard Pryor's character recognizes the villainess because she's wearing Shalimar."

"I don't know what to say, Richard. Sometimes your boundless knowledge and fun facts scare me. You are correct. I am wearing Shalimar. It's my favorite fragrance."

Several months later, remembering their conversation, he gave her a bottle of Shalimar as a Hanukkah gift. He also confessed that he recognized the fragrance because it was his ex-wife's favorite perfume, as well.

"I love what you've done with your study," he said, shifting the conversation. "I'm afraid if I ever went in there to read, I would never come out. You have a real eye for interior design, Shoshana."

"Thank you. I can tell you didn't sit in the chair."

"How so?"

"Because if you did, you'd still be in it. It's that comfortable."

"Gives me something to look forward to. Tell me about the painting. I found myself immediately drawn to it. It's absolutely exquisite. Reminds me of a Motherwell or de Kooning."

"You appreciate art?"

"Yes, very much. I'm passionate about painting as well as sculpture. One of my most prized possessions is a small Marino Marini sculpture of a horse," he said and made a mental note of their shared interest.

"Well, you certainly have a good eye. I adore art, as well. Many years ago in

Chicago, my late husband, Matthew, and I wandered into a gallery in the arts district. I saw the painting and immediately became entranced. It's entitled *The Philosopher's Stone*. I think I loved it because I'm partial to nonfigurative art. But with a price tag of several thousand dollars, it was hardly affordable for us at the time. I was in the fourth year of my psychiatry residency, Matthew had a position as an assistant philosophy professor, and we lived in a tiny studio walk-up on the northwest side with a two-and-a-half-year-old. A few months later, on our anniversary I walked into the kitchen and found *The Philosopher's Stone* resting on an easel with a huge red bow and a card that read *A painting you love, for the love of my life. Happy Anniversary, Your Matthew.*' Sometimes I sit in my study, gaze at the painting, and have an intense sense of longing for him."

Tears glistened in her eyes, and Richard regretted inquiring about the painting. "I'm sorry. I didn't mean to upset you."

"You're not upsetting me. I no longer grieve for Matthew. He passed away over five years ago, but of course I still miss him. My tears are actually tears of joy. When I see the painting I sometimes long for him, but it always makes me happy."

"Do you mind me asking why?"

"Not at all. The joy and love I felt when I saw the painting that morning in the kitchen, knowing how much it meant to me, and most important, how much I meant to Matthew, is one of my happiest memories of our marriage. It renews that beautiful memory and expression of his love every time I see it. The occasional longing I feel is a small price to pay for the great joy it brings me. I'm certain you can understand that."

"I think I do."

"Truth be told, it's quite liberating to have this discussion. I rarely have an opportunity to talk about Matthew. When you are a widow, people avoid bringing up one's departed spouse. I suppose they worry it will only upset me."

"You're right. I've sensed the reluctance in myself when friends have lost a loved one. I can see that you and Matthew loved each other deeply."

"We did. It was love at first sight," she replied, joy shining on her face.

"Can you tell me about it?"

"Are you sure?"

"Even a habitual skeptic like me loves a good love story."

"Well, I was a third-year med student in Boston. It was early spring, and lots of students spent time between classes in the university commons luxuriating in the sun and celebrating the end of a long winter. I was lying on a blanket on the grass when I heard a voice behind me. 'Pardon me, I hope you don't think I'm being forward, but would you mind terribly sharing your blanket? I have a class in ten minutes, and I promise not to disturb you. All the benches are taken, and I'm wearing a suit so I'd rather not sit on the grass.' When I looked up, I saw a gorgeous man with the most beautiful emerald-green eyes and curly auburn hair, a briefcase in one hand and a pipe in the other. He noticed me staring disapprovingly at the pipe. 'No worries, I promise not to smoke,' he assured me. He sat quietly, and after ten minutes he stood up and said, 'My name is Matthew. Thank you for sharing your blanket with me on this beautiful day.' The only two words I could manage to get out of my mouth were 'You're welcome.' After he left, I realized I didn't even think to introduce myself. I felt like an idiot. Needless to say, I spent most of the time during my pediatrics rotation that afternoon thinking about the stunning man with the emerald-green eyes."

"So, what happened?" Richard asked, captivated by her story.

"I decided to return to the commons the following day around the same time and sit on my blanket and see what happened. I felt like a giddy teenager."

"And...?"

"I waited a half hour. I was just about to go when I looked up and found Matthew standing over me with a big smile and two cups of coffee. 'It's another beautiful day, and I took a chance that I might find you here again. I brought you a cup of coffee to thank you for sharing your blanket yesterday.' I invited him to share my blanket again, and much to my surprise and elation, he immediately agreed. We sat talking for the next four hours. He looked a bit older than me, so I assumed he was a graduate student. When I asked what area of study he was pursuing for his graduate degree, he said he was an assistant professor in the philosophy department. I was so embarrassed, but he found it amusing. He asked me out that afternoon."

"Where did you go on your first date?"

"A baseball game. He was a huge Red Sox fan. He even had a Carl Yastrzemski signed baseball."

"Ah, that explains the baseball in your study."

"Yes, it was one of Matthew's most prized possessions."

"Understandably so. The Yaz is one of the BoSox greats."

"I didn't realize you're a baseball fan."

"I'm not, really. When I was in college a friend insisted I join him for a Sox game and I saw Yastrzemski, who was in his early forties at that point, hit a home run. It cleared the centerfield wall by a good forty feet to win the game. Anyway, please continue with your story, Shoshana."

"Well, a few days after our date to Fenway Park, I invited Matthew to dinner. By semester's end, we were inseparable. I had been in relationships before, but had never known what it was to love and be loved with so much intensity. We had each discovered our soulmate. He proposed that summer, and we married a year later, after I finished med school. I received an offer for a residency program in psychiatry in Chicago and accepted. All the fates aligned, and Matthew accepted a position teaching philosophy at a small private college in Chicago, as well. A year and a half later, our daughter Adyra was born."

"What did you do after you finished your residency?"

"I joined a private practice and taught part-time in a pre-med program. Eventually, I took a full-time teaching position and maintained a small private practice on the side. Matthew, who was brilliant, had a very successful career in academia. A few years after Adyra was born, he was offered a university tenure-track position. At the time of his death, he held a distinguished chair in modern philosophy, had published over thirty academic articles, and authored several books, including one of the definitive works on Martin Heidegger. To this day, Matthew is still considered one of the foremost authorities on time-consciousness in phenomenology. I have no idea what that actually means. I just know it's important if you're a philosopher."

Richard chuckled along with her. "Not too shabby. You must have been very proud of him."

"My late husband was never one to let the grass grow under his feet. But all his academic honors were not his greatest source of pride."

"Oh?"

"He was most proud of his work with students, particularly his doctoral students. During his twenty-five years of mentoring Ph.D. students, all but three completed their doctorates. Most of them became tenured professors at colleges and universities. At last count, a dozen held distinguished chairs in philosophy and humanities departments in the States and Europe. I still receive notes and cards from his former students sharing their latest academic and personal accomplishments and crediting their success to their wonderful mentor and friend. Matthew would be overjoyed to see how his legacy has continued to expand even after his death."

"May I ask what happened to him?"

"He was killed in a car accident coming home from the university. A driver fell asleep at the wheel and veered over into his lane. When Matthew swerved to avoid the oncoming car, he hit a tree. He suffered massive head and internal injuries and died three days later."

"I'm so sorry, Shoshana. I can't imagine the sense of loss you must have felt."

"Thank you. Matthew and I had become spiritually and emotional one. When he died, it wasn't just him that I lost. I lost a part of my very being. I found it not only painful, but terribly disorienting. I've never told anyone, not even my daughter, but for the first six months after his death, the only respite I felt came from thoughts of joining him. The depression and grief very nearly swallowed me. However, over time I came to realize grief is a place in which we must all ultimately find a home. Once you dwell there and make it your home, you eventually find peace."

Richard felt honored that she was comfortable sharing with him about the loss of her husband and how it had changed her life.

"Eloquently stated," he said looking into her eyes.

She returned his gaze. "Enough talk of art, love, and loss," she announced. "I'm famished!"

"Me too," he agreed.

When they arrived at the Italian restaurant, he requested a quiet table in the corner. Given the personal nature of the conversation they'd had earlier, he wondered if it was appropriate to bring up her research on handwriting and reincarnation.

She answered before he had time to give it much thought. "So, I have a postscript to your question about potential similarities in handwriting across lifetimes. There's not a lot of information about it, based on what I could turn up. I found some anecdotal accounts where people claimed their current handwriting was very similar to their handwriting in a previous life."

"Sounds pretty vague."

"Agreed. Not much to work with there, but I didn't strike out entirely.

"Go on."

"I found multiple references to a fascinating case in India. A forensic scientist, Dr. Vikram Raj Singh Chauhan, discovered a six-year-old boy, Taranjit Singh, who claimed to remember a past life. His parents said he began talking about a previous life around age two, and as he grew older he became more insistent regarding his past life. He could recall his name, Satnam Singh, his past father's name, Jeet Singh, as well as the name of the village where he lived and the school he attended. Taranjit was also able to describe his untimely death. Riding home from school on his bicycle, he was struck by a motor scooter, sustained serious head injuries, and died the following day."

"You mentioned before about the large percentage of children who recall past lives where they remember dying, often from tragic or violent deaths."

"Exactly. Eventually, Taranjit's parents took him to Chakkchela, the village he remembered from his previous life, but they couldn't find anyone who matched the description of the parents he had described."

"That doesn't sound promising."

"Have a little faith! As it turned out, someone in the village told them there was another village with the same name in a nearby district. At one point, the boy's father visited a school in the village of Nihalwal, the same village in which Taranjit reported attending school in his previous life. At the school Taranjit's father met an old teacher who verified that a boy named Satnan Singh had died in a motor scooter accident. He said the deceased boy's father's name was Jeet Singh, and that he lived in the village of Chakkchela. They located Satnan Singh's parents in the second village. Taranjit's father explained to them that his son claimed the books he was carrying at the time of the accident had gotten blood on them, and that he'd had thirty rupees in his wallet. At this point Satnan Singh's mother broke into tears. She had saved the blood-stained books and the thirty rupees to honor her son's memory."

"Interesting," Richard said. "But how does handwriting figure into the story?"

"I was saving the best for last," she said eagerly. "When Dr. Chauhan first heard the story about the six-year-old boy he didn't believe it and decided to conduct a thorough investigation. After considerable effort, he confirmed the veracity of the story. However, he went one step further. He compared Satnam Singh's writing from a notebook his parents had kept to Taranjit Singh's handwriting."

"I think I know where this is going," Richard interjected.

"Handwriting is kind of like one's fingerprints. No two people have identical handwriting."

"True. Even a damn good forger's work can be detected by a highly trained handwriting expert."

"So, when Dr. Chauhan compared the two writing samples, he found them nearly identical. He attributed the small differences to the fact that Taranjit came from a very poor background and was not accustomed to writing. As a result, he didn't possess the same level of fine motor coordination that develops with regular writing practice. When Dr. Chauhan shared the writing samples with other forensic handwriting analysts, they came to the same conclusion. He later presented his findings at the National Conference of Forensic Scientists."

"Were you able to check Dr. Chauhan out?"

"Yes, he has a substantial Internet presence and is clearly a very reputable forensic scientist who specializes in handwriting analysis."

"Before we discuss this fascinating case you've uncovered may I share a fun fact first?"

"Of course. I always find your fun facts interesting and of course, entertaining."

"Notice how almost everyone seems to have the last name of Singh in your account of Taranjit Singh? Singh is the second most common surname in India and the sixth most common surname on the planet. It comes from the

Sanskrit 'simha' meaning lion. What's truly interesting is that in an effort to create a casteless society many first-generation Indians and Nepalis changed their name to Singh making it a very common, non-caste specific last name."

"Your fun facts rarely disappoint, Richard. I never cease to be amazed. I have an idea. Just for fun let's just play a little word game first," Shoshana suggested. Without waiting for her date's response, she began. "Most common surname in the world?"

"Wang. Mandarin for 'prince' or 'king,'" he responded without hesitation.

"Most common surname in India?"

"Devi, of course. Twice as many people with that last name than Singh."

"Most common surname is the US?"

"Smith."

"Second most common?"

"Johnson, followed by Williams, Brown and Jones in that order.

"Okay, I give up. How could you possibly know that?"

"Exploring names has been a hobby of mine for years. I really became fascinated by names while my ex-wife and I considered names for our daughters."

"And your daughters' names?"

"Fallon Elinor and Harper Blayr. Blayr is spelled B-L-A-Y-R. It's a Scottish variant of B-L-A-I-R.

"Such beautiful and unusual names."

"Thank you! My greatest joy would be that I could see them again one day." Crane felt his eyes begin to tear and immediately changed the subject as he wiped the tears with the pads of his thumbs hoping his date would not notice them. "Do you think Dr. Chauhan's account might give us some insight into George?"

"I've thought a lot about the two cases. They're difficult to compare because they are very different, as are the results."

"How so?"

"I think the evidence is much stronger in the boy's case because his two lifetimes were in close proximity to one another. And he began talking about his previous life at age two and his recollections unfolded very quickly. George's experience is very different."

"Right. His previous lifetime occurred over a century earlier," Richard said.

"When you think about it, Dr. Chauhan had the perfect storm for doing a handwriting analysis. He had actual writing samples from both lives, each verified by the parents. We're working with digitally enhanced photos of a writing sample not definitively written by Jack the Ripper, and from 1888. We're comparing it with writing in blood on a wall at a murder scene. Still, I agree with the FBI handwriting analyst's conclusion that there is a very high probability that they were written by the same person. I also believe that George Lindfield Maybrick and Jack the Ripper are one and the same person."

"I don't ever remember you stating that with such certainty, Shoshana."

"Well, you have now. What I can't explain is the fact that George's normal handwriting is nearly impossible to read. How do you square that? Any thoughts?"

"I've actually given it considerable thought, and all I can come up with is a crazy theory that is pure speculation."

"Now you've piqued my curiosity, Richard. Spill."

"Okay. Try to appreciate that I'm trying to ground my wild idea in the evidence presented, with no particular nod to reincarnation. So, here are the facts as I see them. We have very accurate accounts of how Jack the Ripper killed and mutilated his five victims through the autopsies and police descriptions. Under hypnosis, George provided very graphic descriptions of the murders he recalls committing in Whitechapel. He has also confessed to the two brutal murders he committed in New York City and Hightower, including significant details of how he disfigured and mutilated his victim's bodies after he strangled them and cut their throats. I meticulously studied the documents from the police surgeons, coroners, medical examiners, and witnesses who testified at the inquests, as well as any other documents that provided information pertaining to the murder victims in 1888. I took the cases of Catherine Eddowes and Mary Kelly's murders and created a profile for both murders, incorporating as many details as I could find from the documents of the period and paying close attention to the actual murders and subsequent mutilation of the bodies. Then I took George's confessions of the two murders and created a similar profile, again with as much detail as possible."

"And *then* you compared them? Right?"

"Hold on. You're getting ahead of me."

"Then I took your transcripts from George's accounts during regression of the murders he recalled committing in the London East End. Again, I created a profile with every detail that he related while being regressed."

"And then you compared them," she said enthusiastically. "Richard, you're brilliant. What did you determine when you put them all together?"

"The high degree of correlation between all three sets of profiles was uncanny. However, I focused very heavily on the profiles I put together from the murders in 1888 and those from George's confession and the New York and Hightower medical examiners' autopsy reports. Allowing for differences in police reporting, medical terminology, and autopsy procedures between 1888 and the present, based on the profiles I created from the 1888 documents, I could predict almost exactly how George murdered his victims and what he did to them afterward. I'm telling you, Shoshana, if I didn't know better, I would say that George Maybrick was actually in Jack the Ripper's head when he killed his victims. That's how eerily similar the profiles are."

"That's both fascinating and deeply disturbing."

"I'm sure you're wondering what all this has to do with George's handwriting."

"The thought did cross my mind," she said.

"Think about the two Georges we have come to know. There is George the serial killer capable of brutal murder. Then there is George the deeply wounded, brilliant artist who loves to read and rattles off Dylan Thomas's poetry like a southern Baptist preacher quotes the Bible. We might both say he fits the psychological profile of a psychopath. But we both know he's not."

"True," she agreed.

"So, here's where my handwriting theory comes in. I believe that the George who wrote *From Hell* and *Catch me when you can* was of the same mind as the Victorian killer who wrote the 1888 letter. Think about the two photos I showed you of the crime scenes in Hightower and Miller's Court. Nearly identical. So just as George killed in much the same way as the Ripper who wrote the letter, he wrote in a similar way, as well. It's part of who he was."

"But not who he is now. The George we know as the gifted artist who loves poetry… he just happens to have terrible handwriting."

"Exactly. I don't know if it adequately explains our George with two different handwritings, or if it jibes with past life protocols, but it's the only way I could make sense of it."

She nodded. "Let's call it a working hypothesis. It's an intriguing explanation and definitely worthy of consideration. With that, let's order some dinner."

"I always find a good hypothesis is a great place to begin an evening meal," he joked.

For the remainder of the evening, they set aside any more discussion of George, the Ripper, reincarnation, or handwriting. They talked about their favorite foods, best books, and special travels.

At one point he reached across the table. He could see she thought he was going to retrieve a roll from the breadbasket and was surprised when he placed his hand on hers. He said nothing, nor did she, as their hands rested together for several moments and they looked deeply into each other's eyes.

As they enjoyed their lobster ravioli and veal a la Milanese, he asked her about her faith. Having been raised by nonreligious parents who leaned towards agnosticism, listening to her talk about Judaism touched him in a way he'd never expected. He found himself admiring her deep personal spirituality, guided by religion without being dominated by it. She seemed comfortable with the discussion, so he continued to ask questions.

"What does it say on the wooden plaque in your study with the two lines of Hebrew?"

"The English translation is 'Be still and know that I am God.' It comes from Psalm 46. It's my favorite verse in the entire Jewish scriptures."

He reflected on the verse for a few moments. "On its face it seems simple, yet also profound. One day I'd like to know why the verse is so meaningful to you."

"I would welcome that conversation."

"I'm deeply moved by your quiet spirituality, Shoshana. While I don't completely understand it, I can see that it is a quintessential part of who you are as a person, and I feel drawn to it. Is prayer a part of your spiritual practice?"

"Yes, I pray daily, in my own way," she said. "For instance, I don't pray for material things."

"I take it you're not a fan of those televangelist who preach the prosperity gospel."

"My beliefs suggest otherwise," she said without judgement.

"I thought God was supposed to answer all our prayers," he said, trying to be clever.

"Hmm...the history of religion seems to be pretty clear about one thing."

"And what is that?"

"Job descriptions assigned to God are rarely valid," she stated.

The wisdom and brevity of her response astounded him. In one terse, brilliant observation, she had managed to disarm and dismiss centuries of believers of all religions who battled one another, often violently, in an effort to claim the mantle of truth, arguing that they, above all others, understood God's true nature and purpose.

He would never forget their short exchange regarding prayer, and would forever remain in awe of her beautiful, unassuming spiritual insight.

As they prepared to order dessert, the conversation came around to their children.

"Tell me about your daughter," he said.

"Adyra is a wonderful young woman. Her name in Hebrew means great strength. She and Matthew were very close, and she mourned his loss as much as I did. Neither of us would have made it without the other. Many nights we sat on the edge of the bed and held one another as we sobbed uncontrollably. But we worked through it and emerged on the other side of our grief even closer than before. She's brilliant, just like her father."

"Let's not forget her mother, who is quite brilliant herself," Richard said with a smile. "What does your daughter do?"

"She's a hippotherapist."

"Equine therapy?"

"Honestly, Richard. Is there anything that you don't know?"

"A great deal, I assure you. I had a colleague in New York, fabulously wealthy, who bought a farm and created a not for profit equine therapy center in upstate New York. The center had three hippotherapists and six horses. It specializes in working with children and young adults with PTSD. I had the opportunity to witness firsthand the healing work that the hippotherapists and horses working together were able to accomplish. Adyra has chosen a very special occupation vocation. You must be very proud."

"I am."

"I would like to meet her someday," he said.

"And no doubt, she would like to meet you," Shoshana assured him. "Now, please tell me about Harper Elinor and Fallon Blayr."

"You remembered their names."

"Of course. You gifted your daughters with such beautiful names."

"You have me at a disadvantage. Remember when you asked how I came to Percyville, Missouri from New York City? I told you it was a long story. What I was really saying was I didn't want to talk about it. I would love to be able to tell you about Fallon and Harper, but I can't, because…I don't know."

"I don't understand."

"The truth is, I haven't seen or talked to them in several years." He took a deep breath and told her how a highly regarded Manhattan psychiatrist with all his uber-wealthy patients, admitting privileges at the best hospitals in the city, and a teaching appointment at one NYC's stellar med schools, had lost it all to the ravages of addiction to drugs and alcohol. The collateral damage of destroying his career was the loss of his family. "I could blame Meredith, my ex, for turning the girls against me, and she did, but I really only have myself to blame. The judge granted her sole custody. I was given visitation rights, but I discovered those rights don't mean much when your daughters don't want to see you. Fallon and Harper were twelve and eight when my ex decided to end the marriage. The divorce and my children's rejection only made matters worse.

"I'm so sorry, Richard." she said as she reached across the table and gently touched his hand.

"I didn't think I could sink any lower, but I was wrong. One morning I woke up in a jail cell arrested for public intoxication. And while I was drunk,

I'd tried to buy drugs from an undercover cop. None of which I had any recollection. A Buddhist friend who specialized in addiction psychiatry bailed me out of jail and got me into a residential program. His compassion saved my life. I spent five long months in rehab. I'll spare you the details. That same friend intervened with the state medical board so I was able to retain my license if I could demonstrate that I could remain alcohol and drug free. I quickly learned that most places weren't interested in employing a psychiatrist in recovery. When you think about it, a recovering shrink with a script pad is like an alcoholic working in a liquor store. Who's going to sign on for that?"

"It's such a contrast with my wonderful relationship with Adyra. I can only imagine the pain you've experienced over these years being cut off from Fallon and Harper."

"Thank you. I haven't shared that story with anyone since I came to Percyville thirteen years ago. I worried people would judge me, even question my competence as a doctor."

"How did you end up in Percyville, of all places?"

"The Internet," he replied. "I found a posting for a director of medical services for Percy County. I applied and sent in my resume. Much to my surprise, the county director of public health called me. He was very honest. He really didn't think he would hire me, but he was curious why someone from New York City with my experience and credentials would be applying for a position in a rural midwestern county. I was completely honest with him, and fully expected him to tell me he wasn't interested. Instead, he asked if I would like to come to Missouri for an interview. 'Really?' I asked in disbelief. To which he replied, 'No personal calamity is so crushing that something true and great can't be made of it.' Later I learned he was quoting Bill Wilson, the founder of A.A., and that he had been in recovery for eighteen years. It's funny how things work out. I thought I would spend a few years in Percyville and then return to the city and get back to being a real psychiatrist. I continued to reach out to Fallon and Harper, but I guess they're unable or unwilling able to forgive me. I still send them cards and gifts for Christmas and their birthdays, but they go unacknowledged. Still, I'll never give up hope that one day I'll be reunited with the girls, and that they again see me as their father and know that I have never stopped loving them."

"Thank you again for being so open with me, Richard."

"I hope my tale of woe didn't ruin our dinner. If it did, I apologize."

"Not at all. On the contrary."

When the check finally came, Richard glanced at his watch. It was nearly midnight. He couldn't believe how quickly the time had flown by. They had both shared stories of great pain from their pasts, and their sharing had created a bond that brought them closer together. Sharing his experience of addiction and the loss of his family had been cathartic, showing him the heart was capable of experiencing great pain and joy all at the same time.

He found himself overwhelmed with attraction for the beautiful, brilliant, compassionate woman sitting across the table from him. Feelings were stirring in his heart that he had not experienced since the end of his marriage and family.

His pulse quickened. Should he tell her how he felt?

CHAPTER FORTY-NINE

The presence of someone on the other side of her bed startled Shoshanna as she rolled over, bumping into him. She had not shared a bed with anyone in over five years. Since Matthew's death, she'd rarely dated, in part because of her schedule, but primarily because she'd simply had no interest. It wasn't for lack of offers. She was always impeccably dressed and had retained her youthful figure into her mid-fifties thanks to a routine exercise regimen designed to ward off the effects of middle-age metabolism and the stress of a sixty-hour work week. She smiled as she recalled one of her residents at the hospital, half her age, who'd been relentless in his efforts to get her to go out with him.

An early riser, she looked at the clock. Only six-fifteen, much too early for a Sunday morning. Still, she found it difficult to go back to sleep, so she quietly made her way to the kitchen for a much-desired cup of coffee.

She and Richard had shared so much the night before, and Richard's eager acceptance of her breakfast invitation had delighted her. Slipping on her plush fleece robe, she glanced down at the man in her bed and smiled, overcome with a feeling of joy and contentment that she had not experienced in a long time. Too long. Dr. Richard Crane was as handsome as he was sensitive and intelligent.

Life felt suddenly brighter.

* * *

Richard couldn't tell whether it was the cheerful morning sun piercing through the window or the aroma of freshly-ground coffee that told him it was time to wake up. He opened his eyes as Shoshana walked into the bedroom with two trays filled with fresh strawberries, crème fraiche, scrambled eggs, warm croissants, and two large espressos. She presented one tray to him, slid under the covers next to him, and brought the other tray onto her lap.

"Good morning. Enjoy!"

"You certainly got up early."

"I usually wake just before dawn. I always feel like the day will be kinder to me if I greet her just as we're both starting our mornings."

"What a beautiful thought, and expressed so elegantly," he said. Who lived their life from a place like that? "I must confess, I didn't think you were serious about cooking me breakfast."

"Why not? One of my favorite things is breakfast in bed on a Sunday morning with *The Times*. It makes me feel like all is right with the world."

"Is breakfast in bed better if you are sharing it with another person?" he asked, immediately regretting the nosy question.

"It depends."

"On…?"

"On who it is." She winked.

"And in my case?"

"Trust me, Richard Crane, breakfast in bed is a whole lot better with you in it."

CHAPTER FIFTY

Three years later…

George's trial had garnered considerable media attention. The judicial process had turned into a surreal experiment in criminal justice that didn't fail to disappoint. The Percy County DA, rumored to be up for a big job in Kansas City, had left nothing to chance. Ironically, the confessed killer intentionally insured the DA's victory, getting his death row ticket stamped in the process. As the trial unfolded, it became increasingly clear to Chris that George understood the criminal justice system far better than people realized. He always knew what was coming and had cleverly prepared in advance. As a first degree murder case, Missouri law required the DA to call a grand jury. The DA, who also served as the prosecutor, correctly predicted that an indictment for the murder of Donna Strickland would be forthcoming, given the evidence presented to the jury.

At his arraignment, George astounded everyone. To the dismay of all, including Chris and his two psychiatrists, he refused to make a plea, knowing full well that would force the judge to enter a plea of not guilty on his behalf. George also refused to accept a court-appointed public defender, arguing persuasively that the sixth amendment guaranteed him the right to represent himself. *Voir dire* had quickly revealed how difficult it would be to select a jury. It took three weeks to impanel a jury, given few people said they could be impartial because of all the publicity surrounding the murder and its aftermath. Most of the prospective jurors admitted they had already decided that George Maybrick was a sadistic serial killer. In refusing a lawyer, George had all but insured his conviction on first degree murder, given the reems of evidence that he had murdered Donna Strickland. Had he not opted to defend himself, any lawyer would have insisted on a change of venue, arguing a fair trial was impossible in Percyville.

Richard had reluctantly taken the stand, testifying that in his professional opinion the defendant was mentally competent to stand trial. The prosecutor knew he had scored big points with the jury. He wasn't finished, however. To hammer home the point as to the accused killer's state of mind, he called Shoshana to testify, who had echoed her colleague's testimony as to the defendant's sanity. She had immediately left the courtroom and Chris had found her crying privately, devastated knowing what her testimony portended for her patient's eventual conviction and probable death sentence.

Taking the stand as one of the prosecution's witnesses, George took the fifth twenty-seven times, leading the DA to ask if he had any intention of answering any of the questions under oath.

George simply replied, "That is correct," as the jurors looked on in amazement.

The prosecutor said, "No further questions, Your Honor," grinning ever so slightly as he sat down, no doubt confident that the defendant had sealed his fate and that he had the jurors right where he wanted them.

To everyone's surprise, Donna Strickland's mother, estranged from the victim for many years and living in another state, was attending the trial. No sooner had the prosecutor taken his seat than the victim's mother immediately stood up in the gallery. She pointed at George and screamed, "You're a heartless, coldblooded murderer. You killed my Donna and I pray to God that you burn in hell!" Then she'd collapsed onto the floor sobbing uncontrollably.

Despite the prosecution's confidence in a speedy conviction, the jury had taken three days to render a verdict, after sending three different requests to the presiding judge asking for clarification. Richard, ever the gentleman, who made it a point to never use anything faintly resembling foul language, had called the whole trial "a cluster you-know-what."

Eventually the jury returned a guilty verdict and recommended the death penalty. At his sentencing, George offered an apology, saying, "I am truly sorry for all the pain and suffering I have caused. I accept the sentence, and I believe it serves the cause of justice. I would like to thank the jury and Your Honor. Yours was not an easy task."

The judge thanked George for his statement and when asked if he had anything further to say, George quoted his favorite poet.

"When the morning was waking over the war, He put on his clothes and stepped out and died, The lock yawed loose and a blast blew them wide, He dropped where he loved on the burst pavement stone, And the funeral grains of the slaughtered floor."

Chris learned later that in the sea of confused expressions, only two people had recognized the opening lines from a Dylan Thomas poem—a retired literature professor from the local community college serving as an alternate juror, and Shoshana. She'd told Chris she knew the opening lines of *Among Those Killed in the Dawn Raid Was a Man Aged a Hundred*. She had studied the poem many years earlier and explained to him that Thomas's work acknowledged the reality of death just as George was doing now by quoting him. But what she also understood was the reference to funeral grains on the slaughtered floor, indicating hope for rebirth and renewal. Shoshana had smiled as he recited the poem, and understood George was telling his audience that he believed death was not the end, there was more to come. Something she would scarcely have thought possible when they first met months earlier in the basement cell of the Hightower police department.

That day, the case should have been closed, as George had said he had no intention of appealing the conviction or sentence. But his performance in the courtroom caused an anti-capital-punishment organization, the End the Death Penalty Project, to immediately file an appeal—over George's objection—claiming the trial amounted to little more than a court-assisted suicide since the accused clearly did everything he could to secure his own conviction and death sentence.

"Of course, I did," George explained to Chris, Richard, and Shoshana with a smile the day he was transferred to the Potosi Correctional Center in Mineral Point, where Missouri housed its death row inmates. "Death has no dominion over me. I have no fear of dying. In fact, I welcome it. I'm grateful for your friendship and appreciate all that you three have done for me. If there is such a thing as redemption, you have helped me find it. And now it is time for me to move on."

Chris and his friends understood the deeper meaning of George's declaration. They had occasionally heard from George over the next three years, but that was the last time the three of them would ever speak with the convicted murderer.

CHAPTER FIFTY-ONE

A year after George's trial Richard and Shoshana wed. Chris thought it a bit strange that their relationship was the result of an attempt to shed light on the mind of a serial killer. But his own friendship with the two psychiatrists had also developed because of George Maybrick.

He and his wife, Julia, had attended their wedding. With some sleuthing, Chris had located Richard's two long-estranged daughters and told them about the wedding, urging them to come. Their attendance, a complete surprise to Richard, had made the occasion doubly joyful. Shoshana's daughter, Adyra, had written a beautiful poem honoring the occasion, which she read during the ceremony. The newlyweds had looked profoundly happy as they watched their daughters celebrating their newfound sisterhood.

Today, the drive from Hightower to St. Louis passed quickly. The crisp November day prompted Chris to roll down his window and breathe in the cool, fresh air while the sun's rays stealing through the windshield warmed his hands on the steering wheel. It felt good.

His mind returned to the saga of George Lindfield Maybrick and speculated on where George might be now. He had only learned a few weeks earlier that George had died unexpectedly but had few details regarding his passing on Death Row. Now, Chris found himself very curious about the contents of the letter in his shirt pocket and looked forward to finally opening it in the presence of Richard and Shoshana.

In the living room of their St. Louis home, Chris sipped his coffee. He and his wife, Julia, had rarely visited Shoshana and Richard since the wedding two years earlier and Chris smiled seeing how happy they both looked. At least one good thing had come about because of George.

Shoshana began. "Let's begin with a few moments of silence to remember our dear friend, George." Following the period of silence she continued. "Although we don't yet know the circumstances of his death we mourn his loss and honor his memory."

"Leave it to George to create a little drama and mystery to remind us how important he was to each of us," Richard said. "Chris, why don't you get us started!"

"Okay! Everybody got their envelope?" he asked, waving his. He couldn't contain his curiosity any longer. As Chris opened his envelope, the tension in the room grew. He frowned and removed an index card from the envelope.

"What does it say?"

"Strange... All that's written on the card is a number...or numbers, maybe."

"Huh?" Richard asked, clearly confused.

"The numbers are one six six and seven. But George's handwriting is so bad I can't tell if it's a date, two separate numbers, or four different numbers," he said, holding up the index card for them to see.

"Hmm...curious," Shoshana said, then turned to her husband. "What's in your envelope, love?"

Richard opened his envelope and carefully removed a similar index card.

"More numbers?" she asked.

"No. It looks like a couple of lines from a poem." He read the writing on the card, stumbling through thanks to the awful handwriting. "Father and Mother, they have passed away; Sister and brother, now beneath the clay." He looked up. "Lines from a poem? Do they ring a bell with anyone?"

"Nope," Chris replied.

"Me neither," Shoshana said. "It's definitely not Dylan Thomas."

"Can't wait to see what's in your envelope, sweetheart," Richard said.

She opened her envelope and read the contents to herself, then said, "It's some sort of release drafted and signed by George." She pursed her lips. "He's basically waiving his right to privacy and patient confidentiality. I had asked him for permission after one of our sessions to make transcriptions of our recorded sessions. I wanted to be able to use them in my research. Initially he said no. However, after we established a relationship and he came to trust me, he changed his mind, but he never gave me a signed release. I reminded him a couple of times, then forgot all about it until a couple of days after the trial. By then it was too late." She looked down at the paper. "And... This is curious."

"What's that?" Richard asked.

"He scribbled a note at the bottom. Given George's handwriting, it's difficult to decipher, but I think it says 'You may have more use for this than you realize, Doc.'"

"Well, that was considerate of him," Chris said.

"There's another message from him instructing the three of us to pay a visit to Father James Wheeler, the prison chaplain at Potosi Correctional."

"Okay..." Richard said.

For the next fifteen minutes they tried to make sense of George's cryptic messages.

"The numbers could be a date," Shoshana suggested. "Does 1667 have anything to do with Victorian England?"

"Not really. Perhaps a lock combination? Sixteen, six, seven?" Richard suggested.

"Maybe it's two numbers, sixteen and sixty-seven," Chris offered.

"Who knows? What about the lines of poetry?" Shoshana asked as she Googled the word poem and the lines on her phone. "Hmm. Nothing comes up," she announced, scrolling through the results.

"Maybe it's not poetry. Could be lyrics from a song?"

"Good thinking, Chris," she said and changed the word poem to lyrics in her search. "You're brilliant, Detective," she said excitedly. "It a line from an old song written in 1881 titled *A Violet from Mother's Grave.*"

"Read the lyrics," Richard urged.

"Absolutely," she replied, and read from the screen. "Scenes of my childhood arise before my gaze, Bringing recollections of bygone happy days. When down in the meadow in childhood I would roam, No one's left to cheer me now within that good old home, Father and Mother, they have pass'd away; Sister and brother, now lay beneath the clay, But while life does remain to cheer me, I'll retain. This small violet I pluck'd from mother's grave."

"Why would George send you lyrics from a song written in 1881?" Richard asked.

"Yeah, strange," Chris said.

"Well, I doubt we'll figure out the meaning of the numbers or the lyrics today, but I'm betting they have something to do with Jack the Ripper," she said confidently.

"What does Jack the Ripper have to do with any of this?" Chris asked them, totally confused.

Over the next three hours, they filled him in on how the various lives of George Lindfield Maybrick had come to light and unfolded over the course of three months of regression therapy that Shoshana had led him through in his basement cell. Chris sat in rapt attention as they took turns explaining some of Maybrick's horrible past life experiences. Periodically he would interrupt with a question and a bit of skepticism, but the granular detail that George had rendered in his accounts riveted his attention.

As the story of George's past life regressions began to unfold, Chris grew more excited and curious. "Could I listen to one of the recordings?" he requested.

"Certainly," Shoshana replied. "I now have George's signed release. I also made duplicates of all the recordings, just in case. I keep a set in the study." She got up and retrieved one of the recordings and began playing it.

"Listen carefully, Chris," she said. "This is the murder of Mary Kelly, Jack the Ripper's final victim. Every detail George relates checks out. I'll warn you though, it's really grim."

Richard pulled a copy of a book from the study and paged through it to a photo of the Miller's Court murder scene. "All the other Ripper victims were killed outside on the streets. But Mary Kelly's murder occurred in her room. It is the only Ripper crime scene to be photographed by the police."

"Oh, my God!" Chris exclaimed as Richard showed him the photograph. "It looks just like the crime scene photo from the Donna Strickland murder."

"Indeed. It's uncanny how eerily similar the two murder scenes are," Richard observed.

After listening to the regression recording and looking through the photos, Chris looked from Richard to Shoshana and back again. "You guys were holding out on me," he groused. "None of that was in your psych evaluation."

"Because we weren't able to include it," she explained. "George and I had a therapeutic relationship, and I couldn't violate doctor-patient confidentiality. I hope you're not angry."

"Of course not. I understand. And since we're telling secrets, there's something I'll share with both of you." Chris told them about his visit with Heidi Carson who shared the struggles of the Maybrick family around

George's chronic nightmares.

"Very interesting, Chris. Thank you for sharing that. I don't believe we really considered the full impact George's horrible dreams had on his family."

Chris nodded. "Did you know if she ever tried to talk to her brother about his nightmares?" Richard asked.

"I asked her the very same question. She told me that she had tried to talk to George several times and he was always totally resistant and finally made her promise she would never bring the subject up again."

"Makes sense when you think about it, Chris. George was initially resistant to talk to us, too," Richard said.

"What do you think changed?"

"Could be a lot of things," Shoshana suggested. "Emotional burnout from accumulated years of psychic pain, depression, fear, guilt. Maybe even despair. By any measure, George Maybrick lived a very unhappy, painful existence and your conversation with his sister further confirms that."

"What about hope?" Chris asked. At his friends' skeptical stares, he said, "Think about it. In our own ways, we all extended kindness to George, and he embraced that graciousness. The two of you earned his trust, his confidence, and helped him believe there might be a path out of the darkness that had defined so much of his life. What is that if it's not hope? And where would any of us be in the world if we didn't have hope?"

Shoshana and Richard glanced at each other, then she said to Chris, "Your insight is deeply touching."

Chris felt an unspoken but shared reality that their collective experience had created a sort of calculus of compassion and understanding between them.

"Chris, indeed, your words are beautiful. Thank you," Richard said.

Shoshana dabbed tears from her eyes. "Group hug," she announced.

And they all came together in a shared embrace.

After a couple of minutes of contemplation, Chris's head filled with thoughts of solving the greatest whodunit of all time. He said, "What if—?"

Richard interrupted. "Stop right there, Chris. We know exactly what you're thinking," he said. "Shoshana and I have been asking that same question for three years."

"But it's one of the greatest mysteries in history!" Chris exclaimed.

"Absolutely," Richard said. "Unfortunately, George was unable to recall his name, despite several regressions to his past life in Victorian England."

"God knows, we tried to get him to remember," she added.

Chris was hooked, nevertheless. "We've got to put all of this together and write it up," he announced enthusiastically.

"Not so fast. We still have no proof," Richard cautioned. "There are dozens of theories about the identity of Jack the Ripper, but no one has been able to prove definitively who he was."

"What about all of the details in the recording?"

"George obviously did a lot of reading. Every bit of it he could have gotten from books. We were never able to ask a question that would prove absolutely he was Jack the Ripper in a former life."

"The question that most intrigued us George never answered. But as much as Richard and I were dying for him to reveal his identity, just look at the healing he experienced with regression therapy."

"We all knew he was getting better because of your therapy, but the fact that it was thanks to past life regression is so fascinating!"

"Over time, Richard and I discovered that many of George's nightmares were manifestations of past life experiences. Some of his nightmares were nearly identical to the past life experiences he shared under hypnosis."

"I'm surprised George ever got any sleep at all before your therapy."

"Exactly. Therapy allowed the memories related to his dreams to come to the surface, and once illuminated, his nightmares began to dissipate."

"I don't know much about psychology but that makes sense."

"And yes, I am working on an academic paper about our therapy," she said. "While I absolutely see the power and wisdom of a belief in past lives, Richard is still not completely convinced about George."

"I must say, however, I'm this close," Richard said, pinching his forefinger and thumb nearly together. The evidence is hard to ignore."

"If I'm being honest, the idea that we have past lives is a hard concept for me to wrap my head around. Living one life is hard enough. I couldn't imagine having to do it all over again."

"My initial sentiments as well." Richard nodded in agreement.

"Still, given what the two of you have shared with me now, it's more difficult to come up with alternative explanations."

Then Shoshana picked up her envelope and card from George and indicated the other envelopes lying on the table. "Well, we have answers to some of our questions. I'm guessing we probably also have answers to questions we aren't even aware of that may arise when we visit the prison chaplain. I think we should honor George's request, and all go together," she suggested.

"Yeah, he's expecting us, and he doesn't even know it," Chris joked. "Let's plan something as soon as possible."

CHAPTER FIFTY-TWO

When the three arrived at Potosi Correctional less than two weeks later, a guard escorted them to the chaplain's office. Father James Wheeler, a short, portly man with thinning grey hair and an infectious smile attired in black clerical garb welcomed them.

"I see all three of you received your letters," he said after everyone had introduced themselves.

"Yes, and we are very grateful to you for mailing them, Father," Shoshana said. "As you can imagine, George's death came as quite a shock to us. Are you able to share with us how he died?"

"A heart attack. When the medical examiner performed the autopsy, she discovered that he had an enlarged heart."

"Hmm, hypertrophic cardiomyopathy is not usually fatal," Richard said. Shoshana nodded in agreement. "What were his symptoms?"

"The prison physician explained that in some cases an enlarged heart can go undetected and the first symptom is sudden cardiac death. Sadly, that was the case for George. When the guards went to his cell to take him out for yard time that afternoon they found him on the floor, and he had already been dead for a couple of hours."

"Thank you for sharing this with us, Father," Shoshana said.

"You're welcome. George told me that I should expect a response shortly after I mailed the letters," the priest explained, "but he never told me who exactly it was that I should expect a visit from. I must admit, I became very curious."

"We didn't know that we were going to visit you until ten days ago, Father. Frankly, we're as much in the dark as you are. George just left us each a note and asked us to come together."

Over lunch in the chaplain's office, they reminisced about George and the good things they remembered.

"He wasn't a religious man, but I truly believe he died in peace," the chaplain said.

"I think you're right," Shoshana agreed, and the others nodded. "I corresponded with him and found him tranquil, serene, and very comfortable with what was happening to him."

"I observed the same thing, Dr. Liebman. Acceptance and surrender are two deeply spiritual values," Fr. Wheeler said. "Most of those on death row are afraid to die. George never was. He was one of a kind. About a year ago he asked me to visit him and gave me the three letters and four packages. He asked me to mail the three envelopes in the event that he died, but to hold onto the packages. He expected someone would probably come for them shortly after he passed. If no one came, I was to destroy them after six months." The chaplain got up from his desk and went over to a closet and removed four items wrapped with brown paper and masking tape. "From the looks of them, I'd guess these three are paintings. I have absolutely no idea what's in the last box," he said as he handed it to Shoshana.

"Is that one of George's?" she asked, pointing to a painting hanging on the wall across from the chaplain's desk, a beautiful impressionist landscape of the French countryside replete with hillside vineyards.

"Indeed, it is, Dr. Liebman. Isn't it stunning?" he said. "George told me he once worked on a cargo ship that stopped at the port of Bordeaux at the height of the grape season, and he took a day trip into the wine region. He said it was breathtakingly beautiful. He painted this picture from memory. Can you imagine?"

"George was an amazing talent for sure," she agreed.

"I interceded on George's behalf with the warden to get him paints, brushes, canvases, even an easel so he could pursue his art. Not exactly death row protocol, if you know what I mean. He painted this and gave it to me as a gift. I hung it there so I could look up and see it while I'm working at my desk. It never fails to give me a sense of peace and serenity. I know very little about art, but George clearly possessed a remarkable gift."

"Absolutely," Richard concurred. "Well…shall we open the parcels now, or later at home?"

"I vote later," Chris said.

"That's probably a good idea, Detective Stanford," the chaplain said. "While I must admit I'm curious as to the contents, it's probably better you open them when the three of you can sit together privately."

CHAPTER FIFTY-THREE

"Well, here we are again!" Shoshana announced a week later. She, Richard, and Chris had once again planted themselves in the living room around a mid-century modern wood and glass coffee table that looked as much like an Isamu Noguchi sculpture as a piece of furniture. A massive, four-inch-thick volume on the works of Marc Chagall and a copy of *The Book of Symbols* rested on the coffee table next to a box wrapped in brown paper. The other three parcels sat on the floor resting against the table.

"Where shall we begin?" Richard asked.

"Why don't we start with these," Chris suggested, pointing to the three parcels on the floor. "There are no names on them, so I think we should each choose and open one."

"Please, Chris. You go first," she said.

"Sure," he replied. He swept one off the floor and placed it in his lap. As he tore the paper away, a beautifully painted canvas of a winter landscape rendered in the impressionist style emerged. It was not dated, but the initials GLM had been painted in very small letters in the bottom right corner.

"It's exquisite!" she cried as he held the painting up for them to see. "So reminiscent of a Sisley landscape."

The trio sat for several minutes quietly admiring the masterpiece.

"Why don't you go next, sweetheart?" Richard suggested.

"If you insist, love." She enthusiastically grasped one of the remaining wrapped canvases on the floor. As soon as she unwrapped the painting, she teared up.

A seascape had been captured with the sun in its final few minutes before disappearing on the horizon. The clouds illuminated in orange, red, and pink created a breathtaking skyline while the dying light of the sunset shimmered across the water.

"I don't know if I've ever seen anything so beautiful," she said dabbing her eyes with a tissue.

"Me, neither," Richard said.

Once again, silence settled over the room as they marveled at the incredible beauty of George's canvas.

Finally, Richard took up the last parcel. He tore into the brown wrapping paper, anxious to see what art treasure it might reveal. He recognized the image immediately. George had captured a view of Big Ben and Parliament with the Thames River in the foreground. He had masterfully executed the two famous London landmarks, though the city's signature purple and blue mist obscured any architectural details. Hints of an early morning sunrise positioned just to the right of the clock tower punched through the fog, an orb of soft orange and yellow light, its reflection floating on the surface of the Thames. Richard beamed with pride and immediately began contemplating a placement in the house that would show the canvas to its greatest advantage.

The irony of an image of London painted from George's past life in Victorian England did not escape the group.

"I suspect George chose this subject very deliberately. I think he wanted to create something beautiful in the present out of something very ugly from his past. He succeeded wonderfully."

Richard nodded in agreement. "Can we take a break for a fun fact?"

"Certainly," she replied, but rolled her eyes.

"Cobalt violet and manganese violet were first formulated in the mid-nineteenth century. The impressionists, particularly Monet, fell in love with purple and made the shade popular by introducing it into many of their paintings. They were so fond of using purple that many critics suggested the impressionists were suffering from 'violettomani.' Other critics vexed by the impressionists' heavy use of violet attributed it to some sort of optical or neurological malady."

"That's really fascinating, Richard. But I think it's time for us to open the box now," she said. "I believe we're all anxious to discover its contents. Why don't you open it, Chris?"

"No, Shoshana you do the honors, please," he insisted.

She took the box from the table and enthusiastically began removing the brown paper while Richard and Chris looked on. Inside the box, on top she saw an envelope with all three of their names on it.

"Thank God!" she exclaimed, opening the envelope. "It's a letter from

George, but its typewritten. Can you imagine trying to read a whole letter in his terrible handwriting?"

They all burst out laughing. After the laughter subsided, she began reading the letter aloud.

"Dear Doc, Dr. Crane, and Detective Stanford, If you are reading this letter, you have abided by my wishes, for which I'm very grateful. I trust you had a nice visit with Fr. Wheeler. He was very good to me during my little layover on death row, including procuring this old typewriter for me. By now, Detective Stanford, you must be caught up on everything that has gone on, since the release I signed for Doc allowed my two favorite shrinks to share our little chats in the basement cell of the Hightower police station. I must confess, the death row accommodations here at Potosi Correctional make my basement cell in the Hightower police station seem like the Ritz. I wish I had solved the mystery about the real identity of my past life in England. Believe me, I tried. Nonetheless, I'm encouraged by other developments and I hope the contents of this box may hold the answer. Doc, thanks for sending me the copy of the Brian Weiss book *Mirrors of Time* with the past life regression CD. It worked great and really allowed me to continue to explore PLR therapy on my own. I began keeping a journal in which I recorded my experiences in as much detail as possible. This box contains that journal. I want you to read it. I was able to return to my life in England two additional times. I hope there might be enough information in those accounts to track down my identity one day. I can promise you there is proof that I was the serial killer, Jack the Ripper, if time and the elements have not destroyed the evidence. What a curious claim to fame for a man sitting on death row nearly 135 years later. You once asked me about the murder weapon I used, and I told you I buried it. The clues to where I buried it are on the two index cards and note in the envelopes that Fr. Wheeler mailed to you several days ago. The journal provides an additional clue. I could tell you where I buried it, but what would be the fun in that? Besides, there are no guarantees it would still be there. But it should be a great adventure for the three of you to try and find it. Should you be successful, please compare it to the drawing I made at Dr. Crane's request that day in my jail cell, which now seems so long ago."

She paused, and Richard murmured, "Wow. Interesting. Keep reading!"

So, she did. "I also discovered that I had lived in China a thousand years ago and sailed the Mediterranean as a pirate in ancient times. I may have also learned where my artistic abilities came from. I apprenticed to a seventeenth-century Flemish landscape painter who became a mentor and taught me the art of painting. Again, the details are in the journal. For the first time in all my lives that I can remember, I am going to my death with some measure of peace instead of dying violently or in despair. I can never begin to thank the three of you for your kindness and friendship. If you find Jack the Ripper's murder weapon and solve the mystery of his identity, do with them what you will. With warmest regards, GLM. PS, No doubt we'll encounter each other again. I hope you're looking forward to it as much as I am!"

All three laughed at the PS, then pondered the contents of George's letter.

"Who's going to read George's journal first?" Shoshana asked, digging deeper in the box. Inside she found a spiral notebook and began paging through it. After a few minutes of discussion, they all agreed to leave the journal with her, since she was the authority on past life regression, but that she would have a copy made and overnight it to Chris in Hightower.

CHAPTER FIFTY-FOUR

Chris grabbed his phone on the second ring. "Hi, Richard. Discover anything interesting?"

"Yep. There are couple of developments we'd like to share with you. Anything on your end?"

"I've read through George's journal and he certainly had some amazing experiences. What I found most interesting is that he attended Mary Kelly's funeral. Risky behavior for a serial killer. And he visited her grave a few days later. Go figure."

"Hard to understand. I don't think he planned do that, but I may have found a partial answer to the question. Do you have a minute?"

"Sure."

"I sent you a copy of the Trevor Marriott book. Have you started reading it yet?"

"I'm about halfway through it."

"I believe he makes a very compelling case that Jack the Ripper was a merchant seaman, but that comes at the very end of the book. You might want to skip ahead to the chapter where he looks at possible Ripper suspects. Recall, the night George was killed on the London Docks he was headed back to his ship, the *Sylph*. Marriott found records for the *Sylph* that placed it in London at the time of the murders."

"And?" Chris asked excitedly.

"The *Sylph* had experienced a mechanical failure and repairs took much longer than anticipated. It did not depart London until November 22, 1888. Do you know where I'm going with this, Chris?"

"I think so, but please continue," he urged.

"If you work backward, Jack the Ripper murdered Mary Kelly on the ninth and the funeral took place ten days later on the nineteenth. We'll probably never know why George attended her funeral, but we now have an explanation of why he would still have been in London almost two weeks after the murder was committed.

"Makes sense. The murder was all over the penny press and there was a lot of publicity surrounding the funeral. Hundreds of people lined the streets of the funeral procession, and George's description in his journal is spot on."

"Exactly. His recollection clearly reflects the newspaper accounts of the funeral. He also said he visited Mary Kelly's grave a day or two later, but that may not be as inexplicable as his attendance at her funeral."

"What are you getting at, Richard?"

"Remember when George said he buried the murder weapon but couldn't remember where?"

"Wait. You know?"

"Yes, Shoshana and I may have figured it out, with George's help, of course. That's why I'm calling. Shoshana and I would like to drive down to Hightower this Saturday to catch up with you and Julia, and to show you what we've uncovered."

CHAPTER FIFTY-FIVE

"You got another delivery today, Chris. Another book on Jack the Ripper or reincarnation, no doubt," Julia announced to her husband when he arrived home after his conversation with Richard earlier in the day.

"Can't wait to see which one!"

"Don't you have enough books already?"

"Not really. There are over a hundred serious nonfiction books on Jack the Ripper, and new books are being published all the time. I've only got a handful. As long as the case remains unsolved people are going to continue to write about it."

"And I suppose you're going to be the one to solve it…" Julia joked.

"Would you expect anything less from your brilliant detective husband?"

"Of course not, dear," she replied, kissed him, and asked him to get the kids ready for dinner.

"Oh, by the way, I invited Richard and Shoshana for dinner on Saturday. Sorry I didn't check first, but it's been too long since the four of us have gotten together."

"Great. I'd love to see them. Are they coming for a social visit, or is this going to be an evening where I sit around and listen to the three of you talk about George Maybrick and Jack the Ripper?"

"Both, of course!" he replied and rushed off to the living room to retrieve the latest addition to his library.

Chris found it difficult to contain himself. The excitement and anticipation of the Saturday visit made the week seem to drag on interminably. Had they unlocked the mystery of the numbers? In the five months since they had gathered to open the box and George's paintings, Chris had developed into an amateur Ripper sleuth. He knew Julia found his newly discovered passion somewhat unsettling. "Just being a lifelong learner," he would joke if she said anything.

As he anticipated the weekend, he turned the Mary Kelly murder over in his mind. He replayed Shoshana's recordings of George's past life sessions surrounding the brutal murder and reread the journal. The mystery of the song lyrics had proved easy to solve. A couple of targeted Internet searches revealed that someone upstairs had reported hearing Kelly singing *A Violet from Mother's Grave* over and over again on the night of her murder. What was unclear was how George knew about the song and created the clue accordingly. Was he there in the room while she was singing or standing outside within earshot planning how he would kill the unsuspecting victim? He didn't mention Kelly's singing in either of the recordings or his journal. Maybe he'd read it somewhere? A full account of the brutal murder, including her singing, could be found in half a dozen books. Add another mystery to the riddle of the Ripper.

* * *

"So great to see you two again!" Julia said as she warmly embraced Richard and Shoshana when they arrived on Saturday.

"It's been far too long," Richard said.

Julia didn't know the two as well as Chris did, but they had become good friends, nevertheless. "Good people" was how she described them.

Chris hurried down the stairs and quickly offered their guests something to drink.

As soon as everyone had their drinks in hand, the conversation quickly circled around to the Ripper's murder weapon.

"I assume you've brought Julia up to speed on the whole affair?" Richard asked.

"I have," Chris said with an uncertain smile.

"I must confess I'm not nearly as excited as Chris is regarding the identity of the Ripper, but when he told me about the prospect of you finding the actual murder weapon, that got my attention."

"So, Richard and I spent weeks trying to unravel the clue of the numbers that George wrote on the index card," Shoshana began. "You'll recall George's handwriting left something to be desired. We started with the assumption that the numbers went together, and the clue had something to do with the year 1667. We ran through several databases for important historical events in 1667. We couldn't find any event that remotely connected."

"We did discover that the first blood transfusion in medical history took place in 1667 when a doctor transfused blood from a sheep into a young boy. It was an interesting idea, but the young man obviously died," Richard interjected.

"Then we tried to figure out if the numbers were some sort of geographical coordinates, which turned out to be a bust. Then Richard wondered if it might be the chapter and verse of a biblical reference."

"We struck out again," he said, "but we did discover that 16:67 is a notable reference in the Quran which addresses the importance of abstaining from intoxicating beverages."

"Another fun fact," Chris quipped as he sipped his Guinness, eliciting a chorus of laughter from the group.

"We tried all sorts of possible measures of time like 1667 hours, minutes, seconds. Then we did the same thing with inches, feet, yards, meters. Nothing!" Shoshana said. "Then two weeks ago, we were so frustrated we decided to go to the movies. We got our tickets, and when the young man checked them he said, 'You guys are so lucky!'

"I asked him why. He said, 'Sir, you have the best seats in the house.' How so? I asked. He said we were in row fourteen, seats eighteen and nineteen. The ideal seats are in the middle two or three rows in the theater and three or four seats to the left or right of center, he explained. Which of course made me even more curious, so I pressed him on his explanation."

"What did he say?" Chris asked.

"He said when the theater designers lay out the sound system, they work from the center of the theater and balance the sound from there. But you don't want to be dead center in the theater or you'll get a neutral sound. If you sit a few seats away from the center, it gives the full effect of all the speakers in the theater working together. Plus, where you experience the best sound is typically also the best place visually to watch a movie."

"Richard and I were very impressed with this young man. It was so refreshing to see someone so passionate about what he was doing. But I'll bet you're wondering what this story has to do with the Ripper saga," Shoshana said. "Richard, tell them what happened next."

"We were sitting in the theater watching the trailers, when all at once it hit me!" he announced and then paused dramatically. "The 1667," he replied, "refers to row 16 and either 6 and 7 or 67 as seats, or some kind of place or placeholder. So, we started brainstorming all the possibilities where the use of rows is employed—financial reports, spreadsheets, seating in large public venues, you name it, but nothing seemed to make sense."

Shoshana could see the confusion on Chris's and Julia's faces. "Then I remembered going to visit a favorite aunt's grave many years after her death," she explained. "I couldn't recall the exact location, so I went to the cemetery's administrative office for assistance. They looked up my aunt's name, gave me a map of the cemetery layout, wrote the numbers thirteen and twenty-seven on the bottom of the map, and circled row thirteen, plot twenty-seven in the Jewish section of the cemetery. That's when it hit us! George said he buried the knife. It must be in a cemetery! But where? London is a big place. Over fifty cemeteries operated in the city in 1888."

"Did you figure out which one?" Chris blurted out excitedly.

"We did, because once again we got lucky. We decided to work backward from the murder of the Ripper's last victim, Mary Kelly. Kelly was buried in St. Patrick's Catholic Cemetery. That proved to be a good start. After we pounded the Internet for a few hours, Richard uncovered a short but detailed article on Kelly's funeral on the *Casebook: Jack the Ripper* website. It's a treasure trove of information for Ripperologists."

Richard Googled the article on his phone and handed it to Chris and Julia. "Read this part," he said, pointing to a couple of paragraphs near the end describing the burial.

Chris read it aloud. "Mary Jane's funeral procession arrived at St. Patrick's at two o'clock. The body was met by Father Columban OSF (Order of St. Francis), who was accompanied by two acolytes and a cross bearer at the door to the little chapel of St. Patrick's and the coffin was carried to an open grave in the northeastern corner, listed as No. 16, Row 67. Joseph Barnett and the weeping women who had accompanied him as principal mourners knelt by the graveside while Father Columban read the service. There was still a large gathering of people outside the locked gates who were denied entry while the burial service was taking place. After the service, Barnett and the mourners visited the Burbeck public house, which still stands close to the cemetery gates today. The plot in which Mary Jane was interred is found behind the little chapel of St. Francis in the grounds running northeast toward the perimeter railings. The rows of graves in the public plot started by the perimeter railings at row nought and continued consecutively along to the rear of the chapel, ending at row eighty-nine, a total of ninety rows in all. This numbering pattern was laid down when the cemetery opened in 1861 and remained until 1941. The ground was reclaimed in 1947 and the exact location of the individual rows, including Mary Jane's grave, were lost. When the ground was renumbered in rows and ready for reuse, a revised row numbering system was introduced, which put row one close to the chapel— the opposite end to where it had once been when the cemetery opened. Today there is no row nought."

"So, you've solved the mystery!" Julia said excitedly. "Mary Kelly's burial plot was number sixteen in row sixty-seven."

"Brilliant detective work, you two!" Chris said. "The question now is how does this help us find the murder weapon if Kelly's gravesite was reclaimed and reused in 1947? That's almost three quarters of a century ago." He couldn't help his disappointment.

"Don't get too discouraged just yet," Shoshana cautioned. "We asked ourselves the exact same question. It looked like we had reached a dead end again, but Richard refused to give up. After some additional sleuthing on the Internet, he found a 2017 article in the *Daily Mail* about an effort to find the remains of Mary Kelly. The idea was that if the victim's remains could be found, a DNA analysis could be conducted to test the claim of a doctor who said Kelly was his great aunt. The project was commissioned by Patricia Cornwell, the gifted crime novelist who has also written two books on Jack the Ripper. The group included a group of scientists from Leicester University as well as a geneticist who helped identify the remains found under a parking lot as those of Richard III, who died in 1485. In the end, the group had to abandon the project."

"You've got to be kidding me! Why?" Chris asked.

"Too many complications," she explained. "There was some question as to how accurate they could really be in identifying the location of the grave, so the remains of other people buried in the area would be disturbed. Legally, that meant the researchers would have to get permission from the next of kin for every grave disturbed during the search. In the end, the team determined that meeting all the requirements to get permission for exhumation from the Ministry of Justice would be nearly impossible. And even if the ministry issued a permit, it could take years to complete the analysis, and the cost would be considerable with absolutely no guarantee of success. On top of all that, exhumations conducted in the nineteen fifties indicated the remains in that part of the cemetery had become very waterlogged, so it was questionable whether any DNA extraction would be possible."

"So, you're back to square one," Julia said with disappointment.

"Yes and no," she replied. "The article from the *Daily Mail* still offered a glimmer of hope. The bad news contained some potentially good news, too."

"And what would that be…?" Chris asked.

"Well, Dr. Turi King, the forensic DNA expert who identified the remains of Richard III and also led the Mary Kelly Project team, said her remains were likely to have been dug through when the cemetery reclaimed the burial grounds for reuse in the nineteen forties, so it would be nearly impossible to make an accurate identification of Kelly's remains."

"Sorry, Shoshana, but I'm not seeing the upside to any of this."

Richard said, "We're working on the assumption that George left us two clues to the whereabouts of the murder weapon. First, the lyrics to a song that Mary Kelly sang the night Jack the Ripper killed her. Now the row number and plot number of Mary Kelly's burial site. Despite all the discussion, we have documentation from St. Patrick's Cemetery records that confirm her 1888 place of burial. Correct?"

They all nodded in agreement.

"Then doesn't it seem safe to assume that George was telling us he finally figured out that the Ripper buried the knife he used to murder his victims in his final victim's place of burial? We know that he attended Mary Kelly's funeral. We can speculate why he might have planted the key piece of evidence in her grave, but we'll never know for sure."

"I hear what you're saying, Richard," Chris said, "but how does any of this help us solve the problem of how we find the murder weapon?"

"Well, if Dr. King is correct, and the remains of those buried in the communal gravesite that was reclaimed in the nineteen forties were, to use her words, dug through, then if the knife was still buried in Kelly's grave, it probably turned up during the reclamation."

"You think the knife had remained undisturbed for almost sixty years in Mary Kelly's grave?"

"Why not? The same laws and rules and regulations that made it difficult for the researchers working on the Mary Kelly project to search for her remains would also make it difficult for anyone else to disturb her grave," Richard countered.

"So how can we find out if someone discovered the knife when they reclaimed the gravesites? We're talking seventy-five years ago!"

"We realize it's a longshot," Shoshana said, "but we found the name of the superintendent of St. Patrick's Cemetery on the website. His name is Archie Williams and it appears that he has been at the cemetery for some time. He may have even consulted with the research team of the Mary Kelly project, but Richard has been unable to verify that for sure."

"So, let's call this Archie Williams!" Chris exclaimed.

"I already have," Richard replied with a grin.

CHAPTER FIFTY-SIX

Richard kept looking at his watch. It was nearly three in the morning.

"Relax, Richard, please!" Shoshana pleaded. "You're making me a nervous wreck."

"A whole week and nothing! Then he finally returned my call and I missed it. What an idiot I am."

"Don't be so hard on yourself, dear. You're not the first person to forget to charge your phone. Look, the good news is he returned your call, which means that when you call him back, he'll be willing to speak with you."

"You're right." Richard studied his watch as he calculated. "Three o'clock St. Louis time. Perfect. The UK is six hours ahead of us, which makes it nine in the morning London time."

"Go ahead, make the call, Richard," she urged, "or you're going to drive us both crazy."

That settled it. He hit the key to return the call.

"This is Archie Williams."

"Mr. Williams, this is Dr. Richard Crane in St. Louis, Missouri. Thank you for taking the time to speak with me. I'm sorry I missed your call yesterday."

"Quite all right. I'm terribly sorry for not getting back to you sooner. I've been away on holiday for a week. How may I help you?"

"I was wondering if I might ask you a few questions about Mary Kelly's gravesite?"

"Well, Dr. Crane, I'm quite busy. And anything I could tell you can be found on the Internet." He sounded annoyed.

"I understand, Mr. Williams. I've already spent quite a bit of time searching the Internet but the answers to the questions I have aren't there."

"Okay. Such as?"

"I'm particularly interested in the reclamation effort in 1947 in the communal burial area where Mary Kelly's grave was located."

"What specifically are you interested in knowing?"

"Dr. Turi King reported that when the reclamation took place, the remains of Mary Kelly were probably disturbed."

"Yes, I know Dr. King. You're referring to the Mary Kelly Project. I'm very familiar with it."

"My specific question is, do you know if any objects were discovered when the work was done in 1947?"

"Well, obviously I wasn't the cemetery superintendent when that took place. The superintendent at the time passed away long ago. My predecessor, David Evans, worked on that project. He was a groundskeeper and worked at the cemetery for over fifty years."

"Any chance he's still alive?

"No. Sadly, David died several years ago, well into his nineties. A colorful bloke he was!"

"How so?"

"David's nickname was 'Digger.' When his father died during the depression, David left school and started working at St. Pat's as a gravedigger to support his mother and siblings. He worked very hard and by the nineteen forties he had been promoted to groundskeeper which is why he was involved in the recovery of the burial sites in 1947."

"Do you recall if he ever said anything about the recovery of the communal graveyard in 1947? Anything specifically related to Mary Kelly's grave site?" Richard asked.

"Yes, but what you must understand is that Mary Kelly, and those who were buried around the same time in this section of the cemetery, were actually buried on top of five other previous gravesites. A number of things turned up as the groundskeepers reworked the earth, bones mostly, which were gathered up and reburied in a communal grave elsewhere. But I understand the groundskeepers at the time did recover some objects."

"Like what, Mr. Williams?"

"David kept an old wooden Whyte & Mackay scotch whiskey crate in a cupboard in his office, chock full of things he'd found working on that project. Some of his employees told me that periodically he would pull them out and show them to visitors, usually spinning a yarn to go along with whatever object he happened to be sharing at the time."

"Do you recall any of the objects?"

"Let's see... There was a bunch of old buttons from burial garments, military insignia. Lots of small items, a dice carved from ivory, the remnants of a couple of pocket watches, a belt buckle, lots of old nails, a few pieces of jewelry. He had a small jelly jar half full of coins that he'd also collected from the site. One of the groundskeepers found the remnants of a Lancaster four-barrel pistol of all things, a fairly rare sidearm as I understand it. No idea how that got there! It also ended up in David's wooden box of curiosities. He found a few small hand tools, a pair of scissors, and a couple of penknives, all terribly rusted, of course. He discovered a lot of other things, but I just can't remember all of them."

"You mentioned a couple of penknives. Did he ever mention any other knife found at the site in 1947?" Richard asked nervously.

It was followed by several moments of silence on the other end of the phone.

Then Williams replied, "Oh right. I almost forgot about the copper box."

"A copper box?"

"David loved to tell visitors that when he removed all the corrosion off the box, he discovered a set of initials on the lid, and carefully rubbed some black paint over them to make the initials stand out. Later, after being appointed superintendent, he proudly placed it on his desk, where it became a depository for paper clips, elastics, staples, you know, desk stuff. It remained there until the day he retired."

"What does the box have to do with my question about a knife?"

"Terribly sorry, Dr. Crane. As David told the story, he and one of the other groundskeepers were trying to dig up a large stone when his shovel hit something that sounded metallic. They immediately thought they had found buried treasure. It turned out to be a long copper box. Surprisingly, the hinges and clasp still worked, even though it had probably been in the ground for at least sixty years. He and his coworker spent the rest of the afternoon imagining what kind of valuable treasure the box held and traded stories about what they would do with the money once they sold the buried treasure. But when they opened the box, they only found an old knife wrapped in a piece of disintegrating oilcloth. They were convinced it must be of great value for someone to go to all the trouble to protect it with oilcloth and a nonferrous box."

"Did you actually see the knife?" Richard asked, nearly beside himself.

"Certainly. David took his newfound treasure into the city hoping to sell it in at antique shop. When the shop owner asked if he knew what kind of knife it was, he told him he didn't have a clue, but knew it was an antique and quite valuable. The shop owner laughed and said what he had was a postmortem knife from the eighteen seventies or eighteen eighties. David recalled with great drama how his heart sank when the shop owner only offered him two quid, so he decided to keep it."

"Do you know what happened to the knife?"

"Yes, he put it in his desk and used it as a letter opener."

Richard cringed. "A letter opener?"

"That's right. It became quite the conversation piece," the superintendent said laughing.

"Any idea where the knife is now?"

"Can't say really. I helped him pack up his office when he retired. I know he took everything with him that he found in 1947, including the copper box and letter opener. I haven't a clue where they ended up."

"Did he have family, maybe?"

"His wife passed within a year of David's death. Both buried here at St. Pat's," Williams said proudly. "They had a daughter, but I haven't spoken to her since her mother's funeral."

"You wouldn't happen to remember her name and contact information?"

"Susan," he replied. "I know she had a husband and a couple of children, but I never knew her married name or where she lives now."

"Thank you so much, Mr. Williams, for your time. I've really enjoyed talking to you. You've been most helpful."

"Glad I could be of assistance, Dr. Crane, but I must say I'm curious. I'm assuming all this has to do with Mary Kelly. Is there anything you could share with me?"

"My wife and I are trying to learn more about the life and death of Mary Kelly. It's a very long story, but I promise if we find what we're looking for I will call you and tell you how the story ends."

CHAPTER FIFTY-SEVEN

"How are you, Chris?"

"Pretty good, Richard. Julia's under the weather, but the kids and I have been spared so far. Did you get a chance to talk to the superintendent of St. Patrick's Catholic Cemetery?"

"Indeed, I did!" Richard replied enthusiastically.

"From the tone of your voice it sounds like you made some progress."

"You bet!" Richard spent the next half hour relating his conversation with the cemetery superintendent.

Chris listened carefully and tried to stay focused, but his mind spun out one what-if after another. By the time Richard had concluded, Chris hummed with excitement. He peppered Richard with a battery of questions, none of which his friend could answer.

"Where do we go from here?" he finally asked.

"Shoshana and I have been discussing the next steps, and we think we might just go to London and see if we can track down the whereabouts of the knife. Based on all the information we've gathered and what George told us, we're fairly confident that David Evan's letter opener is the actual murder weapon used by Jack the Ripper. We'll try to track down his daughter, Susan, using the Internet, but finding the knife may well require some good old-fashioned detective work."

"Sounds exciting! When do you leave?"

"Shoshana finishes her semester in a couple of weeks. As soon as she's read her final exams and turns in her grades, we're off. We have enough vacation days to give us time to do some meaningful detective work. Hopefully we can locate the daughter."

"And then discover she boxed up her father's things and stored them in the garage, like most of us do when our parents pass away," Chris said optimistically,

"How ironic it would it be that we never learned the real identity of Jack the Ripper, but we actually recovered his murder weapon," Richard mused.

"If you're successful, it will make for a great story."

"You're quite right, Chris, and you know what they say about a great story..."

"No, what's that?"

"It makes for a great book!"

THE END

ACKNOWLEDGMENTS

Writing one's first novel is rarely a solitary endeavor. I want to thank my wife, Roxanne, and my sons, Christian and Harrison, for their support and encouragement during this long process. Not only did they bolster my confidence in times of doubt, but their suggestions proved invaluable in helping shape the manuscript along the way. Roxanne is always my best critic.

I want to thank Christian and Harrison for creating the AI-generated imagery for the cover and the website, and Harrison for his marketing and branding expertise.

I am deeply grateful to my beta readers for their encouragement, criticism, and editorial suggestions: Ronnie Heynes, Sheryl Piper, Erin Kuhl, Amy Blum, and Merle R. Saferstein.

I want to thank my wonderful friend, Felipe Bautista, for supplying me with ample reading material for so many years on the history of London and Victorian England.

I'm particularly indebted to Nina Bruhns, a wonderful and skilled professional editor whose guidance and criticism helped me take a really good story and make it great.

I want to thank Jenny Menzel for her invaluable assistance in taking my novel from a manuscript to a published version as a print and eBook, and designing the book cover.

Last but not least, I want to thank all the readers who took the journey through *Catch Me When You Can* and found it was time well spent!

ABOUT
THE AUTHOR

J. Philip Davies is a retired educator. The author of two previous books on the impact of media on learning, *Catch Me When You Can* is his first novel. He and his wife, Roxanne, live in Miami, Florida, and enjoy traveling, biking, and pickleball. In addition to writing, he enjoys reading, painting, and spending time with his family. He is currently working on a second novel entitled *Jackson Pollock's Jeans?*

www.ingramcontent.com/pod-product-compliance
Lightning Source LLC
Chambersburg PA
CBHW070635260626
47161CB00007B/2712